On a journey through
uncharted land, they followed their dream
of a new life . . .

THE CHISHOLMS

———◆•◆•◆———

HADLEY: The rattlesnake-toting patriarch, he took his comfort where he found it—in the Bible, the bottle, or the bed.

MINERVA: The lusty, stubborn woman Hadley loved, she shepherded her young through the harsh realities of the way west—and the terrifying passions in their own hearts.

WILL: A brawling, hard-drinking sinner, he sought salvation in the arms of an Indian woman.

BOBBO AND GIDEON: They were mere boys at the start of the Chisholms' journey; they were bloodstained men at its end.

BONNIE SUE: Too young to love, too ripe not to, she was a child forced to womanhood in the wilderness.

ANNABEL: The youngest, her quiet courage was tested in an act of unspeakable savagery.

BOOKS BY ED McBAIN

THE 87TH PRECINCT NOVELS

*Cop Hater** • *The Mugger* • *The Pusher** (1956) *The Con Man* • *Killer's Choice* (1957) *Killer's Payoff** • *Killer's Wedge* • *Lady Killer* (1958) *'Til Death* • *King's Ransom* (1959) *Give the Boys a Great Big Hand* • *The Heckler** • *See Them Die* (1960) *Lady, Lady, I Did It!* (1961) *The Empty Hours* • *Like Love* (1962) *Ten Plus One* (1963) *Ax* (1964) *He Who Hesitates* • *Doll* (1965) *Eighty Million Eyes* (1966) *Fuzz* (1968) *Shotgun* (1969) *Jigsaw* (1970) *Hail, Hail, the Gang's All Here* (1971) *Sadie When She Died* • *Let's Hear It for the Deaf Man* (1972) *Hail to the Chief* (1973) *Bread* (1974) *Blood Relatives* (1975) *So Long As You Both Shall Live* (1976) *Long Time, No See* (1977) *Calypso* (1979) *Ghosts* (1980) *Heat* (1981) *Ice* (1983) *Lightning* (1984) *Eight Black Horses** (1985) *Poison* • *Tricks* (1987) *Lullaby** (1989) *Vespers** (1990) *Widows** (1991) *Kiss* (1992) *Mischief** (1993) *And All Through the House* (1994) *Romance* (1995) *Nocturne* (1997) *The Big Bad City** (1999) *The Last Dance** (2000) *Money, Money, Money** (2001) *Fat Ollie's Book** (2003)

THE MATTHEW HOPE NOVELS

Goldilocks (1978) *Rumpelstiltskin* (1981) *Beauty & the Beast* (1982) *Jack & the Beanstalk* (1984) *Snow White & Rose Red* (1985) *Cinderella* (1986) *Puss in Boots* (1987) *The House That Jack Built* (1988) *Three Blind Mice* (1990) *Mary, Mary* (1993) *There Was a Little Girl* (1994) *Gladly the Cross-Eyed Bear* (1996) *The Last Best Hope* (1998)

OTHER NOVELS

The Sentries (1965) *Where There's Smoke* • *Doors* (1975) *Guns* (1976) *Another Part of the City* (1986) *Downtown* (1991) *Driving Lessons* (2000) *Candyland** (2001)

ALSO BY EVAN HUNTER

NOVELS

The Blackboard Jungle (1954) *Second Ending* (1956) *Strangers When We Meet* (1958) *A Matter of Conviction* (1959) *Mothers and Daughters* (1961) *Buddwing* (1964) *The Paper Dragon* (1966) *A Horse's Head* (1967) *Last Summer* (1968) *Sons* (1969) *Nobody Knew They Were There* (1971) *Every Little Crook and Nanny* (1972) *Come Winter* (1973) *Streets of Gold* (1974) *The Chisholms** (1976) *Love, Dad* (1981) *Far from the Sea* (1983) *Lizzie* (1985) *Criminal Conversation** (1994) *Privileged Conversation* (1996) *Candyland** (2001) *The Moment She Was Gone** (2002)

SHORT STORY COLLECTIONS

Happy New Year, Herbie (1963) *The Easter Man* (1972)

CHILDREN'S BOOKS

Find the Feathered Serpent (1952) *The Remarkable Harry* (1959) *The Wonderful Button* (1961) *Me and Mr. Stenner* (1976)

SCREENPLAYS

Strangers When We Meet (1959) *The Birds* (1962) *Fuzz* (1972) *Walk Proud* (1979)

TELEPLAYS

The Chisholms (1979) *The Legend of Walks Far Woman* (1980) *Dream West* (1986)

*Available in paperback from Pocket Books

EVAN HUNTER

THE CHISHOLMS

A NOVEL OF THE JOURNEY WEST

POCKET **STAR** BOOKS
New York London Toronto Sydney Singapore

A Pocket Star Book published by
POCKET BOOKS, a division of Simon & Schuster, Inc.
1230 Avenue of the Americas, New York, NY 10020

This book is a work of fiction. Names, characters, places and incidents are products of the author's imagination or are used fictitiously. Any resemblance to actual events or locales or persons, living or dead, is entirely coincidental.

This novel is loosely based on an original format and characters created by David Dortort and suggested to Evan Hunter by Alan Landsburg Productions, Inc.

FOR MY WIFE, DRAGICA HUNTER,
WHO RECENTLY BECAME AN AMERICAN CITIZEN:
THIS IS WHAT IT WAS LIKE, DARLING.

CONTENTS

I.
HADLEY
1

II.
MINERVA
35

III.
BONNIE SUE
73

IV:
BOBBO
105

V.
ANNABEL
155

VI.
WILL
205

VII.
GIDEON
249

THE
CHISHOLMS

I

HADLEY

They had put out whiskey and cakes, as was the custom, and had left the cabin door wide for mourners to come and go with their condolences. By a quarter past eleven, half a dozen of the men were drunk. The women sipped more politely, but the whiskey loosened their tongues as well, and their chatter in the cabin mingled with the laughter and the loud voices and the keening of the wind outside.

It was a blustery day, for all the sky's brightness. In April, there was early morning fog here in the mountains, but it generally burned off an hour by sun; Hadley Chisholm had watched it from the cabin window, tearing away in tatters that drifted down the valley. By the bottomlands, there were cowslips in bloom. This was springtime. You didn't think of dying and burying when the land was turning green all around you. But they had put Hadley's mother to rest this morning in a rock-lined grave. He had knelt beside the open grave afterward. Reached down. Picked up a handful of earth. The soil was parched and pebbly. He let it trickle through his fingers onto the pine coffin below.

Benjamin Lowery was coming across the cabin toward him. He was carrying a pewter cup in his hand, drinking whiskey from it as he navigated his way past the table in the center of the room, weaving, stumbling into a split-bottomed chair. He giggled, caught the chair before it fell to the floor, and then reeled to where Hadley was standing by the fireplace. Throwing an arm around him, he said very seriously, "Hadley, are you all right?"

"I'm fine," Hadley said.

"Hadley, I'm worried about you."

"No, I'm fine."

"You're not drinking, Hadley. At a time like this, Hadley, a man's mother passes away, it's fitting for him to have a drop. Hadley, let me get you some whiskey."

"Ben, you needn't bother. I'm just fine."

"Fine then," Lowery said, and nodded, and then caught at Hadley for support. "Hadley," he said, "what did you think of the new preacher?"

"I'll tell you plain," Hadley said.

"Yes, tell me."

"He had no right talking of her like he'd known her."

"*Didn't* know her," Lowery said.

"Didn't know her a damn. Put together bits and pieces of her life, is what he done. Got it from neighbors along the ridges."

"Is *just* what he done," Lowery said, and suddenly sat

on the puncheon bench against the fireplace wall. The cup fell from his hand. In an instant, he was asleep. Across the room, a cluster of men laughed at a joke the farmer Henry Soames had just told. Hadley longed for a drink. Thinking of the preacher had got him mad all over again, and a hit of corn liquor would . . . but no, he could not afford to get drunk. He had not yet told the family of his decision, and he didn't want it spewing out in a cloud of alcohol fumes. He quenched his thirst with anger instead, thinking again of the damn fool preacher talking about his mother like she'd never had no more life in her than a rag doll.

Had all the facts, oh yes, dug them all up and recited them like his alphabet: A is for Antrim, the county whence Eva Chisholm had come in the year 1768, the bride of young William Allyn Chisholm. B is for Boston Harbor, to which Eva's first son had fled two months after Hadley was born. C is for Chickasaw, who had slain Hadley's father when Hadley was but fifteen; wonder the fool preacher hadn't mentioned that William Allyn was drunk at the time and that he and the Indian had been fighting over a black wench on the Bailey plantation.

"Loved that woman like she was my own mother," Minerva said. "Wasn't a day went by she didn't tell me how beautiful I was. Which I'm not, but it was nice her saying so."

Ah, but you are, Hadley thought, and looked at his wife where she stood with the other women, and thought of that heart-stopping moment when first he laid eyes on her. He'd been over to Cedar Creek to deliver some whiskey, saw her walking a cow along the road, big stick in her hand, humming as she ambled along. Bright summer day, hair as golden as the sunshine. Dust rising on the road. Barefooted, she was.

"Hey," he said. "What's a little girl like you doing with such a big cow?"

"What's it *look* like I'm doing?" she said.

"Well, I don't rightly know," Hadley said, and smiled.

"Anyways, I ain't little."

Nor was she. Tallest girl he ever did see; top of her head came almost level with his eyes. Blondest damn hair, sun glinting on it. In the tall grass, flies buzzing.

"How old are you?" he asked.

"Nineteen," she said.

"You want some whiskey?"

"Nope."

"Made it myself."

"So who don't?" she said, shrugging.

"Never saw nobody with eyes so green," Hadley said.

"Well, you're seeing somebody now."

"That I am," he said. "Want me to come visitin sometime?"

"Nope."

"Want to kiss me?"

"Hah!" Minerva snorted.

Hadley smiled with the memory. He would tell her his decision later, when all the well-wishers had gone home. Tell her and the family. He did not know what to expect from any of them. He went to Minerva and put his arm around her waist. She was in the middle of a sentence; she acknowledged his presence with a brief nod.

". . . said he was going to marry me. Well, Eva looked me up and down, head to toe, sitting in that rocker right there near the fire, didn't say a word for the longest time. Then she said, 'You're Ian Campbell's daughter, are ye not?' I admitted as I was. . . ."

Wore her hair long then, Hadley remembered, curled like a shell at the back of her neck. Hands folded in her lap, she'd nodded to his mother and said, "I'm Ian Campbell's daughter, yes, ma'am."

"Your father's a scoundrel," Eva said.

"I love him," Minerva said.

"Aye, as a good daughter should," Eva said. "Which makes him no less a scoundrel." Eva smiled suddenly. "But that's not to say I find his daughter disagreeable."

Minerva was twenty by then. She'd returned Eva's smile and the women had reached across to clasp hands as if they were helping each other to ford a stream. As she related the story now, tears formed in her eyes. Standing close beside her was Millie Bain, who lived not half a mile away on the ridge. She immediately put her arm around Minerva and patted her shoulder.

"Touches me every time I think of it," Minerva said.

"Ain't no sin to weep," Millie said.

"Thirty-some-odd years ago, and I can still remember it plain."

"What about the time with the hoop snake?" Millie said, and laughed. She was four or five years younger than Minerva, forty-eight or -nine, Hadley didn't know which. A short chubby woman with a dumpling face and merry blue eyes, the closest friend Minerva had in all the world. It was she had helped to deliver their first son, a breech birth it had been, Millie and Eva both struggling to bring the baby into the world. He'd been named William Allyn Chisholm in memory of the soft-spoken man who'd been Hadley's father.

"You tell one more time about that hoop snake . . ." Hadley warned.

"Oh, just cause you know all about snakes," Millie said, and laughing, shushed Hadley with one plump little hand. "It was when you was carrying Bobbo, do you recall?" she said.

"Here comes the damn hoop snake," Hadley said, and rolled his eyes heavenward.

"Hush," Millie said. "And we was walkin in the woods with Eva and little Gideon beside us in his pinafore. He musta been six or seven years old—"

"Five," Minerva said, smiling.

"We was out there lookin for ratbane."

"That's right," Minerva said. "Will was coughing up his innards, and we was wanting to brew him a little syrup."

"Walking along in his pinafore, Gideon was."

"I remember it clear."

"Big old hoop snake came rolling across the path, Gideon hightailed it for the nearest tree."

"Think *I'll* hightail it for the nearest tree," Hadley said.

"Now hush, Hadley," Millie said. "Was Eva took after that snake with a grubbing hoe, yelling at Min not to even look at the ugly thing, lest the newborn babe be marked with a circle."

"Didn't look at it, neither," Minerva said.

"People roundabouts claim a hoop snake can kill a full-grown tree just by sticking their tail spike in it," Millie said.

"I don't put much store in that," Hadley said.

"Well, one thing you know is snakes, I guess," Millie said.

"That's for sure," Hadley said, and suddenly wanted these people to be gone, friends though they were, wanted to be left alone with his family so that he could tell them the secret he had carried inside him for more than a month now. He could remember a time—but ah, the land was new then. When he was a boy, when his father was still alive and even afterward, in the years of his young manhood before he met Minerva, the land they owned on this Virginia mountaintop had been rich enough to provide them with all their needs. Not only corn, no, this had always been good corn-growing country. But beans, too, in the field the other side of the cabin, and pumpkins and pattypan squash, and peas, and watermelons on the hillside. And in the land they'd cleared of stumps and cane roots they planted flax, which later they rotted and dried and then crushed in the brake Hadley and his father had themselves built. They shook out the bits of bark they called the shoves, and then Hadley's mother would get to work with the hackle, its iron teeth sticking out of the paddle-shaped board as she stroked and cleaned and separated the fibers into tow cloth, which was good for cleaning out rifle barrels and not much else. The finer fibers she used to spin the thread that went to make their fanciest garments. The seeds were used to make linseed oil; there wasn't much lost in the flax plant, save for the shoves, and a field of it in flower was as breath-taking a sight as a cloudless blue sky.

Flax, aye, and corn enough to feed the squirrel, the crow, and the family besides, with bushels left over for baking bread and feeding the hogs and horses and dis-tilling a little whiskey as well, though in those days Hadley's father made whiskey only for the family and his still was small and hardly industrious. They grew she-corn for hominy, and sweet corn and popcorn, turnips and onions and cabbage and okra. His father even planted a small patch of tobacco, which he did not smoke, but bartered instead for things they could not grow or make. The yard in front of the cabin bustled with chickens and hogs, and there was a single milk cow, earmarked, branded, and belled; a goodly part of Hadley's childhood was spent chasing animals out of the herbs and flowers his mother planted, shooing them away from the doorstep tansy or the lavender and chives. The land was dead now, as dead as the beloved woman they had put to rest on this nineteenth day of April.

Engulfed in sound, Hadley looked about the cabin, searching for his loved ones. He located his three sons and two daughters, and studied their faces for answers to the question he hadn't yet asked.

It was one in the afternoon.

The mourners were gone.

"There's somethin I've got to tell you all," he said. "I been thinkin this ever since my mother took sick a month ago. I knew she was going to die this time, knew there wasn't nothin we could do to save her, she was an old lady heaven bound, God rest her soul. And I thought, when she dies, we ought to leave this place. Well, now she's dead, we buried her this morning, we said our prayers over her grave. There's nothin here no more but land that's as barren as the company of the godless. I want to leave this place."

Minerva was standing at the fireplace, near the Dutch oven. She turned to look at her husband as though he had spoken blasphemy against the dead and the living both. He caught her glance and nodded—in affirmation, or in defiance.

"Where would you have us go, Pa?" Will asked.

Will was almost thirty-two, born on the eve of The War, in June of 1812. He keenly resembled his father, with the same tall, broad-shouldered, wiry physique, the same dark blue eyes and black hair—though Hadley at the age of fifty-six already had more than a sifting of snow on the roof.

"I thought west," Hadley said.

"Where west?" Minerva said at once. "Kentucky, do you mean?"

"Ain't no land to be had in Kentucky, nor anyplace east of the Mississippi," Hadley said. "I'm thinkin of California. Or maybe Oregon."

Minerva shook her head. "No," she said.

"There's nothin for us here no more," Hadley said.

"There's home," Minerva said.

"It ain't home," Hadley said. "It's the Cassadas going to kill us if the land don't first."

"Ain't the Cassadas going to kill us nor the land neither," Minerva said. "I been on this land since I was twenty and you brought me here from Cedar Creek to marry. I can remember when that quarter acre—"

"The land is dead," Hadley said.

"—behind the cabin would yield twenty-five bushels at the least. And I can remember when times was bad, too, during the Panic, when I already had Will and was carrying Gideon, and we lived through that, too. There's trouble now with the Cassadas, but there's always been trouble one kind or another, and I don't see as picking up and moving's going to solve nothing.

You want to go west, then you just git on your horse and go, Had. Ain't a soul on earth can stop you from doing whatever it is you want to do."

"Pa's right," Will said.

"Then you go with him, too," Minerva said. "I'm staying right here."

"I wanted to leave this place when Elizabeth passed on ten years ago," Will said. "Wanted to pack up and go, felt there was nothing to keep me here no more."

"Man's wife dies, it's natural for him—"

"It was more'n that, Ma. It's like Pa says. You got to kill yourself here to wrest a turnip or an onion from ground resists you all the way. Hell, Ma, you saw what—"

"Don't you cuss in this house!" Minerva snapped.

"You saw what happened when we planted that cornfield, didn't you? Had to work inside a ring of rifles, keep the Cassadas from blowing our heads off—"

"Almost did blow mine off," Bobbo said.

He was seventeen, the youngest of the boys, with his father's black hair and blue eyes, his mother's thin nose and jaw, her sensuous mouth. There were those who said there was French blood on Minerva's side, a Campbell back before the Indian Wars taking for his bride the daughter of a trapper. The Cassadas rumored it about maliciously that Minerva had a bit of Cherokee in her as well, discounting as though blind the hair as yellow as corn silk, the eyes as green as grass.

"What do you mean?" she asked.

"Now hush about that," Hadley said.

"What do you mean, Bobbo?"

"I was on my way to town with whiskey to sell—"

"She don't want to hear it," Hadley said.

"I want to hear it. What happened?"

"One of the Cassadas shot at me from in the bushes. Dropped two jugs full, broke em on the ground."

"That was hard-earned cash soakin into the earth," Hadley said.

"Why didn't you tell me this before?"

"Thought Pa told you," Bobbo said, and shrugged.

"You're makin this up," Minerva said.

"It's the truth, Ma," Bobbo said.

"Ma, there's something you just got to recognize," Will said. "If we try to touch an ear of corn we planted—"

"The feudin with the Cassadas'll pass," Minerva said. "A body waits long enough, everything on God's earth'll come to pass. Was Jeff Cassada's mother served as granny woman when Gideon was born. I'm not forgettin that, Had."

"That was more'n twenty years ago, Min! We're talking about—"

"I'm saying we was fast friends then, and we'll be friends again when the feudin is over and done with."

"You don't understand, Ma," Gideon said. "The Cassadas are laying claim to that field; they're sayin it's theirs by deed."

Gideon was twenty-three years old, the middle son, still as curly-haired and blond as he'd been when a baby, his mother's legacy, wasted on his brothers. He'd been named after the Biblical son of Joash the Abiezrite because in Judges 6:15, he said to God, "Oh my Lord, wherewith shall I save Israel? behold, my family is poor in Manasseh, and I am the least in my father's house." Gideon was born in 1821 at the height of the Panic, Hadley believing after years of deprivation that his clan truly *was* the poorest in all this Godforsaken corner of Virginia. Moreover, his newborn son was surely the runt of any litter, blondy-haired and blue-eyed, skinny as a rake, *truly* the least in the family—so Gideon he'd been named. But he had grown to be six feet three inches tall, weighing sixteen stone, with a huge barrel chest, and muscles on his arms as hard as lightard knots. Gideon was Minerva's favorite. She listened more closely to him now than she had her husband or her other sons.

"Ma," he said, "I love this place as well as you, but I think Pa's right, I think we ought to leave it. It ain't worth spilling a drop of Bobbo's blood nor anybody's over even the richest land in all the valley. And, Ma, we ain't got nothin but a mountaintop patch of dirt that was worth our lives to plant, and'll be worth our lives to touch an ear of corn when it's ready to pick. I say we go."

"*Can* we go, Ma?" Annabel asked.

"No," Minerva said flatly.

"We've got kin out there, you know," Bonnie Sue said.

"What kin? Who told you that?"

"Pa did. Man name of Jesse Chisholm. From Tennessee."

"I never heard of no Jesse Chisholm. You made him up, Hadley."

"No, he's kin sure enough."

"Where's he at then?"

"Texas, I suppose," Hadley said. "I wouldn't know him if I fell over him. Anyway, that ain't where I plan to take this family."

"This family's staying right *here*," Minerva said. "Was

my own brother waitin out west with open arms, I wouldn't leave Virginia." She lifted the sole remaining log and threw it into the fireplace. She did not know what she was going to cook for the midday meal. She was close to tears, but she would not show this either to Hadley or to her sons. To her daughters she said only, "We need more wood. Going to have bread, we'll want a fire."

The girls had changed out of their calicos and were wearing simple linen dresses that fell tentlike and loose about their bodies. Their legs and feet were bare; they stood just inside the doorway cut between the two rooms, Bonnie Sue womanly and round at the age of fifteen, Annabel two years younger and just beginning to show buttons of breasts, both girls blond and green-eyed like their mother.

"Fetch me some kindling," Minerva said.

There would have to be bread. With whatever they ate, there would be bread. She would bake it in the Dutch oven after she'd heated the lid and the oven itself on the fireplace coals. The bread would be corn bread, of course. But they were insisting the land was dead. And the land to her was corn.

"Min," Hadley said. He was standing very close to her; she did not turn to look at him. She busied herself with accepting the tinder the girls brought, and placing it under the single log. They had let the fire die. They had buried a woman she loved like her own mother and had let the fire die besides. "Min," he said, "I asked the squire how much he'd be wantin for that blue wagon of his. Be a big enough wagon to make it across the country. He said ninety dollars. We've put enough by to pay for the wagon and the journey, too, and get us some land besides when we—"

"You'd spend what's taken half our lives to save?"

"I'd spend it for the *next* half, Min. Damn it, I'm a farmer ain't got nothin to farm! There's *land* out west. It can be bought cheap, it can be planted. I want to go. Bailey says he'll sell us the wagon. I want to buy it, Min."

"Do what you like," she said, and angrily struck flint into the tinder.

The snake was not as big as some Hadley had handled; he guessed it was maybe four, five feet long—he hadn't measured the creature, and didn't plan to. In his time in these mountains, he had seen every kind of poisonous snake there was, from diamondbacks, like the one in the gunnysack, to copperheads, which if you cornered one hiding in the bushes, he'd shake his tail and make them bushes buzz to stop your heart. He'd even seen a cottonmouth or gapper or trapjaw or water moccasin, or whatever you wanted to call the damn thing, swimming in the Clinch like an eel and nearly scaring him half to death.

He'd been bit by a snake only once, and that one a rattler who'd struck first and only then given warning. Hadley'd gone back to the cabin and swallowed two whole cups of whiskey and then tied a rag tight around his arm between his heart and where the snake had bit him. He poured salt on the fang marks, where the arm was beginning to rise, and then he moved the rag a bit higher on his arm when the rising started to spread. He was alone in the cabin and beginning to get a bad headache and feeling somewhat dizzy and thinking maybe he shouldn't have drunk the whiskey, though some people hereabouts said whiskey was the only sure cure for snakebite. It was then Will came in the house and saw Hadley standing with one hand against the wall, his head bent, and went over to him fast and caught him before he fell down.

Will cut through the fang marks with a knife he'd brought back with him from the fighting in Texas. The knife had a walnut handle inlaid with silver. He sucked out the venom, and spat it on the floor, and then washed out his mouth with whiskey. He gave Hadley more whiskey to drink after he'd bandaged the wound, and then both men sat drinking till sundown, when the rest of the family got home. Hadley was drunk by then and eager to tell them all about how he'd almost died from snakebite, weren't for Will here with his Mexican knife. But they'd all been in town watching a man used to be with the Buckley & Weeks Circus, had himself a dancing bear now, and was selling a medicine supposed to be good for curing snakebite! Never did get to tell them what had happened. When Minerva in bed that night saw the bandage and asked him what was wrong with his arm, he said he'd got bit by a rattler while she was in town watching the dancing bear, and she said, "No, you didn't, Hadley."

That was the first and only time he'd been bit by a rattler or any other kind of snake. It was all in knowing what to expect from the creatures, and also in knowing how to handle them if you were of a mind to pick one up. Hadley picked up most any serpent he ever saw because the way he read the Bible, it said in John 3: "And no man hath ascended up to heaven, but he that came down from heaven, even the Son of man which is in heaven. And as Moses lifted up the serpent in the wilderness, even so must the Son of man be lifted up:

that whosoever believeth in him should not perish, but have everlasting life." Hadley believed in the Son of man and hoped for eternal life and felt that one way to guarantee life forever was to lift up the serpent in the wilderness.

Besides, he enjoyed snakes.

Liked them better than birds, you wanted to know. All birds did was make an infernal racket in the morning when a man was trying to sleep. Messed up the front porch, too. Snakes were clean and polite, and even the poisonous ones wouldn't strike at you less you stepped on them by accident or poked at them with a stick. The way he looked at it, snakes were the most misunderstood creatures on all God's earth. Person saw a snake on the ground, *whap*, he'd hit him with a rake sure enough. Poor thing was just slithering along, trying to make a living same as anybody else. But *whap* came the rake, woman standing on the porch screaming with her skirts up around her knees. Afraid that old snake was going to crawl up there and get between her legs, that was the thing of it. Wasn't no *man* on earth had to be fearful of reptiles, though, less his own pecker was tiny as a worm and could be put to shame by the littlest garden snake.

The bell in the rotting church steeple was tolling as the Chisholms rode into town that Sunday morning. Hadley stopped the mules in front of the open doors to let Minerva and the girls out of the cart. By the time he'd taken mules and cart around back to hitch them to the rail there, his sons had dismounted and were coming across the field, raising a cloud of dust behind them. It had not rained hereabouts for more than two weeks, but the Clinch was running swiftly nonetheless; Hadley could hear the water below, out of sight beyond the knoll. The moment his sons disappeared around the corner of the church, he lifted the gunnysack from inside the toolbox.

Three rows ahead of where Hadley took a seat inside the church, he could see his son Gideon looking across the aisle to where Rachel Lowery was sitting. Benjamin Lowery had come to Hadley one time last year and asked him what his son's intentions were. Hadley had said, "Which son?"

"Why, Gideon," Lowery said.

"His intentions toward what?" Hadley said.

"Toward my daughter Rachel," Lowery said.

Hadley was no fool, he knew what had been transpiring between his son and Rachel for the longest time. But it was rumored at the livery stable—where admittedly the talk was sometimes inaccurate—that Rachel had been fornicating with half the young men in town since she'd turned fourteen, the wonder being she hadn't borne a bastard before now and been publicly whipped for it.

"I know of no intentions he has toward your daughter," Hadley said, and that had been that.

Yet there was Gideon staring across the aisle at her now, his intentions plain as the nose on his face. Though here in church he surely was, it was another temple he longed to enter. God forgive me, Hadley thought, and turned his attention to what the fool preacher was saying. It took him only a moment to realize young Harlow Cooper was reading from the epistle of James.

" '. . . is first pure, then peaceable, gentle, and easy to be entreated, full of mercy and good fruits, without

partiality, and without hypocrisy. And the fruit of right-
eousness is sown in peace of them that makes peace.' "
Cooper cleared his throat. " 'From whence comes wars
and fightings among you? come they not hence, even of
your lusts that war in your members? Ye lust, and have
not: ye kill, and desire to have, and cannot obtain: ye
fight and war, yet ye have not, because ye ask not. Ye
ask, and receive not, because ye ask amiss, that ye may
consume it upon your lusts. Ye adulterers and adulter-
esses'!" Cooper said, and closed the Bible as though he
were slamming a door on an intruder. "That was from
the epistle of James," he said, as though he were riding
into town with fresh news. His eyes were roaming the
church. Hadley remembered those eyes watering on
the wind-swept ridge two days ago, when they'd buried
his mother. He was surprised to find them coming to
rest on him now.

"I chose this passage," Cooper said, "because Friday
morning I commended to God a woman who lived her
whole life through in peace with her neighbors. I chose
this passage because there has been strife in this town,
neighbor against neighbor, Christians behaving toward
each other in ways that are neither peaceable, gentle,
easy to be entreated, nor full of good fruits. I chose this
passage—"

Hadley rose.

"Your Worship," he said, using a term the congregation supposed was common currency among Papists,
and causing them to snicker at once, "I wonder why
you pick your Scriptures the way you do. Is it cause
you're ignorant of the word?"

"Sir," Cooper said, "I—"

"Your Worship," Hadley said, "I'm thinkin of what

you said over my mother's grave this Friday past. Now those words weren't fit for the burial of a woman who—"

"Mr. Chisholm," Cooper said, "I'm sorry if my choice of—"

"Those were words of celebration," Hadley said, "and here in these mountains we don't celebrate at graveside. We mourn those who've passed on, sir, and we were there last Friday to mourn a fine and decent—"

"I assure you, Mr. Chisholm—"

"A fine and decent woman," Hadley said. "You should have quoted not from Psalms, but instead from Proverbs 31, where it's written, 'Her price is far above rubies. The heart of her husband doth safely trust in her,' and so on down to 'She looketh well to the ways of her household, and eateth not the bread of idleness . . . ' "

"Yes, yes," Cooper said, and smiled out at the congregation for approval. " 'Her children arise up, and call her blessed; her husband also, and he praiseth her. . . . ' "

"You know it well enough now," Hadley said, "but where was it last Friday? Does it take a poor farmer to poke and prod you into recollection?"

"I assure you, sir," Cooper said, and saw that Hadley was reaching into his gunnysack. He could not imagine what was in the sack. He had seen a rattler only once, and that one a pygmy he'd almost tripped over in the woods. But yes, Hadley Chisholm was pulling a *rattlesnake* out of that sack, his right hand clutched behind the head, his left arm cradling the hidden body of the snake, his thumb on one side of the jaws, the forefinger on the opposite side, the remaining fingers tight around the . . . neck? Did snakes have necks or did their heads suddenly become their bodies? Cooper saw the snake's mouth opening and the fangs springing down from the upper jaw into striking position. He heard what he thought to be the sound of ominous rattling coming from inside the sack and realized in the next instant that it was only Hadley Chisholm chuckling.

" 'Now the serpent was more subtil than any beast of the field which the Lord God had made,' " Hadley quoted. "Where in the Bible is it written?"

"Genesis 3," Cooper said.

Hadley was standing just before the pulpit now, his eyes on the preacher, whose eyes were on the snake. "That's very good, Your Worship," he said. "Let's see what else you can remember with a little poking and prodding." As he said the word "poking," he thrust the head of the snake toward Cooper, who backed away. " 'Their poison is like the poison of a serpent,' " Hadley quoted; " 'they are like the deaf adder that stoppeth . . .' "

"That's—from . . ."

"Yes, Your Worship? 'That stoppeth her ear; which will not harken to the voice of charmers. . . .' "

"Psalms 58," Cooper said.

"Psalms is correct; you know your Psalms well. It was Psalms you quoted Friday; are you nothing but a psalm singer?" Hadley said, and climbed up onto the small raised platform to stand directly alongside Cooper. The snake was rattling ferociously from within the gunnysack; Hadley's hand still clutched firmly behind the open jaws. "Fear not the reptile," he said, and laughed. "He'll bite only a man who cannot tell his

Scriptures. So then . . . 'There be three things which are too wonderful for me, yea, four which I know not: The way of an eagle in the air . . .' "

" 'The way of a serpent upon the rock,' " Cooper said at once. "Proverbs 30."

"Excellent, sir!" Hadley said. " 'For they cast down every man his rod . . .' "

" 'And they became serpents!' " Cooper said triumphantly, and looked at the open jaws of the snake and quickly added, "Exodus 8."

"Exodus 7!" Hadley corrected.

"Exodus 7, just so, yes," Cooper said. "Exodus 7."

"It gets more difficult," Hadley said, and brought the snake up level with Cooper's face. "Look into them beady eyes, Your Worship. He's waitin to bite you should you slip on the word. Now then, are you ready?"

"You know, do you not," Cooper said, "that you are blaspheming in the house of—"

" 'For behold,' " Hadley said, " 'I will send serpents, cockatrices, among you,' " and thrust the snake forward and immediately pulled it back and said, " 'The serpent beguiled me, and I did eat,' " and again the snake's head came toward Cooper, who was about to say, "Jeremiah," its jaws opening, its fangs slanting down— he swore he could see droplets of venom on them. Hadley was now quoting from Matthew, yes, the passage about "I send you forth as sheep in the midst of wolves: be ye therefore wise as serpents, and harmless as doves." The eyes of the snake glared at Cooper malevolently. He backed away, Hadley and the snake following, the snake seeming much more interested in what was happening now, possessed of a will of its own.

Hadley shouted, " 'Ye serpents, ye generation of vipers, how can ye escape the damnation of hell?' " and the snake hissed and rattled, and Cooper turned and ran from the pulpit and the platform, toward the door on the back wall of the church. He grasped for the knob, his hand slippery and wet as he tried to twist it, certain the snake and Hadley were behind him, equally certain the snake would bite him on the seat of his indignity. He somehow managed to open the door and flee. Behind him, he heard the congregation laughing. Hadley thrust the snake triumphantly into the gunny-sack and threw his head back and laughed, too.

Squire Bailey was wearing a coat of the finest blue cloth, a darker blue velvet on the lapels, opening in a V over a waistcoat of cream-colored cashmere. The collar of his linen shirt showed above the white-cascade neck-tie crossed over his chest and held in place with an amethyst stickpin. His trousers were full at the hips, narrow from knee to ankle, the instep cut to accommo-date his highly polished boots. In his left hand he was holding a palm-leaf hat made on the island of Cuba. All in all, he looked the way his grandfather must have looked two generations back when the settlement was new and the term "squire" meant country gentleman and something more, a learned man of humor, intelli-gence, and charm.

He came down the church steps with a bull of a man named Jeremy Stokes, hired some three years back to oversee his sprawling plantation. Stokes had fought side by side with Andrew Jackson in the battle of New Orleans, or so it was rumored in the town, and the scar across the bridge of his nose had allegedly been put there by a British bayonet. He was decked out as splendidly as was his employer on this sunny April morning. Looking at them both as they sauntered down the church steps, Hadley could imagine them emerging from a fancy whorehouse after an hour or more of houghmagandy. Nor was the notion far-fetched; everyone in town knew that Horace Bailey's single failing—or at least the one failing to which he openly admitted—was women. There were people in town who "Squired" him to death, bowing and scraping not in respect for his wisdom and wit, which were nonexistent, hut only for the wealth he'd inherited along with his title. Hadley was not one of them.

"Good morning, Bailey," he said.

"Good morning, Chisholm."

Hadley took a small leather pouch from the pocket of his coat. "Here's the ninety dollars," he said, and jingled the coins in the pouch.

"What ninety dollars?" the squire said.

"For the wagon."

"And what wagon is that?"

"The wagon you agreed to sell me," Hadley said. "For the journey west."

"I think I'd prefer keeping that wagon," the squire said. "Mind you, I have no objections to you leaving these parts. I'm merely suggesting you do so in your own—"

"Bailey, let's stop the horseshittin," Hadley said. "You promised to sell me your wagon, and I'm here to pay for it."

"I recollect no such promise."

"Now come on, Bailey, we talked about it last Wednesday night."

"I recall no such conversation."

"I rode over to the plantation, the wagon was tied to a post just this side of the barn. We agreed to ninety dollars for it. That was the price and here's the ninety," Hadley said, and lifted the pouch again, and again jingled the coins in it. "We've got a verbal contract, Bailey. We agreed on a—"

"I had a verbal contract with that young preacher Harlow Cooper, too. I promised him he'd find a God-fearing people in this town, and not the kind who'd come in the Lord's house throwing snakes at a man. I reckon if one contract can be broken, then another can be broken just as easy. Wouldn't you say so, Stokes?"

"I would say so, Squire."

"In which case, good day, Chisholm."

Hadley stepped into the squire's path, his choices multiplying like the fishes and the loaves. He could punch the squire in the nose and cause him to bleed all over his cream-colored waistcoat and fancy white tie. Or he could drag the man squealing and bawling down to the Clinch, where he would baptize him proper. Or he could . . .

"A contract is a contract," he said simply.

"Go to law if you like," the squire said, and Hadley stepped aside and allowed them both to pass.

The law he went to was the Bible.

And in the Bible, in Galatians, he found the words: "Brethren, I speak after the manner of men; Though it be but a man's covenant, yet if it be confirmed, no man disannulleth, or addeth thereto." The way Hadley looked at it, he'd made a covenant with Horace Bailey, and now the squire was trying to annul it. Not only was that unlawful in the manner of men, it was also in direct conflict with what was written in the Bible, which was the law of God Almighty.

The Bailey plantation was laid out so that the main house was on high ground overlooking the fields and the slave quarters to the north, the barns and stables to the south, more fields to the east. Behind the house, the ground sloped sharply to the river below; the land here was rock-strewn and scrubby, unfit for planting. But fish could be seined from the river for yet another crop, and in the wintertime ice could be cut from it and stored in one of the plantation's three icehouses. The cotton hadn't yet been planted; it was still a bit early. Next week sometime, or perhaps the week after, the slaves would begin putting in seeds mixed with ashes to soften the hulls and help in the growing. Everyone in these parts knew when the squire was planting his cotton. The voices of the slaves singing could be heard all up and down the valley. The fields to the east were left to wild rye for pasture; the squire owned forty-one mules and horses, three hundred sheep, and seventy-four cows. He also owned one hundred twenty-two hogs and more chickens than anyone had ever bothered to count.

At the main house, Hadley and Will peeked through guillotine windows into the room beyond, lighted with fourteen blazing tapers in a hanging brass chandelier. The squire was dining. The Chisholms had taken their supper before sundown, but neither did they have a pair of house niggers to serve them. A wainscot of what appeared to be pine stained a darker hue ran around the entire room to a height of some four feet from the pegged wooden floor. Across the room were two windows identical to the one through which they spied goggle-eyed upon the squire, each window hung with what was either calico or printed linen, they could not tell.

The walls were covered with wallpaper the color of brick, a complicated design of birds and boughs and leaves upon it, red against a deeper red. There was a fireplace of intricately carved marble, and the chairs around the table were the finest Hadley had ever seen. In the corner, on a cherrywood lowboy, he recognized a napkin press. The squire was dining on what looked to be plates of real London pewter, not the newfangled lead stuff, and there was a sparkling white linen napkin tucked under his jowly chin. As they watched, a slender black woman poured wine from a decanter into the squire's long-stemmed glass goblet.

The clouds shifted, the moon broke through. Hadley and Will moved swiftly away from the house, heading below and to the south where Gideon was waiting with mules and horses, close by the Squire's stable. A man named Alexander Buchanan was sitting on a puncheon bench in front of the unlocked stable door, his rifle resting against the wall. He was whistling a tune Will had first heard in Texas, when he was riding with Lamar against the Mexicans. The tune had been sung by a lanky Texan astride a horse without a saddle, said he'd learned to ride that way from the Kiowa. Fellow said the tune was called "Zip Coon," but Will had heard it again a year or two later, same tune called "Turkey in the Straw" this time around. He sometimes wondered about things like that; like if a fellow made up a tune, could just *anybody* go around singing it and changing the name of it however he liked? Seemed akin to horse-stealing somehow.

Alexander Buchanan was whistling "Zip Coon" or "Turkey in the Straw," or whatever a body chose to call it, as Will came around the side of the stable, his father behind him. He had seen Buchanan often enough in town, had once bloodied his nose for him when the man boasted in the tavern (*and* in his cups) about having been abed with Rachel Lowery; Will hated livery-stable talk, specially when it moved from the stable to the tavern. It was no doubt true about Rachel; Will in fact knew that his own brother Gideon had sampled her quim. But talking about her that way was another thing. You enjoyed yourself with a woman, why then you shut up about it; you savored the pleasure, you anticipated it again, you didn't go spoiling it by sullying it.

He was glad it was Alexander Buchanan sitting here in front of the squire's unlocked stable door. No need for a lock on it, Will surmised, since anybody all up and down the Clinch'd have to be clear out of his mind to even attempt stealing a blade of grass from the Bailey plantation, what with Stokes and his armed patrol roaming the night. Alexander Buchanan was the squire's lock, sitting here on a puncheon bench and whistling a tune to the night. Will smiled, and put his knife to Buchanan's throat. The whistling stopped abruptly. Buchanan knew what the blade of a knife felt like, though he'd never had one pressed up against his throat before. The blade was laying flat just below his Adam's apple, but all a person had to do was turn the knife and there'd be a nice sharp cutting edge against his skin. He swallowed his whistling and sat there very still on the bench, backing away from the knife, trying to melt right into the silvered pine siding on the wall of the stable.

"That's a good boy," Will said, and stepped around Buchanan, turning the knife so that now the tip of the blade was against his throat. Buchanan peered at him in the darkness, moving only his eyes, his head still, his hands still, even his heart seemingly stopped.

"Is that you, Will Chisholm?" he asked.

"That's me, friend," Will said.

"What you want here?"

"We come for our wagon."

"You ain't got no wagon here."

"Don't argue with the man," Hadley said, coming around the side of the stable. "Just slit his throat and toss him over there in the bushes."

Buchanan's heart lurched, causing his Adam's apple to bob, scaring him half witless when he realized he might easily have been the cause of his own death, allowing it to bob up that way against the tip of the knife blade. Were they really here to take a wagon they somehow thought was theirs? Were they really going to slit his throat and toss him in the bushes?

"Your pa's kiddin, now ain't he?" Buchanan said.

"That's right. I ain't going to slit your throat," Will said. He paused and then said, "What I'm going to do is cut off your balls."

"Now come on, Will," Buchanan said, and swallowed, and again his Adam's apple bobbed up against the tip of the knife blade.

"Toss your *balls* over in the bushes," Will said. "Squire's hogs'll find them in the morning. Big balls like these have got to be Buchanan balls, the hogs'll say. Must be this Buchanan's a real lover-man. Must be he boasts around town bout lifting a girl's skirts."

"Now come on, Will," Buchanan said.

Hadley had opened the stable doors and was hauling out the squire's blue wagon. He glanced at Buchanan and said, "Ain't you slit his throat yet?" and Will said, "I was thinkin of cuttin off his balls, Pa," and Hadley said, "He ain't *got* none, Will."

He hung something on the door hasp then, little leather pouch with leather drawstrings, and came back to where Buchanan was sitting motionless, the knife still at his throat.

"I thought I told you t'slit the man's throat," he said to Will.

Buchanan was sure they were joking now.

He guessed.

But he was enormously relieved when they tied him hand and foot and stuck a piece of tow cloth in his mouth and wrapped a rag around that, and left him propped against the stable wall, then hauled the wagon downhill.

Sean Cassada had crept through the cornfield and lay hidden now in the staghorn bushes east of the Chisholm cabin, watching the family pack the wagon. They had unhitched the mules the moment they rode into the front yard; mules were cantankerous and unpredictable, as likely to bolt as bray, and Sean surmised they wished no mishap while they were loading. They moved in and out of the cabin like a line of ants, male and female alike carrying what appeared to be all their worldly possessions and putting them into the wagon willy-nilly; or at least if there was rhyme or reason to how they loaded it, Sean could fathom none. Tinware platters, plates and mugs, candle molds and chamber pots, rifles and hunting knives all went into the wagon, each Chisholm carrying something out of the cabin, and going back into it empty-handed to return a moment later with yet another load. Wool sack coats and cotton dresses, pantaloons and buckskin pants, butcher knife and— Ah, Bonnie Sue, carrying tight against her sweet bosom a mantel clock; how often had he unfastened her bodice and reached inside to touch those tender breasts?

Will Chisholm, who had threatened to strangle him one morning outside church, was loading into the jockey box at the front of the wagon all the family's smaller tools—axes and mallets, jack plane and adze, gimlet and augur, level and square. Gideon was lashing the family plow to one side of the wagon, Bobbo carrying shovel and spade to the opposite side. There now came Bonnie Sue from the cabin again, this time carrying three, nay, *four* grubbing hoes, which she handed to her brother Bobbo. She looked directly into the bushes then, and Sean was certain she'd seen him, and yet the night was so dark; had she heard the pounding of his heart? Were the Chisholms truly leaving? Sean could not believe this, and yet the evidence was there before his eyes to see: tonight he was losing his Bonnie Sue, whose breasts he had kissed, and once tickled the nipples of with a blade of grass, her skirt and petticoats up around her knees, naked beneath she was but would not let him higher than where her drawers might have reached had she been wearing any.

She did not come out of the cabin again for the longest time. Sean lay there crouched in the bushes, wondering what she could be doing inside there, and then realizing when he saw her in the door with a broom that she was sweeping the place out before they left it. He recognized with a sickening lurch that the time of departure was nigh; they were truly leaving this place behind, and with it Sean Cassada's broken heart. He could smell the choking dust from where he lay in the bushes. It rose from the wooden cabin floor in a smothering cloud; a lot of good a proper floor did except to keep out snakes, and even that not so well. Bonnie Sue stood in the doorway with the broom in her hands, and looked again into the bushes, and this time Sean opened his eyes wide to show the whites, and she nodded briefly, and he knew for certain she had seen him.

Gideon, the biggest of the lot, was leading the mules toward the wagon now. The wagon was painted a blue the color of chicory in bloom. Sean had never seen such a wagon before, a good four feet wide and half again as long, or maybe more, ten or twelve feet, he guessed, with iron tires on the wheels, and wooden bows above for a cover, but none in place now. A grease bucket was hanging from the rear axle, and Bobbo was filling it now with pine tar and pork fat; he could smell the tar clear over here in the bushes. Annabel Chisholm, who looked so much like Bonnie Sue that Sean could hardly wait for her to grow up, was climbing up into the wagon over the lowered tailgate and plopping down on the pile of quilts and pillows stacked inside near the butter churn. Old Hadley Chisholm came out of the cabin and tested the lashing on the plow and the other tools, and lifted the lid on the jockey box and looked on in there, and then tested the harness on the mules. Sean heard Gideon ask, "All right, Pa?" and Hadley nodded and went back in the cabin. When he came out again he was carrying four gallons of whiskey hugged against his chest, and he went in the cabin three more times and came out with another dozen gallons that he packed in the wagon.

Sean knew she was behind him there in the sumac even before she rested her hand on his shoulder. "Shhh," she said, and lay down beside him, and moved into his open arms. His hands went at once to the cotton bodice she wore, his fingers unbuttoned it, he reached inside and cupped her right breast in his hand, and kissed her on the lips. His heart was beating wildly, he frantically clutched her to him and kissed her entire face, her cheeks, her nose, her closed eyes, fearful he was making too much noise, terrified Will would come thrashing into the bushes to separate them, but knowing she was leaving, and wanting to kiss her, to touch her, to hold her. He released her breast and then grabbed for it again and released it at once and lowered his hand to where the hem of her cotton skirt had climbed to her shin, and lifted skirt and petticoat both and slid his hand up over her legs. She would stop him at any minute, her brother would find them any minute, God would strike him dead with a lightning bolt, something would happen before he touched the silken softness of—he could not believe his hand was, he could not believe she had allowed, he felt a wild excitement he had never before known, and he rolled, he tried to roll her over onto her back, but she sat up instead, abruptly and swiftly, her hand clamping onto his wrist. Moving his hand from between her legs, she lowered skirt and petticoat, and then leaned into him to kiss him on the mouth. He brought his hand to the back of her head, and felt her long hair cascading over his fingers, and then her lips were on his for what he knew was the last time, she was rising, she was standing, she was smoothing her dress, she whispered, "Never forget me, Sean," and was gone.

He lay there watching.

Hadley Chisholm sat on the wagon seat with Minerva beside him. Both girls were inside the wagon now, Bonnie Sue looking out at the bushes behind which he was hiding. On horseback out in front of the wagon were Gideon, Will, and Bobbo.

Sean thought: *They're going. She's really leaving.*

He wanted to step out from the bushes and stand on Chisholm land like the man he was and yell for them to leave Bonnie Sue behind. Yell that he loved her. But if he done that, why then Will would just turn his big old gelding around and come riding up to where Sean stood like a damn fool with tears in his eyes, and he'd as soon strangle Sean as spit on him. Else Gideon would raise his old rifle and take careful steady aim in his easy slow way and blow Sean's brains to hell and gone.

He lay in the bushes instead and tried to get a glimpse of Bonnie Sue, but she was looking ahead, toward the front of the wagon, she was looking west. He knew he would never again see her as long as he lived, and he told himself it was important that he remember this departure, remember it as the night Bonnie Sue moved out of his life. His eyes were accustomed to the darkness now, he could see as sharply as a cat.

Minerva Chisholm turned her head for a look at the cabin. And brought her hand to her mouth. And held it there an instant, the fingertips gently touching her parted lips.

It was this Sean would remember.

II

MINERVA

"You think I'm going down that river, you're crazy," she said.

They stood on the banks of the Ohio, just above the Falls, and watched the water crashing in waves ten feet high on the rocks below. It had taken them almost two weeks to get here. They had traveled through a countryside as civilized and as settled as any back home. The trail through the Gap and across Kentucky was trafficked with farmers and merchants coming and going with produce and goods to sell. The Chisholms drank fresh milk and ate fresh vegetables. At one farm along the way, they purchased a suckling pig and roasted it that night on the banks of a stream. Wherever there was a barn, they asked a farmer for permission to spend the night in it. Sometimes they were asked to pay a little something for the roof over their heads. More often than not, the people living along the road were generous and hospitable. Two weeks to get here, Minerva thought. That meant it'd take only two weeks to get right back where they belonged.

"Person'd drown out there in a minute," she said.

"There're channels go through," Will said.

"I don't see no channels," she said, and took a step back from the edge, refusing to look again at the river below, boiling with logs and stumps and broken steamboat paddles.

"Your son's *been* here, he knows this damn river," Hadley said.

"Cussin ain't about to get me on no vessel intendin to come down that waterfall. Wild Indians couldn't—"

"There's chutes, Ma," Will said. "You go through one of the chutes."

"I don't care if there's chutes or channels or secret underwater passages known only to the men who founded this garboiling town. I want to go home, Hadley. First thing in the mornin, I want to turn around and go home."

"First thing in the mornin, we're going west," Hadley said.

"*You*'re goin west maybe," Minerva said.

"We're *all* goin west," Hadley said.

"You went over these falls, Will?"

"You don't go *over* them, Ma. You go *through* them, sort of. I took a skiff downriver, and then got on a steamboat in Shippingport."

"Then let's *us* get on a steamboat downriver, too," Minerva said.

"Cost too much," Hadley said, and shook his head.

"How much?"

"Fourteen dollars apiece almost. Plus whatever they'd charge for the wagon and animals."

"Doubt if they'd even take those aboard, Pa," Will said. "Weren't none on the steamboat to N'Orleans."

"Hadley," she said, "I'm goin home. If I got to hire out to a traveling circus . . ."

"Min . . ."

"As a trapeze artist or a bearded lady . . ."

"It ain't really dangerous," Will said. "The current's fast, and the river changes width a lot. . . ."

"I'm sure happy to hear that," Minerva said.

"And there's islands and rocks all along the way. . . ."

"Soundin better all the time."

"But look down below there, Ma. Look at all them kinds of craft floatin on the river down there. Now *they* made it safe through the Falls, didn't they? Ain't no reason we can't do the same."

Below, there were flatboats and keelboats, galleys and barges; bateaux, pirogues, dugouts, and skiffs; scows and arks and rafts and canoes; steamboats and schooners and even brigs that had sailed from Europe. She could scarcely name a third of the vessels she saw down there on the river, but the very profusion of them filled her with a new dread. Even if they did make it safely over the Falls—or *through* them, as her son insisted—wouldn't they then collide with one or another of the craft below, so clotted was the river?

"No," she said, and shook her head.

"Let's find a livery stable," Hadley said, and sighed.

The city frightened her as much as had the river.

Back home, she knew what to expect, there were no surprises. You came into town on a wide dirt road lined with board-and-batten buildings. There were several smaller dirt roads branching off it on either side, likewise lined with wooden structures, some of them dating back to the time of the first settlement. The town proper started just beyond the branch to Bristol. The wide main street of the town was, in fact, the old Wilderness Road itself. They had followed it west when they left on the twenty-second—she would never forget that date—and it had taken them clear to the Cumberland Gap. There were four hundred some-odd people ("some of them *mighty* odd," Hadley said) in the town Minerva called home. There were twenty thousand here in Louisville.

The noise alone was enough to make her ill.

She hurried her daughters along the sidewalks, clinging to their hands, one on either side of her, fearful they would all be trampled underfoot if they did not keep pace with a population that rushed and pushed and jostled shoulder to shoulder everywhere around them. The sidewalks were lined with lampposts. The streets were paved with limestone blocks. In the streets there were men riding horses, jackasses, and mules. Carriages and coaches clattered and rattled, carts and wagons rumbled by—it was worth a person's life to try crossing to the other side! Here now came a burly black man pushing a wheelbarrow and shouting to another man lounging in the doorway of a saloon. The city was a blur of noise and motion, horses neighing and mules braying, peddlers shouting their wares to passers-by, delivery men banging crates on the sidewalk, even babies bawling louder than any Minerva had heard in her life. The din everywhere called to mind for sure the passage in Revelations, where John beheld a great red dragon, having seven heads and ten horns, and seven crowns upon his head, and his tail drew the third part of the stars of heaven, and did not cast them to the earth, and none of that could have made more commotion than was here in this noisy, noisome city of Louisville, Kentucky.

The girls wanted to dawdle, oohing and ahhing over whatever caught their fancy in shopwindows along the way. But Minerva briskly pulled them along past silversmith and coppersmith, tailor shop and pharmacy, a saddlery selling fancy Spanish saddles for forty dollars each, a furniture store and three mercantile stores, one of them advertising dry goods from Boston and New York. They rushed past theaters and dining rooms, taverns and more saloons than a thirsty man could drink his way through in a year. When at last Minerva found a store selling the staples she needed to replenish their dwindling supplies, she threw open the door as though she and her daughters were being chased by highwaymen, and closed it immediately behind her.

Silence.

Blessed silence.

The proprietor was a ruddy-faced man with a bald head; he regarded the three of them with mild amusement, his eyes twinkling behind gold-rimmed spectacles, a faint smile on his mouth. Minerva suddenly saw herself through his eyes—she was scared of this city, and was certain her fear showed on her face. The man's smile annoyed her because she felt it indicated ridicule or pity, and she could abide neither.

"What do you find so amusing?" she snapped.

"Ma'm?" he said, and his eyes popped open wide behind his glasses, and she knew she'd made an error in

judgment, and blushed as she hadn't since she was
Bonnie Sue's age. In apology, she told the truth. "The
streets frighten us," she said.

"Not me," Annabel said.

"Hush," Minerva said. "We're far from home, and
have never seen a city this size."

"It's a good city," he said, "though the waters are
stagnant and the inns infested with varmints. Will you
be staying at one of the hotels?"

"No," Minerva said, "but much obliged. Is that coffee I spy?"

"That's coffee."

"How much the pound?"

"Fifty cents."

"Fifty cents!" she said.

"That's not a bad price," he said.

"It's an outrageous price. Back home I can get it for
thirty."

"It's been thirty-eight here, even before it got
scarce."

"I'll need it anyway," Minerva said. "But you
couldn't do better with a pistol and a mask on your
face."

The man laughed.

"We're going west," Annabel said.

"Are you now?" he said. "How many pounds will
you be wanting, ma'm?"

"Make it two. But *just*," she said. "We're not going
west, Annabel."

"Sure we are," Annabel said.

"Where west, young lady?"

"California," Annabel said.

"Or Oregon," Bonnie Sue said.

"We haven't decided yet," Annabel said.

"We're going *home*, is where we're going," Minerva said.

"And wise you'd be. How are you for cornmeal, ma'm?"

"How do you mean wise?"

"You'd be foolhardy to attempt the trip this time of year."

"The Falls, do you mean?"

"Well, the Falls aren't so bad. I'm talking about running into snow in the mountains. Did you say meal?"

"Five pounds," Minerva said. "What snow?"

"In the Rockies. You're late starting. Were you hoping to meet a wagon train in Independence? Cause they're all gone by now, you see, and there's nothing would please the Indians more than to come across a lone wagon on the prairies. Those bloody savages'll—"

"You needn't worry," Minerva said. "We're going—"

"—scalp your menfolk, burn your wagon, steal your horses, take you and your daughters captive. . . . How are you for molasses?"

The saloon was a long narrow room with a bar along one side of it and a cluster of tables at the far end. A mounted elk's head was hanging in the center of the far wall, and there were five or six men looked like tough customers sitting at the tables there drinking hard liquor. Gideon and Will stood at the bar, drinking beer, three or four other men ranged along the bar beside them. A mirror framed in dark wood hung behind the bar, together with some portraits of what looked like riverboat pilots. There was also a picture of a showboat called the *Delta Maiden*, with a black dwarf wearing a checked suit and a straw skimmer, standing on the dock alongside the paddle wheel.

"Man was all out of linchpins," Will said, and shook his head.

"Kingbolts, too," Gideon said.

"You'd think a town this size . . ."

"I just hope Pa had better luck finding a cover."

"We could maybe still get the chain and rope we need."

"We'd do better in Evansville, I'm thinkin."

"Or maybe Independence."

"We ever *make* it that far."

The man standing at Gideon's elbow suddenly turned to them and said, "Excuse me, gentlemen, but if you plan to stock a wagon, it's Independence will be better."

He looked to be about Gideon's age, maybe a year or two older, handsome enough fellow with black hair partly hidden by the blue felt wide-brimmed hat he wore tilted over his forehead. His eyes were a brown the color of wild ginger, and he was smiling now and showing teeth that had never once been yellow.

"Cause Independence is the jumping-off place," he said. "That is, if you was planning on going west."

"We was," Gideon said.

"My name's Lester Hackett," the man said, and extended his hand.

"Gideon Chisholm," Gideon said, and shook hands briefly and cautiously. "My brother Will here."

Will nodded.

"You're startin a bit late, though," Hackett said. He was leaning casually against the bar, one elbow on the polished mahogany top. The saloon was a drab and dreary place; he twinkled in it like a blue jay flashing through the treetops. Dressed in blue from tip to toe: the blue felt hat, and then a blue jacket with velvet collar and cuffs, blue string tie hanging over the front of his ruffled shirt—only thing wasn't blue on him, that and the brown boots. "Trains start making up late April, early May."

"That's what this is," Gideon said. "Early May."

"May the third, you want to know," Will said. He resented Hackett's intrusion. Back in Virginia, strangers didn't come breaking in on tavern talk unless they were politely wanting directions to Bristol or Fincastle or westward to the Gap.

"The third it is, right enough," Hackett said, and nodded. "But in Evansville downriver, it's already the sixth. And in Independence, which is clear the other side of Missouri, it's now the middle of June."

"I don't follow you," Will said.

"I'm telling you, sir, that with any luck you'll reach St. Louis by the end of the month, and you've got to figure at least another two weeks on top of that for the trip to Independence. That'll put you the second week in June. All the trains'll have left a month or more before you get there."

"There's bound to be some late travelers," Gideon said.

"Not likely," Hackett said.

"We'll find some."

"There'll be none left, Mr. Chisholm. You did say Chisholm?"

"I said Chisholm."

"Gideon, was it?"

"Gideon."

"Gideon, I'm telling you they'll have gone long since. You'll not find anyone foolish enough to risk snow in the Rockies. They've got to be well beyond them before the fall. You get snow sometimes early as the middle of September. You got any idea how many miles you're talking about? Where do you plan on heading? Is it California or Oregon?"

"We ain't decided yet," Will said.

"Well, sir, when do you hope to make your decision, would you tell me? When the Indians have scalped all in your party and are dancing on your graves?"

"I don't see as that's any business of yours, sir."

"Pardon me then," Hackett said, and turned away.

"Besides, sir, how do you know so much about the journey west?"

"Let it pass," Hackett said, his back still to them. "It's no business of mine, you're right, sir."

"You're the one as opened the discussion," Gideon said.

"And I'm the one as now is closing it," Hackett said, but turned to face them again. "Thank you, gentlemen, for passing the time of day with one who's only been guiding parties west since the year 1837, and who's familiar not only with Independence as a jumping-off place, but also with Westport and Fort Leavenworth, and St. Joe fifty-five miles to the northwest."

"If you're a guide," Will said, "you'd best be hurrying, Mr. Hackett. It's already the middle of June in Independence."

"Well put, sir," Hackett said, and began laughing. "Well put. I've already missed the wagons this year for sure. Believe me, were it not for business I've had here in Louisville, I'd have been somewhere on the Missouri border this very minute. This is when the trains are leaving, friends. You'll be late by a month when you get there. Take the advice of a well-meaning stranger. Go back to where you've come from." He lifted his whiskey glass, drank, smacked his lips, and then wiped the back of his hand across his mouth. "Where might that be? I'd guess someplace upriver if it wasn't for the sound of your voices. That's neither Ohio nor Pennsylvania I'm hearing."

"It's Virginia," Gideon said.

"Then you're less than two weeks from the Gap. Turn around. Go back."

"We've come this far—"

"This *far*?" Hackett said. "Why, when you get to Independence, you'll *still* have two thousand miles to travel before you reach the west coast, whether it's Oregon or California you choose. Turn around now and save yourselves a lot of grief."

"I think not," Will said, and shook his head.

"Then let me buy you both a drink," Hackett said. "For you're either heroes or madmen, and I've never before met either."

It was late afternoon and the lamplighter was making his rounds. Behind the glass panels on top of each post, the lamps sputtered into light, flickered, and then began to glow more boldly, casting warm circles onto the sidewalk. The city seemed less frightening now. The crowds had thinned, there was less traffic and less noise.

The wooden sign outside the hotel creaked in a brisk breeze blowing in off the river. The grocer had warned Minerva that the hotels in Louisville were bug-infested, but she didn't plan to sleep here, and besides, the sign told her that a woman was the proprietor. Laden with groceries, she marched her daughters through the lobby to the front desk. A clerk there was writing something into a leather-bound book. She waited till he was finished.

"I'm lookin for Alice Pierson," she said.

"Yes?" the clerk said.

"Yes. Is there an Alice Pierson here?"

A woman in her sixties, sitting and reading a newspaper in a chair near the desk, looked up sharply and said, "I'm Mrs. Pierson. What is it?"

"Are you the one whose name is on the sign outside?"

"That's me," the woman said. She had not risen from the chair. Her hair was white, and she wore a long black dress, four strands of pearls draped over her bosom. She looked up at Minerva and the girls along the length of a nose too long for her face.

"Is it you that's proprietress of this place?" Minerva asked.

"It is," Mrs. Pierson said.

"Then my daughters and I are wantin baths."

"Put your parcels down," Mrs. Pierson said, getting out of the chair. "We'll find you some tubs and hot water."

"How much will it be for each of us?"

"Fifteen cents for a bath and clean rinse."

"Does soap come with it?"

"How else would you get the grime of travel off you?"

"Ah, is it that plain then?" Minerva said.

"Where are you coming from?"

"Virginia. And headin back in the morning."

"Take your bath first," Mrs. Pierson said.

In three wooden tubs, they soaked luxuriantly, washing their hair with scented soap, pouring buckets of hot water over their slippery bodies, watching the suds cascade away as frothily as had the Falls of Ohio. To think of even attempting those Falls! No, she was armed with knowledge now; the storekeeper had given her priceless information. Hadley might be stubborn sometimes, but he was never foolhardy or wasteful. It would be senseless to continue on to Independence with no hope of finding a wagon train when they got there. What was the point of risking the Falls and then trekking clear across the state of Illinois, only to reach a town on the edge of nowhere, with nowhere to go from it? Be like getting to a party a day late. Hadley would see the foolishness of it, she was certain of that.

She would talk to him when she got back to the livery stable. He'd made arrangements to spend the night there. Wouldn't be nothing like sleeping in a fine hotel, but at least it was a roof over their heads, and besides, who but a rich man could afford the prices in this city? She'd seen a sign in the window of an inn, said breakfast, dinner, or supper could be had for twenty-five cents. But it was costing them forty cents to corn and hay each of the animals! Shouldn't complain, she supposed, since the family would be sleeping there as well, free of charge. Man said it'd be all right to cook their supper in the yard outside, too. Be good to get back home again. Cook inside her own house, take a bath in front of her own fire, have a cup of hot sassafras tea afterward, crawl into bed under quilts Eva Chisholm had made, bless her heart.

The clock on the wall read ten minutes past four; they would have to be hurrying back. Minerva got out of the tub and began drying herself with one of the towels Mrs. Pierson had provided. Bonnie Sue was lying back in her own tub, her knees islands in the water, eyes closed, hair trailing over the tub's wooden sides.

"Bonnie Sue?" Minerva said. "Got to go now."

"Mmm," Bonnie Sue said.

"Come on now, honey."

Across the room, Annabel had already dried herself and was putting on her underdrawers.

"Bonnie Sue?"

"I could stay in this tub forever."

"You can take baths aplenty when we get home."

"Are we really goin home, Ma?"

"You heard that man, didn't you? Indians'd eat us alive, we got out west there."

"Mmm," Bonnie Sue said.

"Out of that tub—come on now."

From across the room, Annabel said, "Mama, there's blood in my drawers."

"Let me see," Minerva said. She put down the towel, pulled her petticoat over her head, and then walked barefooted to where her daughter was scrutinizing the underdrawers. Minerva took them from her.

"Is it the pip coming?" Annabel asked.

"Looks like the start of it, sure enough," Minerva said.

"Whooooop-eeeee!" Annabel shouted, and began dancing around the room naked, twirling her towel over her head, and setting the oil lamps to shaking.

"Ain't nothin but a lifelong chore," Bonnie Sue said from her tub. "I got mine when I was twelve."

"It's nothin to grieve about," Minerva said, "nor nothin to rejoice in neither."

"Just a lifelong chore," Bonnie Sue repeated.

"Get on out of that tub. I'll find somethin for you to bind yourself, Annabel. You'd best wear the stained drawers till we get back to the livery stable."

Annabel danced around her sister as she got out of the tub. Then suddenly, she stopped dead still, and looked at her mother, and asked, "Can I have babies now?"

"You ain't careful," Minerva said.

"I've been guiding parties west for seven years now," Lester Hackett said. "Made the trip to the coast and back a total of five times. It's not difficult, if you do it right. You're planning to do it wrong, lads."

They'd been drinking steadily for the past hour or more. There was a glazed expression on Gideon's face, but he still seemed to be listening intently to every word Hackett uttered. Will had lost interest long ago. Across the room, a painted whore had taken a seat with three tough-looking men appeared to be desperadoes. Every now and again, a garter flashed. Made Will wonder when it was he'd last had a woman.

"Are you Irish?" Hackett asked.

"Who?" Gideon said.

"You," Hackett said.

"Are you?"

"Isn't everybody?" Hackett said, and laughed.

"By way of Scotland," Gideon said. "Scotch-Irish."

"That's decent, too. Long as you're not Dutch. Let me buy you another drink. Whereabouts in Ireland?"

"County Antrim."

Six graves on that ridge now, Will thought. *Grandma Chisholm from County Antrim, alongside her husband William Allyn; my two brothers born after me who never saw the light of day; and my wife and baby.*

"Would you like to know how I happened to miss the wagon trains west?" Hackett asked.

"How?" Gideon said.

"I came to Louisville in pursuit of a poker game heading downriver on a steamboat out of Cincinnati. Came from Carthage with four hundred dollars in cash, hoping to build it into a small fortune I might invest in California. Lost all of it save thirty dollars. Would've lost the thirty, too, hadn't had it tucked in a pocket I rarely use."

"That's a lot of money," Gideon said.

"Lost my pocket watch besides, and a ring my daddy willed to me, not to mention a horse and saddle, a fine Kentucky rifle with brass and silver inlays, and a pair of Spanish pistols."

"That's a lot of money," Gideon said again, as though he'd completely missed Hackett's listing of all the other things he'd lost.

"I've got three dollars and fifty cents to my name," Hackett said. "Do you know what I plan to do with it?"

"What?" Gideon asked.

"Drink it away in this fine saloon with you two Irish gents from Virginia."

"*Scotch*-Irish," Gideon said.

"Aye, after which I'll wander down to the Falls and throw myself in the river."

"No, you won't," Gideon said, and grinned.

"Yes, I will," Hackett said, and grinned back at him.

Died when she was eighteen, Will thought, *her and*

his newborn daughter both, the baby gasping out her final breath scarce before she'd taken her first, Elizabeth suddenly raising her head from the pillow to search the room for him, seeing him, reaching out her hand to him—and then falling back again on the pillow, dead. He'd gone to stand alone behind the cabin, shouted his rage to the universe, and then wept in the night till his father came up beside him and, weeping too, put his arm around him, and led him inside, and put him to bed.

"Here's what I'll do for you," Hackett said.

"Drink up," Gideon said.

"Cheers," Hackett said. "If you're mad enough or courageous enough to want to continue west after all I've told you—"

"Ma wants to go home," Gideon said.

"And right she is. But what does Pa say? Is there a father with you here in Louisville?"

"Oh, yes. Yes, indeed. Hadley Chisholm himself."

"Here's to Hadley Chisholm then."

"Here's to him then," Gideon said.

"What does *he* say?"

"About what?"

The question took Hackett aback. He stared at Gideon. Gideon stared back at him. "About *what?*" Hackett said.

"That's right," Gideon said, and drank.

In the middle of a chore, he'd remember something he wanted to ask Elizabeth. He'd start back for the cabin thinking to find her there, and remember suddenly that she was dead and gone, he could no more talk to her again than he could move mountains. And he'd start to crying. His hand on the plow or the ax, he'd cry. Annabel was but three years old then; she came up to him in the field one day, blond little thing in a pinafore had been her sister's.

"Will," she said, "you has got to stop."

Sobbing, he said, "I know, darlin."

And she said, "Cause my heart is broke when I hear you weep."

The whore cut loose with a laugh deep from her belly. Frizzy-haired brunette, he could smell her perfumed tits clear across the saloon. One of the men at the table had his hand on her leg, just below the garter, squeezing her white-powdered thigh. She laughed again, and Will thought suddenly of all the whores he'd fucked from Texas clear back to Virginia when he'd finished fighting with Lamar. Gone there to forget Elizabeth, something he never could have done in a million years anyway. Rode through the Gap and across Kentucky to right here in Louisville, this was in April of '36—he'd left home soon as news of the Alamo massacre reached Virginia. Down the Ohio to where it joined the Mississippi, and then on to New Orleans. Caught up with the Texas cavalry on the nineteenth, rode two days with them to the San Jacinto ferry, where Houston was waiting to ambush the Mexicans.

A Georgian was commanding the cavalry. Will almost laughed out loud when he heard the man's name—Mirabeau Buonaparte Lamar. In the grove of oak trees there was the low whinny of horses, the pawing of hoofs, and then a sudden hush. Will heard someone whisper, "There they are," and then Lamar gave the order to charge. Saw more damn blood that day. Fucked his way back to Virginia. Fucked every whore he ever met on the way back. Couldn't forget Elizabeth and neither could he forget ten thousand men yelling, "Remember the Alamo!" Sabers slashing. Blood on the neck of his raindrop gelding. Fucked every whore.

"Does your pa want to continue on west?"

"Oh, yes," Gideon said.

"Then here's my proposition," Hackett said. "I'll guide you to St. Louis. How's that sound?"

"Sounds good," Gideon said.

"No charge," Hackett said. "Free of charge. Just tuck me in the wagon someplace, and give me a little bit to eat every now and then. How's that sound?"

"Sounds very good," Gideon said. "How's that sound, Will?"

"I'm sorry," Will said. "I wasn't listenin."

"Help you find a vessel to take you down the Ohio, and then guide you to St. Louis," Hackett said. "I've got friends there'll get me a job. Once I earn myself the price of a good horse, which I figure to be about a hundred fifty dollars including a bridle and saddle—"

"That's a bit high," Gideon said. "High by twenty dollars, I'd say."

"No, that's the price in St. Louis."

"Back in Virginia—"

"Well, maybe a hundred forty."

"A hundred thirty, Lester."

It seemed to Will that time was their chiefest enemy. He did not want to go back to Virginia; there was nothing for him there but painful memories and tavern whores. But neither did he want to cross Indian territory alone. If the wagon trains had already left or were leaving, then the best they could hope for was to catch up somewhere along the trail beyond Independence. If

Hackett could help them save time, then he'd be worth all the food he could eat between here and St. Louis.

"About your proposition," Will said.

"What proposition is that, Will?"

"The one you just put to us. About—"

"What*ever* it was, I've got a better one," Hackett said. "Now you may have noticed that sweet young lady across the room, who happens to have a dozen or more sisters down the line. Why don't we ask her to take us three little darlins home?"

"Sounds good, Lester," Gideon said, and clapped him on the back. "Let's go get some women, Will."

"Let's go get some coffee," Will said.

Last thing on earth she wanted was a fight with her son.

She'd convinced Hadley, told him everything the storekeeper had told her, and of course he'd seen the sense of it, and had agreed to turn back. Now here was Will with a stranger who'd offered to guide them to St. Louis.

Supper was cooking in the yard outside the stable, the rich aroma of frying pork blowing in to mingle with the stench of horses, mules, hay, and manure. It was cold in the stable, but they kept the doors cracked a bit anyway; the stink would have been intolerable otherwise. Lester Hackett was smoking a long cigar, his booted feet up on the watering trough, his hat tilted back on his head.

"What I can get you is a broadhorn," he said. "Now what she is, she's similar to a flatboat, but not quite so crude. She's got a deck, and a cabin for the ladies to set in, but she's only got two men handling the long oars— that's where she gets her name—and the patroon at the rudder in back, and that's it. The patroon I have in mind is a man named Jimmy Jackson, no relation to the former president. Patroons is what they call these riverboat captains. He owes me a favor; I think I can get him to take the wagon and the entire party for an even twenty dollars. That's inexpensive, if you know riverboat prices."

"Would that be all the way to Evansville?" Will asked.

"Yes," Lester said. "I've not talked to him, yet, mind you, but I'm sure that'll be the destination and the price."

"That's very nice, Mr. Hackett," Hadley said, "but it happens we ain't *goin* to Evansville. Where we're goin is back to Virginia."

"Now who in hell decided *that*?" Will said.

"You cuss one more time in this house—"

"It ain't but a stable, Ma," Will said. "Who went and decided we're turnin around?"

"*I* did," Hadley said. "I'm still head of this family, son, and I ain't about to lead it into danger. Now I know it cost us a penny to get here, but what I plan to do is sell the whiskey we brung with us, make up the loss that way. You know what kind of prices they're getting here?"

"Pa, I found us a man can get us to St. Louis in no more'n ten days," Will said. "Ain't that right, Lester?"

"That's right."

"And if we travel fast when we leave Independence—"

"Wagon trains've already *left* Independence," Minerva said.

"I know that, Ma. But we can catch up with them, ain't that right, Lester?"

"It can be done, yes," Lester said.

"Common rum's selling for four dollars a gallon here," Hadley said. "Brandy's fetchin six. I want to sell my whiskey high, and head back home fore the Cassadas take over my still. That's what I want to do," Hadley said.

"Aye," Minerva said, and nodded.

"Let's put it to a vote," Will said.

"We don't need no vote. I already decided," Hadley said.

"There's others in this family," Will said.

Hadley looked at his son.

"Yes, Pa," Will said. "I got a life, too. I want to go west. I want to start livin my life, Pa."

Hadley looked at him a moment longer. Then he turned away and said, "Go on and vote then."

"Pa?"

"I said go on and vote."

"What's your say?"

"You know my say. I want to go home."

"Ma?"

"Aye. Home."

"Gideon?"

Gideon looked into his father's eyes.

"West," he said.

"Bobbo?"

"West."

"Bonnie Sue?"

"West."

"Annabel?"

"West."

"I vote west, too," Will said, and paused. "Pa?" he said.

"I heard it," Hadley said, and walked suddenly to the wagon and pulled his gunnysack from the toolbox. Moving to where Lester was standing all fine and fancy in his frills, Hadley said, "You've been west and back a dozen times, is that it?"

"Five times, sir," Lester said.

Minerva watched. She knew what was in the gunnysack. She suspected that Lester knew as well, though there was no sound from inside the sack, nothing to betray the coiled cool secret within. She'd heard that some men could smell the presence of danger, and she watched Lester's eyes now and saw something other than intelligence sparking them, saw too the slight flaring of his nostrils. He either knew there was a rattlesnake inside that sack, or else he was reacting to Hadley's stance and manner. Whatever was in that sack, Lester was sniffing hostility in the air, over and above the strong stench of horse sweat and mule dung.

"Five times or six, there's small difference," Hadley said. "What I'm driving at is I'm sure you're a man skilled in the ways of the trail."

"That I am, sir," Lester said. His eyes were still on the sack.

"And being skilled in the ways of the trail, I'm sure you've many times seen what I've got right here in this old sack." Hadley opened the sack, and reached into it, and came out with his hand clutched behind the rattler's head. He squeezed gently and the jaws gaped wide.

Lester looked at the snake. "Yes, sir," he said, "but of the western variety."

"A brother or a cousin, aye," Hadley said.

"It might be put that way."

"Have a closer look at him," Hadley said, and put

the snake down on the hay-strewn floor, directly at Lester's feet. The moment he released his grip, the snake began rattling and hissing.

Lester took a step to the right just as the snake struck, its fangs sinking into the leather of his left boot. The snake withdrew, was slithering into an S as Lester moved swiftly behind it and reached down and grabbed it back of the head, just as Hadley had done when pulling it from the sack not two minutes before. Lester was smiling. He lifted the snake up close to his face, the jaws gaping wide, venom dripping from the fangs. Looking into the snake's mouth, he said, "Shall I break his back, sir, or did you still want him for a pet?

The barge—for such she was, there was no disguising her name or her plainness—was carrying downriver a full load of flour and hemp, feathers, and soap, pork in bulk, dried beans, ginseng and Seneca oil, seven score chickens in cages, and a dozen slaves in chains. The slaves huddled near the stern, peering at the churning river below, wailing and moaning in despair—or else praying; Minerva couldn't tell which. The Ohio was full; it had been raining on and off in Louisville for the past two weeks. Otherwise they could not have come through the chute on the Kentucky side, impassable when the river was low. The current was swift, too, the water choked with floating debris, jutting logs, pieces of timber buried in the silt below. Another barge had broken up on the rock ledge stretching across the river, and the sight of it did little to calm Minerva's fears. She squeezed her eyes shut as they approached it, and then opened them again immediately when she heard Jimmy Jackson's voice over the noise of the Falls.

"Is she afraid of the river?" he shouted.

"Mind your steering!" she shouted back.

"I've made this trip a thousand times before! I can do it blindfolded!"

"Do it in silence, would you please!"

"The drop's but twenty-two feet—"

"Look out!" she yelled.

The barge veered sharply away from an island midriver. Jackson laughed. Behind them, the Falls pounded and roared. The slaves were moaning in unison now, a dirge that drowned out the cackling of the chickens in their cages. Over the moaning and the clucking and the braying and the pawing, Minerva could hear the patroon still laughing.

Then suddenly, all was still.

They had come through the passage alive; miraculously, it seemed to her. She looked ahead to where one of the slaves, a buxom girl in a hempen dress, was staring out over the river. The moaning had ceased now. The slaves were as silent as the water through which the boat moved.

"See those steamboats ahead?" Will said.

"Aye," Minerva said.

"That's Shippingport."

"Is she still frightened?" Jackson yelled.

"What's wrong with him?" Hadley asked. "Is the man daft?"

"It would seem so," Minerva said, puzzled.

She had never met a man the likes of Jimmy Jackson.

He was six feet four inches tall, and weighed two hundred and eighty pounds. As bearded and as shaggy as a grizzly, he made even huge Gideon seem small beside him. He wore a shirt with the sleeves cut off so that his massive arms were free to tug and pull at the rudder. His trousers were too small for his enormous hulk; they stretched tight across his thighs and groin and were short by at least four inches, his thick hairy shins showing between the trouser bottoms and the high tops of his shoes. He stood grinning out over the water, his face and his beard wet, a soggy woolen cap pulled down over his forehead, a small gold earring in the lobe of his right ear.

Minerva suspected he'd been flirting with her on the trip through the Falls, suspected she'd been flirting back a bit—but only the way she did when there was a barn-raising or a baptism, and everyone was feeling gaysome. Even then, it was "Jeremy, that's the *brightest* cravat I ever did see. Was you plannin to start a fire?" Bantering more than flirting. On the ridges where she'd lived all her life, a man's wife was respected by the men who were his neighbors, and passing strangers were careful not to cast glances that might be taken wrong. Minerva was fifty-three years old, and the banter she enjoyed was no more akin to darting eyes and flashing ankles than was a possum to a skunk. Liked sassing a man, liked to hear him sass her back. The tone she'd used with the patroon was the same she'd have used with Benjamin Lowery in his mercantile store if he'd tried to charge two dollars a yard for calico instead of a dollar seventy-five. Her best friend, Millie Bain, was the biggest flirt she knew, carried on with the greengrocer like it was a royal romance, batting her lashes over the peaches and pears, enough to make Minerva blush clear across the shop. Harmless, though. There wasn't a woman on the ridges had ever . . .

Well, yes, Charity Lewis, who'd come from England three years before, and who'd lived up to her name when it came to bestowing favors. Andy Lewis never did know what was going on till he came back home one day and found six brawny young men sitting on the front step of his cabin. Wanted to know what was going on here. Fellows didn't know this was Charity's husband. They'd rode over from Damascus, where the news had already spread there was a lady doing things up there on the ridges. Came clear from just this side the Tennessee line, across Copper River and over Copper Ridge. Andy Lewis stood there asking them what this was all about, six hulking fellows sitting on his step. One of them told Andy they were waiting their turn with the English lady. Said Andy should take a seat like the rest of them. Andy went to get his rifle from the wagon. He stormed into the cabin and shot at the one on top of Charity, who scarcely missed a beat, or so the ladies on the ridges said while quilting. The six outside ran for their lives, Andy Lewis chasing them, and firing as fast as he could reload. He later divorced her, first divorce Minerva ever could recall on the ridges, though there'd been several in town. Charity went back to London to live with her father, who was an ironmonger there.

So yes, there was banter and there was also flirting, and here and there a pat or two (she'd seen Hadley with his hand on Fanny Carter's behind one time, asked him in bed that night did he enjoy feeling Fanny's fanny?), but none of it serious—except when you got somebody crazy like Charity Lewis, who was after all a foreigner. These were God-fearing people who'd no more dream of coveting their neighbor's wife than coveting his ox.

She knew at once, however, that Jimmy Jackson was not the sort of man you'd joke with about the moth-eaten woolen cap he kept pulled down over his forehead, or the single gold earring in his right ear. There was a fierceness in his eyes and a lunacy in his laughter. What she had thought to be banter, she suspected he considered brazenness.

She decided to stay far away from him on the journey downriver.

"Is she lonesome?" he asked.

He sidled up beside her as stealthily as a cat, startling her. She was looking out over the side at the farms lining the riverbanks. The sight of women bustling about their yards filled her with a longing for her home in Virginia. Jackson had almost reckoned her mood correctly; she wasn't feeling lonesome, but she *was* feeling homesick, and the two were akin.

"Good day," she said. There was only one way to discourse with this man, and that was on the plainest level. Give him a hint of humor, and he'd take it wrong. She glanced up forward to where Hadley was in conversation with the man who owned the slaves. "Where are they bound?" she asked Jackson.

"Is she interested in slaves then?" Jackson asked. "New Orleans," he said. "The man talking with your good husband there is breaking up his farm in the Shenandoah. Moving north, bought himself a mill there. Carried the niggers by wagon to Louisville."

"Will he sell them in New Orleans?"

"That's his plan. He'd damn well *better* sell them," Jackson said, and burst out laughing. "He's paying me five dollars a head for transporting them, which is more'n I'm getting for you and your entire load. Offered to hire me his strongest bucks for two dollars apiece on the trip downriver, told him I already *had* two in crew, didn't need any damn niggers underfoot. What d'you think of the shape on the wench there?"

"Pardon?" Minerva said.

"Teats on her like a broodmare," Jackson said. "Like to hire *her* for two . . ."

But Minerva had already walked away.

He referred to her constantly as "she," as though he were talking about a person other than Minerva herself.

"Does she see the sawmills?" he asked when they passed New Albany. "Are there any like that in Virginia?"

"There's sawed lumber aplenty back home," she snapped, and realized at once that he'd been teasing and had elicited from her the angry response he'd expected. She paused a moment, and then continued in a calmer tone, as if she were talking to a reasonable man and not someone crazy. "When I was a girl," she said, "you couldn't get sawed lumber for less than five or six dollars a hundred feet, depending on how far it'd traveled down the Clinch."

"But now there's fine and fancy furniture in her house, ain't that so?"

"Our house back home was plain but cheery," she said calmly.

"Was it bigger than the cabin there in the middle of the boat?"

"Quite," Minerva said.

"With all in it homemade save for the cherrywood dresser she's carrying west."

"How'd you . . . ?"

"I spied it through the open cover," Jackson said, and laughed. "There's enough in that wagon to furnish the governor's mansion! Pewter plates and wooden bowls, shot bags and—"

"You didn't spy all that through the cover," Minerva said. "Have you been inside our wagon?"

"Only to sniff at her pillow," Jackson said.

"Would you like to be sniffing it through a bloodied nose?" she asked, and moved away from him at once.

But she was trembling.

On the third day out, she stayed close by Hadley and her sons, keeping Jackson constantly in sight, making certain she was never alone in the cabin or by its exterior sides sheltered from view. But along about three that afternoon, Lester asked the men if they wanted to play some poker.

"Don't know the game," Hadley said.

"Be happy to teach you, sir," Lester said, and Hadley burst out laughing.

"You're a sharper for sure," he said. "Do you plan to win from us all you lost on the steamboat?"

Lester turned toward where Jackson stood at the rudder, the woolen cap pulled over one eye, the golden earring glinting in the sun. "Hey, captain!" he shouted. "Can we have a fistful of those beans you're carrying?"

"For what purpose?" Jackson shouted back.

"To use for money."

"Be a trick I'd like to see," Jackson said. "Help yourself, but don't go spilling them all over my deck."

"Let's find a spot in the sun," Lester said, and the men rose, and Minerva rose with them. Hadley took her aside.

"What is it, Min?" he asked.

"What do you mean?"

"Is something ailing you?"

"No," she said.

"Then what is it? You're clinging to me like . . ."

"It's the farms and all."

"The farms?"

"Seeing them along the river."

"Well, Min, we're about to play some cards here."

"I know that."

"There's apt to be talk I wouldn't want you hearin."

"Ain't no talk in the world I haven't heard. Could give you some talk of my own would blister your eyeballs."

"That's the truth," he said, and smiled. "But I know you don't like cussin, Min, and there might be some if the cards run wrong one way or another."

"I don't mind cussin," she said.

"That's news," he said.

"I suppose it is."

"But *I* mind your hearin it. Now you set yourself down right here, and leave us play the game in peace. Be enough trouble us trying to learn it without havin to worry over every word we say."

"Hadley . . ."

"Yes, Min?"

"Nothing."

"What is it?"

"Nothing," she said.

She watched them as they walked to where the beans were stored up forward in hempen sacks. Lester scooped up a hatful of them and the men went to sit in the sun on the starboard side of the boat. She was coming around the side of the cabin, thinking to find her daughters and sit with them, when Jackson stepped suddenly into her path. He was grinning wide, tobacco-stained teeth showing in the black beard, brown eyes glinting under the woolen cap tilted onto his forehead. She noticed at once that the earring was missing from his ear. He held out his clenched fist, and then opened it. The golden circlet caught the afternoon sun, glowed as though alive on his palm.

"Does she want it?" he asked.

She shook her head.

"She'll take it," he said, "want it or not," and moved swiftly to where she was standing. Holding the earring between thumb and forefinger, he dropped it into her bodice. She felt it moving over her breasts, sliding down inside her petticoat. In a moment, it fell from the bottom of her skirt and clattered onto the deck.

"Ah, and I thought she might catch it between her legs," he said, and threw back his head and laughed.

"Leave me alone," she said.

"I think not," Jackson said, and was moving toward her when Annabel came around the corner of the cabin.

"Ma!" she shouted. "Come look! There's a ferry crossing the river, all red, yellow, and blue!"

"Coming," Minerva said, and picked up the earring and threw it overboard.

On a rusted iron stove in the cabin, Minerva cooked their supper and brewed a pot of coffee from the precious two pounds she'd bought in Louisville. This was the night of the sixth; they would be in Evansville tomorrow morning. The air was almost balmy, more like August than May. On the deck outside, the men were talking with the Shenandoah farmer. Their voices drifted out over the water. From the banks of the river Minerva could hear the lowing of a solitary cow. Lifting the coffeepot from the stove, she listened, transfixed, the sound of the cow calling to mind sharply and vividly the cow Bonnie Sue had made her pet years back. Couldn't slaughter the animal to eat when times got bad because Bonnie Sue fussed and cried at the very mention of it. Finally had to sell her for less than what they'd—

"Is she pouring?"

She whirled from the stove. Jackson was standing in the open doorway of the cabin. The deck outside was dark, the cabin itself was dark except for the cherry-red glow of the iron stove.

"I'll have some, thank you," he said, and went immediately toward the stove. From a shelf on the cabin wall he took down a tin cup the size of a tankard. On the side of the cup, painted in blue, were the initials J.J.

"Put the pot down," he said.

She would not let go of the pot. The coffee had cost her fifty cents a pound, and whereas Minerva was a generation or more removed from ancestors who kept their siller in a kitchen kist, there was much of Scotland still in her blood.

"Put it down, I say," he told her, and caught her by the wrist, moving her hand back to the stove and forcing her to put the pot down on the glowing lid. "Thank you," he said, and poured his cup full to the brim. "Is there no sugar?" he asked.

"That coffee's fifty cents a pound," she said.

"Aye, coffee's dear," he said, drinking.

"The way you're swilling it—"

"Shut up," he said, and threw his arm suddenly sideward, splashing the contents of the cup onto the rough wooden wall of the cabin. "There's for your shitty coffee," he said. She moved around him swiftly, making for the cabin door, but he seized her from behind, and turned her to face him, and then pulled her in tight against him. His right hand closed on her buttock, fingers and thumb tightening on her flesh. He would not release her. He kept squeezing till she thought she would swoon. And when finally he let her go, he warned, "Keep your tongue in my presence, woman."

"My husband'll kill you," she said. She knew nothing else to say.

"Will he?" Jackson answered, and laughed.

She did not tell Hadley.

She wondered instead what Eva Chisholm would have done, who'd fought wild Indians in the cabin that had been her home, loading rifles in the dark beside Hadley's father. She wondered beyond that to a time when ancestors she knew only by name crossed over from Scotland to northern Ireland to fight against wolves, weather, and worse. Would Glynis Campbell have allowed an Irish widcairn to seize her bottom and hold her fast? She'd have brained him on the spot, no question of it.

Minerva had always thought of herself as a strong woman. Knew she was going to be big even when she was just coming along, always a head or two taller than any of the other girls her age. Jackson made her feel weak and puny, and she cursed him for that now, and cursed him, too, for the knowledge that the only way she could stop him from hurting her again was to stab him or shoot him. Wasn't no other way to do it, had to handle him the way she would an animal in the woods coming at her and trying to hurt her. He was bigger than her by nature, that was the damn thing of it, that was the thing'd never change in a million years. Wasn't no other way to protect herself against somebody his size except by hurting him back. He tried to come near her ever again, she'd *kill* him—and the Lord have mercy on her soul.

Before she went to sleep that night, she asked Will for the knife he'd brought home from Texas.

"What you need it for?" he asked.

"Lost my paring knife."

"You going to be paring this time of night?"

"First thing in the morning," she said.

"Well, I'll give it to you in the morning then."

"Give it to me now," she said, "and be still."

"It's sharp as a razor, Ma," he said, and handed her the knife.

"I'll be careful," she said.

She slept close beside Hadley that night, but she didn't think that would stop a crazy man like Jimmy Jackson. Hadn't been anything of desire or lust in the way he'd grabbed her; he'd wanted only to inflict pain. She held the knife clutched in her right hand. The slaves were singing. Their voices filled the night. From somewhere on the riverbank, the smell of fresh-cut grass wafted toward the barge. The man from the Shenandoah told his slaves to shut up, and the night was still except for the gentle slap of water against the wooden sides of the vessel, that and Hadley's gentle snoring. She wondered if she should have told Hadley after all, let him and her sons handle the matter. She decided she was doing only what Eva Chisholm or Glynis Campbell might have done. She could not imagine either of those two women running to their menfolk for help.

Patiently, she waited.

He was suddenly there in the darkness, stretching out full length beside her. She could smell his sweat and the stench of his breath. He reached around from behind her and clutched her breast, squeezing it as fiercely as he had her buttock.

"Is she waiting?" he whispered.

"Aye," she whispered back, and turned into his arms, and put the point of the knife against his belly. "Do you feel that?" she asked.

"Wh . . . ?"

"It's a knife. It's my son's knife he brought from Texas. It's sharp as a razor."

"Now . . . now what . . . ?" He had already taken his hand from her breast.

"Keep away from me," she whispered.

"I meant no . . ."

"Do you hear?"

"Yes, but . . ."

"Now go."

"Ma'm, I . . ."

"*Go!*" she said.

He went at once. He got to his feet and tripped, and then stumbled his way toward the stern.

In the darkness, she smiled.

There were thousands and thousands of pigeons in the air. White and brown and purple-gray, they filled the sky over Evansville with a fluttering whisper of sound.

Minerva caught her breath.

"There're more pigeons in Indiana than there are people," Lester said. "I've seen them roosting in trees, the branches'll break from their weight. Sometimes, the sky's so full of them, you'd think it was clouds passing overhead. And when they go by, there's a whirring of wind you can feel on the ground, and the leaves in the trees'll shake like the rattler your husband's got in that sack of his."

"They're beautiful," Minerva said.

"Great Pigeon Creek, it's called."

"What's them other birds?" Annabel asked.

"Turkey buzzards."

"So why ain't it called Turkey Buzzard Creek?"

Minerva kept watching the pigeons as Jackson and his crew maneuvered the broadhorn in toward the dock. Beside her, Hadley said, "You never saw nothin like that home, did you?"

"No," she admitted.

She watched as Hadley and the boys took the wagon and the animals ashore. The town beyond seemed a good-sized one. She was ravenously hungry and would ask if they might not take their noonday meal at an inn. As she stepped onto the makeshift gangway, Jimmy Jackson pulled his woolen cap from his head and said without a trace of irony, "Pleasure having you aboard, ma'm. Real pleasure."

The pigeons overhead seemed wheeling in celebration.

III

BONNIE SUE

Illinois.

Mules plodding along. *Ca-chok, ca-chok, ca-chok, ca-chok.* Breakfast, nooning, supper, and bed. Traveling through a countryside not so much different from the one back home where it came to houses and farms and towns you went through. Food to buy along the way, or shoot in the woods. Mostly rabbit. Hated rabbit even back home. It was, she thought, a lot like going to visit one of the neighbors a mile or so down the ridge. Except that you did it forever. And there was rain. The rain began the moment they left Evansville. It plopped on the new canvas cover, and soaked it nearly through, despite its protective coat of linseed oil. It mired the mules and the wagon wheels. It covered the country-side with a uniform grayness that was as flat as the ter-rain itself.

There were three horses. Bobbo, Gideon, and Will

rode them alongside the wagon. The rain was relentless. They wore their hats pulled down over their eyes, rode slumped in their saddles, swore whenever a horse lost its footing in the slime. On the wagon seat up front, Hadley and Lester sat side by side. "Ha-ya!" Hadley yelled from time to time, and the mules plodded through the mud, ears twitching. Inside the wagon, Minerva dozed. Beside her, Annabel was working on a sampler she had started before leaving home. It depicted a log cabin on a grassy knoll. There were flowers in front of the cabin door. A single fat white cloud floated in the sky above the cabin. To the left of the cabin were the words "Home Sweet Home." To the right, Annabel had penciled in the date they'd left Virginia: April 22, 1844. In bright red thread, she was now stitching the A in April.

Leaning back against the side of the wagon, Bonnie Sue propped her journal against her knees and tried to think of something to write in it. She had bought the blankbook in Evansville, thinking maybe there'd be Indians or something in Illinois, and she could set down what they looked like and what kind of things they ate and all that. But her father showed her on the chart where there wouldn't be Indians till they got past Independence, which was clear the other side of Missouri. First you had to go through Illinois. And Illinois was nothing but rain and a landscape as flat as the backside of a barn.

The rain riddled the wagon cover; she looked up apprehensively at a widening wet spot. Monotonously, the wagon rolled, jostling into each pothole, ridge, and rut. Annabel's needle slipped. She pricked herself, muttered, "Damn," and glanced immediately at her mother, whose eyes were still closed. There was a drop of blood on her forefinger. She sucked at it, scowling. Up front, through the open puckered wagon cover, Bonnie Sue could hear the lulling voices of Lester and her father, melting into the steady rattle of the rain.

". . . Galena in 1822," Lester said, "when I was eight."

"Still the west in those days," Hadley said.

"My daddy went there hoping to make a fortune mining lead. Indians'd been stripping it from the limestone there for as long as anybody could remember. Used to pull it to the surface in deerskin bags. I can recall them still doing it that way when I was a boy. The Panic wasn't yet over. . . ."

"Those were terrible years," Hadley said. "I never want to live through anything like that ever again."

"That's why my father left Boston," Lester said. "His blacksmith shop went under; he figured there was nothing to do but try again someplace else."

"Did he make a go of it?"

"Not in lead. Too *many* people trying to mine the earth there. But he started a furniture store and might have done well with it, his heart hadn't stopped of a sudden one day."

"Your mother still alive?" Hadley asked.

"Yes, sir. Living in Carthage."

"Buried mine just before we left Virginia, bless her heart. My pa's been dead since eighteen aught three— got himself killed by an Indian."

"I didn't know there was still Indian trouble late as that," Lester said.

"There wasn't. Wars'd ended almost ten years before, in fact. Townspeople had already torn down the pickets around the old fort. My pa was drunk, is all," Hadley said.

Inside the wagon, Bonnie Sue looked up. She could see Lester in profile in the puckered opening of the cover, the wet gray sky behind him. She had not known that her grandfather William Allyn Chisholm was drunk when the Chickasaw killed him. She had thought till this moment that he'd died a hero in one or another of the skirmishes with local Indians.

"Chickasaw was a no-good redskin used to hang about the livery stable. Him and my father got drunk one night, went down the plantation—that's the Bailey plantation, owned by the man sold us this wagon."

"It's a good wagon," Lester said.

"Cost ninety dollars."

"That's a fair price."

"He's got seventy-two slaves, Bailey has. They must be worth close to fifty thousand dollars, wouldn't you say?"

"Not that much. You know the ones Jackson was carrying to New Orleans?"

"What about em?"

"He said the bucks'd fetch six hundred each, and the wenches somewhere in the neighborhood of three."

"Then the squire ain't as rich as I thought he was," Hadley said. "Though he's plenty rich enough, I guess. Lord knows how many slaves his father had in the old days. Bailey's a man about my age, maybe a mite older. Sired hisself a little pickaninny by a nineteen-year-old house nigger he's got. Likes women, the squire does. Specially colored ones."

Bonnie Sue hadn't known *that* either. She put down her blankbook.

"Anyway, my pa and this no-count Chickasaw got drunk together one night, and went down the Bailey plantation thinkin to sneak in the henhouse, you take my meanin. Was a wench from the Barbados there, white as you or me, must've had lots of Spanish blood in her. My pa and the Chickasaw got in a fight over who'd mount her first. Chickasaw stabbed him four-teen times in the chest, then raped the slave girl in the bargain. Was her who told who'd killed my pa, not because she liked him all that much, but only cause she wanted to get back at the Indian. Bastard had torn her insides all up."

"They ever catch him?" Lester asked.

"Found him two weeks later in a Tennessee cave. You know where the Great War Path crosses the Gap?"

"I'm not familiar with it, no."

"That's where they caught him. Carried him back to Virginia and hanged him outside where the old fort used to be." Hadley paused. "Funny thing," he said. "I wouldn't believe that story for the longest damn time. I was fifteen when my pa got killed; wasn't till years later I'd believe what everybody in town was saying about him. Wasn't till my first son was born, in fact. Will out there. My son Will. Named him after my pa." Hadley was silent for several moments. The rain drilled the wagon cover. "Ha-ya!" he shouted to the mules.

Lester had estimated the distance from Evansville to St. Louis at a hundred and fifty miles. The road was wide and well-traveled; they should have averaged close to twenty miles a day, even without pressing. But the rains slowed them considerably, and though they'd left Evansville on the seventh of May, they had by the fourteenth come only seventy-four miles, with almost half the journey still ahead of them. The clearing skies did nothing to dispel their gloom. To the south was the Ozark Plateau, a wilder place of river bluffs and verdant valleys, wooded hills where they might have felt a trifle more at home. But here there was only flatness.

"How do you spell 'boring'?" Bonnie Sue asked.

Back home, it was never boring.

Wasn't Bobbo getting shot at on his way to town with whiskey, it was something else. Always something. That day he ran home, Gideon was hitching one of the mules to the plow, tightening the cinches. Bonnie Sue was sitting in the doorway of the cabin, shelling peas. Saw Bobbo come running over the brow of the hill, up the rock-strewn path that led to their house. The cabin was on the high ground, where William Allyn had built it to be safe from Indians. Only once did he have to take his family down to the old fort, and that was when a thousand or more of them descended on the settlement from God only knew where. Chickasaw, Choctaw, Chickamauga, Cherokee, or Creek, it could have been any or all of them together, seemed every Indian in the world was burning and pillaging that night, leastways the way her pa told it.

Hadley'd been eight at the time. Grandma Chisholm had bundled him up and carried him down to the fort. Half the people in the settlement made it down there safe. The rest, except for a handful caught at milking, ran to the old Bailey plantation, which was big enough to be a forted station. In the morning, most of the settlement was a smoldering ruin, but William

Allyn's cabin on the mountaintop, and that of the Cassadas beside it, stood unharmed. This was nearly half a century before the feud between them started; both families had put out their latchstrings and offered food and drink to those less fortunate than themselves. Now here came Bobbo running up the road and yelling, "Where's Pa? I just near got killed!"

"What happened?" Gideon said.

"Shot at me from the bushes!"

"*Who* did? Now settle down, you hear me?" Gideon said, and shook his younger brother. Bonnie Sue'd been shaken by Gideon only once in her life, when she was joshing him about Rachel Lowery. Like getting caught in a tornado, she supposed, Gideon picking her up and shaking her that way. He wasn't shaking Bobbo quite that hard now—only hard enough to addle his brains. "*Who* shot at you?"

"The Cassadas."

"Where?"

"On the way to town. You know where the old Settlement Road goes by the branch to Abingdon?"

"Yeah?"

"Where the woods are? On the north side of the road?"

"Yeah?"

"Shot at me from there. Pa's going to throw a fit, Gideon. I dropped and broke two whole gallons of whiskey."

"Did you see who done the shooting?"

"The Cassadas, I just told you."

"Which *one* of them, Bobbo? There's ten of them over there; which one was it shot at you?"

"Was two of them, Gid."

"Which two?"

Don't let it be Sean, Bonnie Sue thought, and split open a pod with her thumbnail, and watched the peas rolling into the colander, and held her breath.

"Phillip and Brian," he said. "Or anyways Brian for sure, and I *think* Phillip. I only got a good look at Brian."

"Let's go on over there right this minute," Gideon said. "I been wantin to bust Brian's head for the longest time."

Damn near *did* bust it, too. Both of them went over to the Cassadas without waiting for Will or Pa, could've got themselves killed that afternoon. They found Brian alone in the Cassada cabin, and dragged him outside and beat him to within an inch. Phillip came running up from where he'd been squatting in the woods; way Bobbo later told it, he hadn't even got his pants pulled all the way up yet. They set upon him, too, knocking him to the ground and kicking him till he was black and blue. Never told Minerva a word about it. She'd been over to the church at a cake sale, came home to find Bobbo and Gideon sitting in front of the fire. Bobbo was whittling, Gideon reading out of the Bible to Annabel. Everybody in the family knew what'd happened that day, except Minerva. When later they were plowing the cornfield, she couldn't understand why the Cassadas were suddenly so riled. Had to cover that field with rifles, three of them around Hadley behind the plow.

Never boring back home, that was for sure.

She must have dozed.

She heard what sounded like a gun going off, and

her eyes popped open. She was alone in the wagon. She sat upright. Her journal was in her lap. Lightning flashed against the blackened sky. She blinked. The deep rumble of thunder again. Where . . . ?

They had nooned in a grove alongside a church, white clapboard and brick. She could remember eating the sausages and bread they'd bought from the farmer ten miles back. Will standing in the rain haggling with the man. Had no eggs to sell, he'd told her brother. She'd helped her mother cook the noonday meal, climbed into the wagon afterward to write in her journal. *The rain has stopped. There's bloodroots blooming, and crinkleroots, and flowers I don't know the name of. It's going to be a nice day after all.* Mighty fine writing, put her straightaway to sleep.

More lightning. Thunder again.

The mules brayed and bolted.

She fell back, and bounced hard on the wooden bed, and yelled, "Ow!" and went rolling toward the rear of the wagon. Great huge plops of rain more like melons hit the wagon cover and came in through the front end. The butter churn rolled toward where she lay on her back near the tailgate, and she tried to get up but was knocked flat again, slamming her shoulder against the bottom of the box. The mantel clock ripped loose from where it was tied to one of the hickory bows, smashing its glass front. One of Annabel's rag dolls from when she was a toddler came sailing through the air for all the world like an aerial performer Bonnie Sue had seen one time in Bristol. Jars of preserves bounced all over the wagon like hoppy toads jumping across a road when it starts to raining hard, which it was doing now for sure. There was a sudden high wind, too, almost drowning out the panicky braying of the mules. Somewhere in the distance, she could hear her brothers yelling. She tried to grab hold of a wooden chest that came loose and fell on her ankle. A spider skillet came clanging down on the wagon bed, jumping up and down like it was alive. A keg crashed from one side of the wagon to the other, and finally burst wide open and sprayed cornmeal in the air like flying snow.

She rolled over on her side, and crawled to the rear of the wagon on her hands and knees. Rain was coming in over the tailgate, turning the cornmeal to mush. Through the flapping open end where cover met tailgate, she could see a man riding after the wagon. She recognized the horse; it was Will's raindrop gelding, an Appaloosa standing sixteen hands high, black leopard spots on a roan background, an altogether handsome animal with white-rimmed eyes and hoofs marked with black and white stripes.

The rider was Lester Hackett.

He scarcely glanced into the wagon as he came past the tailgate and then around the left-hand side. She turned to look through the front end, but all she could see was the sky ahead, as blue as a robin's egg, while behind her it was still scowly and black, the rain pouring down to drown a person. Lester yelled, "Whoa, you ornery bastards!" and the wagon came to a jolting, bone-rattling stop. She was thrown again toward the tailgate, hitting her elbow hard against it. A chamber pot came flying down from where it had been tucked in among the patchwork quilts and pillows, smashing into a thousand pieces on the wagon bed, a good porcelain pot had come from England and was decorated with daisies and blue flowers. She lay against the rough wooden flooring, breathing harshly. The rain drummed steadily on the twill cover.

"Bonnie Sue? Are you all right?"

He climbed into the wagon. He was drenched through to the skin, his hair stringy and wet, his cheeks red with wind and water. He moved to her swiftly, and said again, "Are you all right?" and then he took her in his arms and rocked her as though she were an infant.

Her brothers were riding up.

"She's unharmed," Lester said, and in rising placed his hand upon her knee. He did not look back at her as he climbed out of the wagon.

Bonnie Sue's heart was pounding.

The rain was behind them at last, the wagon moved again on a road negotiable and firm. Dutchman's-breeches and dogtooth violets bloomed along the wayside. Above, the sky was bloated with clouds as white as her sunbonnet. She sat beside Lester on the wagon seat, her face in shade beneath the peak of the hat. Inside the wagon, her mother and father were sleeping. Annabel was riding with Will on his gelding, sitting sidesaddle just in front of him. She pointed to something on the horizon and Bonnie Sue turned to look, too. A flock of sheep, some goats, she couldn't tell from this distance. There were flies on the backs of the mules, biting. Lester snapped the reins, and they buzzed angrily into the air.

"What's that book I see you writing in all the time?" he asked.

"Just a journal," she said, and shrugged.

"What's it for?"

"So when we get to California, I can look back in the pages and remember it all clear."

"Can't you remember it without a diary?"

"It ain't a diary, it's a journal."

"That's the same thing, isn't it?"

"A diary's more personal," she said.

"Oh, then your journal isn't personal, is that it?" he asked, and smiled.

"Not as personal as a diary," she said.

"Do you write about Virginia?" he asked.

"Not so much."

"Don't you miss home?"

"We're going to a new home," she said.

"Don't you have friends in Virginia?"

"Yes, I do."

"Don't you miss them?"

"Just my girlfriend," she said.

"Who's that?"

"Rebecca Hanson."

"Do you have a boyfriend, too?"

"No," Bonnie Sue said.

"I'll bet you have."

"No, honest, I don't."

"Pretty girl like you," he said.

"Thank you," she said.

"Lovely girl like you," he said.

In her journal, she wrote:

What we do is set in the waggen. Ma and me and Annabel. My back is sore, and Ma complains all the time about havvin to pee. We has to stop offen. Cause Ma simply muss pee. Pa said the other day when we git to Saint Loois, he will bye her a cork. Ma dinn find that funny. Lester talks to me sometimes. I keep wondrin why he

⌐□□ᒪ□⊐ ⊐Ŀ ⱶ□□□.

Back home, she'd go down to the Clinch, sit there with her reading books or her diary—which was a *real* diary and not a journal like what she wrote in here. The way she felt about it, a diary was something you had to devote a lot of time and thought to. You didn't just jot down in it flowers you saw along the way, like she was doing here. Or about Ma having to pee all the time. In a diary, you wrote things important to you. That's why she used to take it down to the river with her. Sit there and listen to the water. See a fish jump every now and then. Mallard come by, look her over, dig for a bug under his wing. Tall grass on the riverbank swaying in the wind.

She felt secret down there.

Felt she could write secret things.

In truth, there wasn't much secret to write about except kissing Sean and letting him touch her breasts. She wrote that in code because if there was one thing Bonnie Sue had learned in her fifteen years, it was that you couldn't trust nobody on earth, especially your little sister. She kept a bow around the diary, tied it different each night, just to make sure no little fingers opened it—nor no big clumsy ones either, belonging to her big oaf brothers who'd as soon bust Sean's head as any of the other Cassadas'. Still and all, a bow was no protection if somebody took a notion to open the thing and read what was in it.

So all the stuff about Sean was written in code. When he touched her breast that first time, she wrote in her diary

which looked a lot like the Egyptian hieroglyphics she'd seen in a picture in the Bible, but which only meant "Sean feeled me." The key to the code was hidden in a candy tin she kept other secret little things in. She figured anybody putting the two together would have to be curious enough to open the diary and the candy tin—which she wouldn't put past Annabel, but which she hoped her sister wouldn't do.

The rest of her diary, the parts that were *sort* of secret, but not terribly secret, she wrote in straightforward English. She went to school only on and off because it was hard to keep schoolmarms in the mountains back home, especially in the wintertime. Mostly, you got your teachers in the fall and in the spring, when the mountains were lovely. Minute it got to be close on November, the teachers'd disappear like the leaves on the trees, wouldn't see hide nor hair of them again till the Clinch was running free of ice. One of the teachers said she wrote real fine, but had to improve on her spelling. Seemed to Bonnie Sue everybody spelled just as bad or as good as she did, and she couldn't understand why it mattered so much. Long as a body made her meaning clear, that was enough.

She sat by the Clinch sometimes and thought she might become a writer. Trouble was, she couldn't think of any stories to write.

Oh, she could sure enough set down things that had

actually happened, but that wasn't making up stories, that was just setting things down. Time Gideon picked up the hog and carried it in the house. Had a bet with Bobbo he could pick up that old hog and carry it clear inside the house. Ma was standing there setting the clock, she turned and saw Gideon staggering through the door with the hog in his arms. She picked up the broom and started swatting him with it, and Gideon dropped the hog and went out the front door, and the hog went running over every piece of furniture in the cabin till Minerva finally got him outside. Wouldn't let Gideon sit at table that night. Said he'd have to eat out back with the friend he'd had in the house that afternoon.

But that was real.

"Good morning," Lester said.

She was washing her hair in a shallow sparkling stream, using soap they'd made themselves back home, wearing only a petticoat and expecting no company. It was still but morngloam; she had awakened before the rest of them. She threw her soapy tresses back and squinted up at him. There was early morning sunlight behind him. He was smiling.

"Did I startle you?" he asked.

"No," she said. "It's only . . ."

"You're not dressed for visitors."

"Well . . ." she said, and paused. "There's nothing you can see, I suppose." She wrung out her hair. Suds washed away in the stream.

"Is there something I might see otherwise?" he asked.

She did not answer. She busied herself with rinsing

her hair. Then she piled it on top of her head, and holding it massed there, wrapped a towel around it, rose, and began walking up the bank toward the wagon. In the distance she could see her brother Will in his underwear, stretching his arms over his head.

"No, wait," Lester said.

She turned.

"Do you know how old I am?" he asked.

"Aye."

"Almost thirty. I'll be thirty come September."

"Aye."

"You're but fifteen."

"I'll be sixteen in July," she said.

"Even so." He hesitated. "Bonnie Sue . . ."

She waited.

"Give it no thought," he said, and turned, starting up the bank ahead of her. She looked up at him as he went, then sighed, lifted the hem of her petticoat so that the early morning dew would not wet it, and climbed the bank to where they all were stirring now.

"What day is it?" Annabel asked, and yawned.

Back home, there was an outhouse you could go to, wipe yourself afterward with pages from the Bristol paper. Here you went in the woods, wiped yourself with leaves less you'd remembered to pick up the local paper in whatever town you'd gone through. The towns all looked alike, the farms, too. She sometimes walked alongside the wagon because she got sick to her stomach inside there with the thing rocking back and forth and the wheels squeaking no matter how much grease was put on them. Didn't know how Annabel could stand it, working on her sampler in there, hot as blazes under that cover, air as still as death, flies buzzing.

You walked alongside, you had to keep up with the mules, but they weren't about to race their way to California now that they'd already bolted once. Walking along, she kept thinking of Lester putting his hand on her knee. Thought maybe she'd imagined it. Mules plodding. Will and Gideon on horseback, roaming wider than the road out of sheer boredom. Bobbo out hunting quail or rabbit. Up ahead, her Ma and Pa on the wagon seat. "Ha-ya!" he yelled to the mules. Paid him no mind. Just kept plodding along. Inside, Annabel had stitched her way clear through April 22, and was working now on 1844.

Lester suddenly came up beside her. She'd thought he was with Bobbo, she'd thought . . . but no, there were only three horses. She didn't know what she'd thought; he was there beside her now, matching his stride to hers.

"Penny for your thoughts," he said.

"Ahhh," she said, and smiled.

"Private thoughts, secret thoughts?"

"Silly thoughts."

"Like what?"

"Like those a fifteen-year-old girl might think," she said, and glanced at him sidelong.

"Almost sixteen," he reminded her.

"Aye, almost."

"Have you been wondering where I was?"

"No."

"I was dozing in the wagon."

"Has she come through 1844 yet?"

"I don't follow," Lester said.

"My sister. Her sampler."

"Ah. I didn't notice."

They walked along in silence. She stooped to pick a wildflower, brought it to her nose. There was no scent. "Is it true all the things Bobbo's told me about you?" she asked.

"I don't know what he's told you."

"That you're a big riverboat gambler—"

"Hah!" Lester said.

"And a sharpshooter had himself a Kentucky rifle and two Spanish pistols."

"I had the guns, true enough," Lester said, "but I couldn't hit the side of a barn with them."

"Went off to fight in the Black Hawk War . . ."

"Yes, that's true."

"What war was that?" Bonnie Sue asked.

"Why, the war against Black Hawk," he said, and smiled.

"An Indian?"

"An Indian."

"I never heard of him," she said.

"You weren't more than a toddler. I was only seventeen myself," Lester said.

"Did you kill anyone?"

"I killed my share."

"How many?"

"Three braves and a woman."

She turned to look at him.

"She was an Indian same as the others," Lester said flatly. "When I shot her she was about to stab a soldier on the ground."

Bonnie Sue said nothing. They stood in the road, she looked up into his face. In the tall grass a cricket chirped. Ahead, the wagon creaked and rocked and the mules' hoofs pounded a steady rhythm on the hard-packed dirt. A cloud passed over the sun. They were suddenly in shadow.

He kissed her. She clung to him an instant, and then pulled away. "No, please," she said, but threw herself into his arms again at once and again kissed him. And looked swiftly toward the wagon ahead. And scanned the horizon for any sign of her brothers on horseback. And kissed him again, fiercely.

When it rained the women slept inside the wagon, and the men slept under it on ground cloths, with blankets hanging from the sides to keep out wind and water. The wagon was long enough and wide enough to accommodate four men beneath it. Two would lie side by side, fully covered by the wagon bed above them. Another two would lie with their heads against the feet of the first pair, their own legs jutting out beyond the tailgate. There were five men counting Lester; when it rained they drew straws to see who would have to build a sapling lean-to under which to sleep.

When the weather was good, all of them—men and women alike—slept on the ground around a fire, radiating from it like the spokes of a wheel from its hub. They fed the fire to blazing before they retired, and it was either dead ashes or scarcely smoldering embers by morning. The women usually went to bed first. For all the men's grumbling about saddle sores and rein blisters, the women were most tired by day's end. Usually, the men sat around the fire an hour or more after the women were asleep.

She lay beneath her blanket, listening for Lester's voice.

In the cabin back home, you could hear every sound. There were two rooms and a sleeping loft. Her mother and father slept in the bigger room, and she and Annabel slept in the room next door. Her three brothers shared the loft. At night, you heard whispers. Noises. Someone getting up to use the chamber pot. Beds creaking. When Elizabeth was alive, she and Will used to use the underbed in the bigger room. Pull it out each night, drag it across the cabin to the other side of the room, near where Minerva's good dresser stood against the wall. Part of her dower, only sawed-lumber piece of furniture in the house, eight slats of thick cherrywood with the hinges hidden on the underside of the cover.

Used to moan a lot, Elizabeth. Bonnie Sue was just a little girl, thought her sister-in-law was sick first time she heard her moaning in the night. When she died in childbirth, Will went back to sleeping in the loft again. Three beds up there, all of them sitting right on the floor without a headboard or footboard, but comfortable anyway. At night, she'd hear her brothers talking up there before they fell asleep. One time, Gideon and Will were teasing Bobbo about taking him to meet some woman. Said they'd arranged with Squire Bailey to go downriver with him next time he traveled to New Orleans. Told him the squire knew a nice little redhead would teach Bobbo all there was to know. Aw, come on, Bobbo said. Or he knows some nice blondes, too, Gideon said. Aw, come on, Bobbo said.

She listened to them now.

Though the mules had bolted three days ago, they

were still arguing the matter, Lester maintaining flatly
that oxen did not stampede as easily as mules. Will
counterarguing that when oxen *did* stampede, they ran
much wilder. Her father asked how Will happened to
know, since there'd never been an ox in the Chisholm
family from the time they'd moved down the Delaware
to Virginia. . . .

In a little while, she fell asleep.

In her dreams, Lester Hackett made passionate love to
her.

Not the way Sean Cassada had, his hands alone
inside her bodice or under her skirt, but instead a thor-
ough consummation blazing fiercely hot as all the fires
of hell. In her dreams, her lips were a thread of scarlet,
her breasts young roes that were twins feeding among
the lilies. In her dreams, Lester was a bundle of myrrh
that lay betwixt her breasts, Lester was a cluster of cam-
phire, Lester leaped upon the mountains and skipped
upon the hills, Lester's hands were as gold rings set
with the beryl, his belly was as bright ivory overlaid
with sapphires, his legs pillars of marble, his mouth
most sweet—he was altogether lovely. She longed to go
out early with him to the vineyards, to see whether the
vines had flourished or the pomegranates budded forth.
She longed for him to go down to his garden, to the
beds of spices, to feed in the gardens and to gather
lilies. *I am my beloved's,* she said in her dreams, *and my
beloved is mine; he feedeth among the lilies.*

They came to within a half day's journey of St. Louis by
the nineteenth of May, which was a Sunday, and
attended church services in a small clapboard building

set on a grassy knoll. There was an organ inside the church. Fat sonorous notes floated out on the air as they came down the church steps and onto the sloping path to where they'd hitched the wagon.

"Nice sermon," Lester said.

"Yes," Bonnie Sue said.

"Your father seemed to enjoy it, too."

"Nothin he likes better than a good one," she said. "Nor worse than a bad one," she added, and smiled.

"We'll be parting company tomorrow," he said. "I suppose you realize that."

"Yes, Lester."

"I feel I scarcely know you," he said.

"I feel I know you well."

"Do you now?"

"Yes, Lester."

"And yet . . ." He hesitated. She waited. He shook his head. "It doesn't matter," he said.

"What were you about to say?"

"I have no right; you're still a child."

"I'm a woman."

"Then . . ."

"Yes?"

"When they're asleep tonight—no, never mind."

"Lester . . ."

He moved away from her suddenly, walking ahead of her to the wagon. Annabel came running up to clutch her hand.

"Bonnie Sue?" she said. "Do you like going west?"

"Yes," Bonnie Sue said, staring off after Lester.

"You do?"

"What?" Bonnie Sue said. "I'm sorry."

"I thought it'd be more exciting," Annabel said.

• • •

At sunset, they pulled the wagon off the road and unhitched the mules, picketing them and the horses on good grazing ground. They built themselves a blazing fire then, and took their supper in the gathering dusk. There was a crescent moon showing even before the sky was black. Stars appeared.

Bonnie Sue lay awake in the darkness, her feet toward the fire, the blanket covering her to her chin. She had taken off her bodice, skirt and shoes, and wore only her petticoat and underdrawers. She'd not put on a pair of stockings since they'd disembarked at Evansville, her mother telling her the open road was no place for good cotton hose, especially with the weather so warm. That was before the rains hit them, though certainly enough the weather had turned fine again afterward. She listened to the sounds around her and judged everyone asleep, but she waited, not wanting to make a move that could be rightly read by anyone still awake. She hoped, she prayed that Lester alone was still awake, and still desiring her. She waited.

When she'd judged that fifteen minutes had passed—counting her own heartbeats sixty to the minute, nine hundred of them all told, nearly beginning to panic once when she lost the count and couldn't remember for the briefest tick of time whether the heartbeat of that instant signaled *three* hundred and four or *two* hundred and four, settling on the higher figure in her eagerness for the time to pass swiftly—when she'd counted at last to nine hundred, she raised herself on one elbow and glanced from one huddled shape to another in the light of the blazing fire. Her father was asleep, sure enough, and her mother and her brother

Will, too, who snored almost as loud as her father did. On the other side of the fire were Gideon and Bobbo—his mouth wide open to catch any passing varmint—both of them asleep. And there lay Annabel, also asleep—*We have a little sister, and she hath no breasts: What shall we do for our sister in the day when she shall be spoken for?*—but some ten feet around the circumference of the circle, where Lester should have been, there were only his ground cloth and blanket.

Her heart lurched.

Rising, remembering to take her blanket with her, she ran barefooted toward a small stand of birch near where the mules and horses were picketed. She glanced back over her shoulder once before entering the woods. No one was stirring. She was certain Lester would be here waiting for her, so certain that she almost called his name. But the woods were empty, moonlight shone on pale gaunt trunks, and in the brush an insect clicked and then fell silent. She could hear the mules and horses in the field beyond. A log hissed and spat on the fire and then all was still again.

His arm came out of the darkness, circling her waist from behind. He pulled her in against him, and she felt immediately the stiffness of him inside his trousers and against her buttocks. Still behind her, he reached up with both hands now and clutched her breasts, and lowered the petticoat straps to free them. Holding them naked in his cupped hands, he bent his head to kiss the side of her neck. She was trembling violently. She turned to him and put both arms around him and squeezed him fiercely, as though she might stop the trembling that way. But what she'd earlier felt pressing the curve of her backside was now firm against the mound between her legs, and the hands that a moment before had held her naked breasts were now clutching her buttocks, the fingertips nudging her cleft from behind. She knew she would swoon. He bent slightly and put his left arm behind her knees, and with his right behind her back he lifted her from the ground and carried her through the stand of birch to where the woods became more dense.

It was almost pitch black here in the deeper woods. The fire was too distant even to be seen, and only dappled moonlight filtered through the heavily laced branches of the huge old trees. He carried her to a pale green glade, her head against his shoulder, and then lowered her gently to the ground. The ground was moist; she realized suddenly she had dropped the blanket somewhere back among the birches. She felt the wetness through the thin cotton petticoat, and on the backs of her naked legs when he raised the petticoat above her waist. She did not resist him when he lowered her drawers to her knees, and then eased them past her ankles and removed them entirely and put them on the ground beside her with a curious delicacy, as though he were placing an expensive timepiece on a polished fruitwood dresser top. He had not said a word thus far, and she wondered when he was going to say something, *Thou art beautiful, O my love as Tirzah*, something, *the joints of thy thighs are like jewels*, anything at all. But his hands were gently urging open those jewellike thighs, and she realized with a start, but without particular alarm, that he had unbuttoned the fly of his trousers.

"Open," he said, which she supposed was somewhat poetic, but not quite so flowery as what she'd been expecting. He was pressing against her now, this very moment, trying to place his dove in the clefts of the rock, in the secret places of the stairs, and she felt an uncontrollable urge to giggle. And then, suddenly, there was an implosion of flesh, his and her own, her nether lips clinging resolutely and then receiving him all at once, so that his entrance seemed an unexpected surprise. She opened fully to him, legs apart, petticoat thrown wantonly back, arms flung wide like those of a crucified whore. His hands were under her, his fingers spread upon her buttocks, lifting her to him with each stroke until—learning the motion, discovering that even the slightest tilt against him caused her to quiver below—she cunningly initiated a responding thrust of her own and together they fell into a jagged tempo that was surely the beat of the devil's own jig, played on a fiddle out of tune.

"Do you love me?" he whispered. "Tell me you love me, darlin girl," the words rolling off his tongue as easy as Irish whiskey.

She whispered against his ear and into it, cautiously at first though her passion urged otherwise, "I love you."

"Louder," he said.

"I love you, yes."

"Again."

"I love you," she said, boldly this time, "I love you, yes I love you," she said, "oh Jesus," she said, melting inexorably into her own cleft, climbing each relentless stroke, gliding to the root of him, grinding there, "oh Jesus," she said, "oh Lester, I love, oh Jesus, oh yes, I love you, I love you."

In the morning Lester was gone.

And with him Will's horse.

•   •   •

She thought at first the commotion had to do with
someone having seen her and Lester in the woods the
night before. When she heard the angry voices, she was
sure that her brothers had dragged Lester out from
under his blanket and were now going to skin him alive.
It was first light; the fire had turned to ashes blowing
off fine in a thin wind from the east. She squinted
through the veil of ashes to where her brothers were
standing near the horses and the mules, and looked for
Lester because she thought they'd have him by the
throat or the scruff of the neck, but Lester was nowhere
in sight. That was when she got the gist of what they
were saying.

Lester had run off in the night.

Lester had stolen Will's raindrop gelding.

"Didn't trust him from the minute I laid eyes on
him," Hadley said.

"What do you make of these tracks?"

"They ain't heading west, that's for sure."

"For *all* his knowing snakes," Hadley said, and spat
on the ground.

"How long you think he's been gone?"

"No way of telling."

"Anybody hear anything during the night?"

"Heard some thrashing out there in the woods,"
Bobbo said, "but I figured it to be some critter."

Bonnie Sue got to her feet and smoothed her petticoat. Her sister Annabel was watching her shrewdly, or
seemed to be. Had she, too, heard thrashing in the
woods, and had she gone to investigate? They'd been
out there half the night, Lester holding her in his arms
till he was ready again to claim what she'd already

declared was his. Now he was gone. And they were calling him a horse thief. Quickly, she dressed.

"Ought to string him up," Hadley said.

"Got to catch him first, Pa."

"He *knows* we're late, figures we can't spare no time
chasin him."

"That's a fine horse he stole."

"We go after him, we won't make Independence till
Independence *Day*. I say we forget the bastard."

"And forget my horse, too? Worth a hundred fifty
dollars or more, that horse."

"Those tracks are plain enough headin north,"
Bobbo said.

"To Carthage, more'n likely," Gideon said. "His
mother's there in Carthage, didn't he say?"

"How far's Carthage from where we're at now?"

"A hundred miles or thereabouts," Will said.

"It's more'n that," Hadley said. "A good hun' twenty
at the least."

"I can travel that in four, five days," Will said.

"That's *if'n* he's headed for Carthage, which ain't
likely. Man tells you his ma's a certain place, he ain't
about to steal no horse and head straight *for* that place."

"Nobody says a horse thief's got to be smart, Pa."

"Nor necessarily dumb, neither. Lester didn't strike
me as no fool."

"Either way, I'd have a fair chance of overtakin you
in Independence."

"How do you figure, son?"

"I'd be travelin faster, just me on horseback."

"Still be a hard pull."

"I'd like to go after him, Pa."

"What'll you do if you catch him?"

"Take him to the law."

"Where?"

"In Carthage, if that's where I find him."

"Suppose you find him in the woods someplace, cookin his supper or skinnin a cat?"

"I'll ride him to the nearest place there is law."

"I don't like you goin out alone after no horse thief."

"I'll go with him," Gideon said.

"Leave me alone with Bobbo and the mules, huh? I'll tell you, boys, I don't like the whole idea. If there's wagons still in Independence, we'll have to leave when they do. And if there *ain't*, we'll have to move out straightway and try catchin up with them's already gone. Suppose you ain't there yet?"

"Then you just go ahead without us," Will said. "We'll catch up wherever."

"I don't know," Hadley said, and shook his head.

"Man stole my horse," Will said.

"I *know* what he done, damn it!"

Bonnie Sue wished they'd ride out after Lester and bring him right back here, where she'd declare her love for him and save his life. At the same time, she wished they'd ride out after him and hang him on the spot instead, in punishment not for having stolen Will's horse but only for having deserted her. Her cheeks still burned with the memory of their ardor, burned with anger, too, and with what she supposed was shame— was she only imagining Annabel's intense scrutiny? Or was her fornication as evident as the mist on the meadow beyond, where the picketed mules and horses stood sniffing the morning air and pawing the ground?

"Pa?" Will said.

Hadley nodded.

"We can go?" Gideon said.

"I reckon," Hadley said, but he looked troubled.

Minerva hugged her sons close.

"Be careful," she said.

"He ain't even armed. Ma," Gideon said. "Lost all his hardware in that poker game."

"So he said. But it's my experience a horse thief'll lie about anything, includin his own name. You don't know for sure he ain't got one of them little pistols tucked in his boot."

"We'll watch out for one of them little pistols," Will said, and grinned.

"Don't be so smart," Minerva said.

"Ma, you needn't worry. There's two of us."

"Just be careful," she said, and kissed them both, and then climbed up onto the wagon seat. Only thing that worried her was Lester. She knew her sons could take care of themselves anywhere, and Illinois was as civilized a place as anyone had a right to expect. It was Lester bothered her. Will's raindrop gelding was branded and earmarked both; there was no way Lester could disprove their claim to the animal once they caught him. He was a man threatened with the noose, and that made him dangerous. She watched silently as her sons studied the tracks again, and mounted their horses. Will waved to her and turned the horse he was riding, Bobbo's black mare. From astride his piebald, Gideon called, "See you in Independence!" and then the two rode off toward the north. She watched them through the dust raised by the horses' hoofs, watched till she could no longer see anything *but* dust, and then not even that.

From inside the wagon, Bobbo said, "One of the rifles is gone, too, Pa."

"He's armed then," Minerva said, almost to herself.

Sitting beside her on the wagon seat, Bonnie Sue burst into tears. Minerva looked at her in surprise, and then put her arm around her and hugged her close. In a little while, Hadley cracked his whip over the backs of the mules, and yelled "Ha-ya!" and the wagon lurched forward with a jolt toward St. Louis in the distance, and Independence far beyond.

Bonnie Sue was still crying.

IV

BOBBO

He had to find his father.

This damn Independence wasn't so big that a man couldn't locate another man when he needed to tell him something. Had to find him fast, too, before the opportunity drifted away like early morning mist back home. Pretty much like home, this town was. Bigger and more sprawling, no mountains, of course, but the same easy mix of houses and business establishments, same grid pattern of streets and cross streets. There were sturdy brick buildings everywhere Bobbo walked, chimneys smokeless now in June, steeples and steps, doorways arched in stonework—a right proper town except that just outside its doorstep was the wilderness. What all the charts called Indian Territory. Or unorganized Territory. Meaning there was nothing between here and the Pacific Ocean but a few trading posts and lots of—

"You've killed my snake, y'bloody bastard!"

The voice was his father's, and it was coming from inside a saloon dark as a dungeon. Bobbo pushed open the doors to the place and saw first his father standing at the long bar, and then the bartender with a blood-stained meat cleaver in his fist. Hadley's rattlesnake was wiggling on the bartop, its body in three separate pieces.

"Come bringin no damn poison snake in *here*," the bartender said. He was a squat solid man in striped shirtsleeves and apron, a thick handlebar mustache under his nose and curling downward over his mouth. "Now pick up that shitty quiverin thing," he said, "and get it the hell out of here."

On the bartop, the snake's head lay motionless, but the other two severed parts were still wiggling and jumping. Hadley looked down at all three parts, and then reached across the bar and seized the bartender by the front of his shirt. The bartender's apron was flecked with the rattler's blood, the bloodstained cleaver was still in his hand. As Bobbo moved quickly forward, the bartender raised the cleaver over his head, and Bobbo's heart lurched into his throat.

Hadley said, "*What!*"

There was indignation enough in his voice to have stopped a stampeding herd of cattle, no less a mere bar-keep with a cleaver in his fist. Bobbo knew that voice well. It had dogged him all the years of his youth; he had heard it razoring across mountaintops and mead-ows, gullies and gulches. It was the voice of Hadley Chisholm himself, whose ancestors had fought wid-cairns in Ireland, that could cut you dead to the ground with the icy edge of it, sharper than the blade on the cleaver in the bartender's hand. That cleaver hesitated somewhere behind the man's ear now. His eyes went wide, the brows shooting up in arcs that echoed the arc of his handlebar mustache.

"You *dare* to raise a weapon?" Hadley asked.

The cleaver still hung there undecided. The bartender felt he'd rightly and justly slain a wild creature placed on his bartop for no reason he could fathom. He'd reflexively reached under the bar for the cleaver and *snick-snack*, there went the head, and there went the body neatly cut in two. He wasn't in the habit of having his shirt front gathered in a stranger's hand. He was, in fact, widely reputed for his vile disposition and the meanness with which he wielded the cleaver he kept under the bar. But he held back the cleaver now, and stared into Hadley's indignant blue eyes, and hesitated. He wasn't afraid of the man, he certainly wasn't afraid of him—but there was something told him to belay separating his head from his body as he'd done the snake's.

"Put that cleaver down," Hadley said. "Do it now."

Across the room came another one, broader and taller but unmistakably kin, with the same blue eyes and fierce look could cut a man down like a scythe through wheat. The bartender decided to drop the cleaver after all. He let it fall from his hand to the floor behind him, and immediately wondered who was going to clean up the mess on his goddamn bar.

"You all right, Pa?" Bobbo asked.

"Aye," Hadley said. "Join me, son. This man here was about to set out whiskey for us." He looked into the bartender's face, and then released his shirt front. A round of applause went up from the gathered customers, initiated by a man sitting at a table against the wall. There was a framed portrait of President Tyler over the table. Two small United States flags were crossed over it.

"Pa," Bobbo said, "I met some men while I was getting my hair cut, they told me . . ."

His father wasn't listening. He was staring instead at the man who sat under the portrait of President Tyler. The man was still applauding though everyone else in the bar had already stopped. He wore a flat black hat and wire-rimmed spectacles. His beard was the color of rust on a rain barrel's rim, big red bushy thing that sprang from his cheeks and his chin and seemed to grow wild into his eyebrows. Sitting at the table with him was an Indian woman. Still clapping, the man got up and walked to where Hadley was waiting for the whiskey to be set out. Applauding him face to face, grinning in his beard, he said, "Bravo, sir, well done," and extended his hand. "Timothy Oates," he said.

"Hadley Chisholm," Hadley said, and took the offered hand.

"Bobbo Chisholm," Bobbo said, and also shook hands with the man.

"Have a drink with us, won't you?" Hadley said, and poured whiskey from the bottle the bartender had set on the bartop. The bartender was scowling. "I was fixin to turn the critter loose," Hadley told him. "You had no cause to cut him up that way."

"You *did* turn him loose," the bartender said.

"He got out the sack, that wasn't no fault of mine."

"Carryin a damn poison snake in a bar," the bartender said.

"Have a drink with us," Hadley said, and grinned.

"Who's paying for this?" the bartender asked, pouring himself a whiskey glass full.

"You ruined a perfectly good snake, didn't you?" Hadley said.

"What's that mean?" the bartender asked. "Ain't a snake on earth worth a pile of rabbit shit."

"This one was a pet," Hadley said, and winked at his son.

"Well, you can find yourself another pet just beyond town. Hundreds of them out there. Sometimes they come wiggling right up the street."

"Better not come in here," Hadley said. "There's a man in here'll chop em up like green beans."

The bartender smiled through his scowl.

"Drink hearty," Hadley said, and raised his glass.

"Pa," Bobbo said, "these men I talked to are fixin—"

"You live hereabouts?" Hadley asked the bearded man, and Bobbo sighed. There were times he wanted to yell his father down, same way he would anybody *else* was irritating him. Wouldn't, of course; had too much respect for him. But here he was busting to tell what he'd learned, and he had to keep quiet instead till the head of the family ran out of steam. Times like this, when his father treated him like he was still in rompers, he felt like a big awkward dummy. Everybody always thought of him as dumb anyway. Was being seventeen did it. Having pimples.

His father and Timothy Oates had told each other where they were from, and now they were telling each other where they were bound. Bobbo waited patiently for a break in the conversation, but it didn't look like one'd be coming before Christmas.

". . . have already left, you know," Timothy said.

"Most of them anyway. There're some strays like your-self still coming in, though, and I'm hoping to join up with whatever kind of train can be put together."

"Then you're bound for California, too."

"Not so far as that," Timothy said. "I'm going only to the Coast of Nebraska, to take my wife home before her heart breaks." He gestured with his head toward where the Indian woman sat under the portrait of President Tyler. "She's Pawnee," he said, "and far from home."

Bobbo looked across the room.

The woman's face was large and massive, thick black hair pulled tightly to the back of her head and braided there on either side. She was wearing a worn and greasy two-piece garment, skirt and cape of elkskin hide orna-mented with porcupine quills, many of which had fallen loose. Hadley was looking at her, too, over the top of his glass. Bobbo leaped into the momentary silence.

"I've found some others as well," he said in a rush. "Two families headin west, Pa. A carpenter from Baltimore with his wife and three children, and a man from—"

"We don't need young'uns underfoot, thank you," Hadley said.

"The sons are thirteen and fourteen; they can pull their own weight."

"Which means the third one's a daughter, eh?"

"Well . . ."

"Ain't she?"

"She's an infant in her mother's arms," Bobbo admit-ted. "But, Pa—"

"Just what we need's an infant."

"The sons can handle guns as good as you or me,"

Bobbo said. "The wagon's ox-drawn, and they're traveling with four good horses besides. Mr. Comyns said he'd allow one of us to ride that extra horse, was we of a mind to. That's his name, Pa, the carpenter. Jonah Comyns."

"Has an extra horse, eh?"

"Yes, Pa."

"Mm," Hadley said. "And the other family?"

"Does it sound interesting, Pa?"

"You said there were two families."

"Aye. The other's a man named Willoughby and his two daughters. He's a widower, Pa, decided to move from Pennsylvania when his wife passed on."

"How old are the daughters?"

"One's just Annabel's age. Be somebody for her to play with, Pa. She's been hurtin for company."

"And the other one?"

"A toddler two or three years old."

"With no mother to take care of her."

"Most well-behaved little child I ever did see," Bobbo said. "Sat on a bench along the wall all the time her pa was gettin shaved, never made so much as a peep."

"Mm," Hadley said.

"There's that extra horse to think about, Pa. Mean less of a load in the wagon; mules'd have an easier time of it."

"Mules made it all the way here from Virginia, I reckon they can make it beyond as well. 'Sides, your brothers ain't here yet."

So *that* was it.

"Pa," Bobbo said, "we told them—"

"I don't want to leave without em," Hadley said.

"We said we'd wait only till we found some wagons going out. Either that or—"

"They'll be here any day now," Hadley said.

"Pa, we don't know *when* they'll be here—that's the plain truth of it. I found us two wagons we can join up with—"

"Three, if you'll include me and mine," Timothy said. "I've got but a small one drawn by a pair of mules, and no horse to contribute. But I'm a good shot, and I own a Hall percussion carbine. I know Indians well, sir, the good ones and the bad. I've been to the Rockies and back as many times as I've got fingers and thumbs. I know the terrain, and I know what—"

"We met a fellow in Louisville, had no horse neither," Hadley said. "He's got one now."

"Eh?" Timothy said.

"How far'd you say you were going?" Bobbo asked.

"The Coast of Nebraska."

"Where's that?"

"This side of the Platte."

"Pa?" Bobbo said.

Hadley knew the mileage from Carthage by heart—Gideon and Will should've been here by now. This was the ninth of June; they'd parted company outside St. Louis on the twentieth of May. His every instinct told him to wait here for his boys, but he knew he couldn't delay the rest of the family any longer. Bobbo was right, this was a fine opportunity. Counting Oates here, there'd be four wagons, which maybe wasn't a proper train, but enough of them to form some kind of circle at night, keep from getting scalped. Didn't much like the idea of an Indian right in their midst, woman or not, but Oates seemed a decent enough fellow, and

Hadley supposed you couldn't go around blaming every redskin in the world for something had happened to your father forty-one years ago. Besides, it wouldn't be charitable to let a man struggle across the plains all by himself, just him and his wife in a little old wagon. He sure wished Gideon and Will were here. Seemed like all he had to do anymore was make decisions all the time, each one harder than the one before. Back home, a man woke up of a morning, why the day just seemed to unfold of its own accord, and you didn't have to go making up your mind every time you took a breath.

"Pa?" Bobbo said again.

"Yes, son, yes," Hadley said wearily.

They left Independence shortly after sunrise the next morning. As they moved out in single file, Bobbo saw his mother look back over her shoulder. It seemed to him in that minute that she was looking clear to St. Louis or beyond. Evansville maybe, or Louisville, or straight through the Gap to Virginia. Timothy's wagon was in the lead; they had charts, but he alone had made the trip before. The wagon behind Timothy's was that of the carpenter, Jonah Comyns, followed by the Pennsylvania widower and his two young daughters. Last in line was the Chisholm wagon, Bobbo riding the borrowed horse beside it. The day was clear and bright; they could not have wished for better weather. They could see Independence behind them for the longest time.

Then suddenly it was gone.

This was the wilderness.

Not at all what Bobbo expected. No dense forest to hack through, no underbrush ripping clothes and flesh, no wild animals crouched to attack. Just . . . nothing. No houses, no fences, no barns. Emptiness. Except for every now and then an Indian going by on the horizon.

Bobbo rode up alongside Timothy's wagon, slowed his horse.

"Is that the same Indian I see out there all the time?" he asked.

"How's that?" Timothy said.

"See an Indian going by all the time, thought maybe he's scouting us for a massacre." Bobbo smiled. But he was serious.

"I think it's several different Indians you're seeing," Timothy said. "They're peaceful farmers. You needn't worry."

"Mm," Bobbo said. He supposed Timothy knew; he'd made the journey west often enough. In the back of the Oates wagon, Timothy's Indian wife huddled as if chilled. "Is your wife all right?" Bobbo asked. "She ain't ailing, is she?"

"No, she's fine, thank you."

"She looks so sad all the time," Bobbo said.

"She *is* sad all the time," Timothy said.

"Why's that?"

"Misses her people."

"You met her out there west, huh?"

"That's right."

"Well, I hope she gets to feeling better," Bobbo said.

"She will, I'm sure," Timothy said, and smiled.

Bobbo turned the horse about, and rode back to where his father and sister were sitting beside each other on the wagon seat.

"Pa," he said, "you want to swap places awhile?"

"Don't mind if I do," Hadley said, and tugging at the

reins, stopped the mules. "Backside's beginnin to wear thin. How's that horse, son?"

"Good one, Pa."

"Well, get on off him," Hadley said.

Bobbo dismounted and handed the reins to his father. Hadley swung up into the saddle and adjusted his rump to it. He said, "Come on, horse," and clucked gently to the animal. Watching him ride ahead past the lead wagon, Bobbo climbed onto the seat and picked up the reins. "Ha-ya!" he shouted, and the wagon rolled into motion again. Beside him, Bonnie Sue was silent.

"What's troublin you?" he asked her.

"Ain't nothin troublin me."

"Then how come you don't say a word to nobody, just sit around moping all the time?"

"I ain't moping," she said.

"It sure *looks* like moping," he said. "Looks like *wilting*, you want to know."

"Bobbo, it ain't your business," she said.

"Well, it *is* my business," he said.

"No."

"Cause I love you half to death, and can't bear to see you unhappy."

She looked at him.

"That's right," he said.

"Well," she said, "I ain't unhappy. It's . . . I'm scared, is what it is."

"What of?"

"There's smoke goin up in the distance there. I'm sure it's Indians sendin some kind of message, tellin each other to come scalp us."

"Bonnie Sue, that ain't it," Bobbo said.

She looked at him again.

"That just ain't it, Bonnie Sue. I know you better'n I know myself, and it ain't Indians troublin you. Now, Bonnie Sue, what is it?"

She did not answer.

"Bonnie Sue, please tell me. I want to help you, Sis. Please."

"You can't help me," she said.

"What?" He'd hardly heard her.

"I said you can't help me, Bobbo."

"Always been able to help you before," he said.

"But not now," she said.

Always *had* been able to help her, too.

Closer to her than anybody in the whole family. Closest to her in age, and closest to her in temperament, too. Was a time, when they were both just tads, nobody in the family could bust in on one of their conversations. You come upon them talking together, you'd think it was one person talking to himself out loud. Chattered like magpies. Give Bobbo a thrashing, as Pa'd done often enough, Bonnie Sue'd bust out crying. Same the other way around. Ma said when Bonnie Sue wet her pants, it was Bobbo's you had to change. Inside the family, they got to calling them "Them two." You said "Them two," you knew it was Bobbo and Bonnie Sue you were talking about and not Will and Gideon or a pair of mules. Those days, when they were both coming along, Bobbo eighteen months older than his sister, wasn't anybody in the family could stand up to them. No way to do it. You got into an argument with them two, it was like trying to rassle a pair of bears. One'd give ground only long enough to let the other one get a hold on you, and then he'd swing you around into the grip of the second one. That was then. When they were both just coming along.

Now she was looking more mournful than even Timothy's wife, and she'd told him he couldn't help her nohow. He'd have given his life to have helped her. He'd have given that much.

"I've never made this trip before except in the company of the military," Timothy said. "What we did at suppertime, we arranged all the wagons and carts in a rough circle, oh, some fifty to sixty yards in diameter. Pitched our tents inside, hobbled the animals outside to graze."

It was their first night out of Independence. The men were standing around the fire. Comyns and his two young sons. Willoughby. Bobbo and his father. Timothy there, closest to the fire, the light from it glowing in his red beard, making it look like his chin was aflame. Bobbo liked the man, liked the gentle way he talked to his wife in Indian, liked his sure knowledge of the trail. Hadn't got a chance to talk to any of the others yet, and didn't know as he wanted to. There was a fierce look about the carpenter Comyns, and his two sons were a mite young for Bobbo. Willoughby was altogether too mournful a man; spend any time around him, you'd bust into the weeping shivers.

"When it got dark," Timothy said, "we'd drive the animals inside the circle, and then picket them on long halters. Gave them freedom to forage in the night, and also kept them safe from Indians. Now, I don't know quite what to do with this party," Timothy said, and smiled. "This isn't exactly what you'd call a wagon train, not by any stretch of the imagination, and I'm thinking that however we arrange ourselves, we're going to be vulnerable somewhere."

The carpenter Comyns was listening intently. Fifty years old or thereabouts, massive head, mane like an elderly lion's. Brown eyes fierce as a prophet's under shaggy white brows. Nose like a wedge, lips thick and purple as calf's liver. There was something scary about him, reminded Bobbo of when his father messed with his damn snakes, though with Comyns it seemed the usual and not the peculiar. His sons were by his first wife. They resembled their father in every respect save the white hair and brows.

"So what I'd like to do, with your permission," Timothy said, "is arrange the camp each night with a fire in the center, and a wagon at each of the four compass points. We'll keep the animals inside, same as the military did, and mount the first guard at nine o'clock."

"Till when?" Comyns asked.

"Till sunrise."

"That's a good nine hours."

"Yes, and there're seven of us here," Timothy said. "I thought we'd relieve every three hours, two men to the watch, each of us having a night off once a week. I can't see any other way of doing it, not with so small a party."

"That sounds fair to me," Comyns said.

"You think we need be so careful, this stage of the journey?" Willoughby asked.

He was a tall thin man with a tanned and weathered face. Dressed in brown the color of earth, he looked altogether like what he was, a farmer plain and simple. The firelight flickered on his hands. He was wringing them as he spoke, kept wringing them as he waited for

Timothy's reply. Made Bobbo nervous, the way he fidgeted all the time.

"Well, there's not much danger of Indian attack just now," Timothy said. "But there might be an ambitious brave out there itching to get his hands on some horses, so caution won't hurt. Besides, it'll be good practice for later on," he said, and again smiled.

They moved the wagons and posted the first guard, the two young Comyns boys roaming the perimeter from side to side. The night was still save for the crackle of the fire and the low murmur of the wind. At the fire, Willoughby sat beside Hadley, staring into the flames. He said nothing for the longest time, just kept wringing his hands like he was washing them. Some twenty feet beyond, Minerva stood staring out over the prairie, her arms folded across her waist as protectively as the ring of wagons surrounding the fire. Willoughby sighed at last and nodded to himself, and Hadley knew he'd made a decision about something or other. But he didn't suppose the man was about to share it with him, and was surprised when he did.

"I'm not sure I want to continue on," Willoughby said.

It seemed to pain him to say the words. They came from his lips with some effort, as though he were trying to strangle them back He kept wringing his hands in the light of the fire, but the rest of his body was still as granite. Only the hands moved.

"I'm fearful for the young'un," he said. "My older daughter and me can endure. But I'm not sure about the young'un." He nodded again, affirming his decision, strengthening it. "I should've waited till next year.

I knew the damn wagons'd be gone by now, but I was hopin to catch up. I had to get away from Pennsylvania, you see. My wife passed on not long ago, I had to get away. Did you know my wife had died?"

"Yes," Hadley said. "I knew that."

"And you see, I thought to get away. The house there, the farm, it was far too big for just the two girls and me; I needed to get away from it. Start again someplace. But now I'm fearful for the young'un. Your eldest daughter is grand with her, by the way, I'm thankful to you, she relieves the burden. But you see, it's just . . . I keep imagining the Indians laying hold of her. Raising her up like their own. I've read tales of that, have you not? Wouldn't recognize her as mine fifteen years from now. Look just like Oates's squaw there in the wagon," Willoughby said, gesturing with his head. "And I keep thinkin the older one's none too safe neither, the Indians decide to attack. We're a small party, that can't escape their attention if they're of a mind to come raiding. They'll have counted the men and the animals, they'll know for sure we're vulnerable. Seeing all the young girls—there're lots of young girls in this party— they might consider it a tempting proposition, as well they might anyway, even without the promise of reward greater than livestock. I'm frankly worried, I'm thinking of turning back."

"Alone?" Hadley asked.

"Or with as many as'll come with me. We're but fifteen miles from Independence, and the Indians behind us are friendly, or so Oates has said. I'm not afraid to risk it alone if I have to. I'm thinking it's the wisest move." Willoughby hesitated, and then turned to look into Hadley's face. "What do you think?"

"I don't wish to advise you," Hadley said. "Was you to get scalped on the way back to Independence, I wouldn't want that weighin on me."

"Well, there's not much danger of that."

"True enough, the real danger's ahead, not behind."

"Which is just the matter of it," Willoughby said.

"I'm not following."

"They'll think me cowardly."

"Who will?"

"The others. And maybe you as well."

"I judge not that I be not judged," Hadley said. "You're to do what you think right, Willoughby. If there's a man here can say how he'd act was a band of wild Indians to come riding in off the prairie, I'd like to meet him."

"I'm not afraid for myself, you know," Willoughby said. "It's for the girls I'd be doing it. Especially the young'un."

"Aye," Hadley said, and the men fell silent.

Willoughby was wringing his hands again.

"Guess maybe I'll have to think it out a bit more," he said.

"As you wish," Hadley said.

"Don't want to wait till it's too late, though."

"No."

"Get much farther from Independence . . ." He let the sentence trail. Sighing, he rose ponderously. "Good night, Chisholm," he said, and Hadley said, "Good night, Willoughby," and watched as the man walked over to his wagon and peeked inside to where the little one was sleeping. He came back to the fire then, took off his boots, and crawled under a blanket. In the flickering light, Hadley could see his hands pressed together in prayer, his eyes closed. The night was cool, not a star showing, the moon obscured by heavy clouds that rolled in off the prairie. Hadley rose, and stretched, and walked to where Minerva yet stood, tall and silent, staring out over the prairie ahead.

"Look at it," she said. "It stretches to nowhere."

"It stretches to California."

"I prefer Virginia, thank ye."

"Willoughby's talking of turning back," Hadley said.

"Then let's go with him," Minerva said at once.

"I think not."

"Do you not miss home?"

"I miss it."

"Do you not long for Virginia?"

"With all my heart, Min."

"Then, Hadley, darlin . . ."

"I think we've got to make this journey, Min, or else learn how to die on land won't support us."

"Won't we learn to die out there as well?" Minerva asked, and turned again toward the empty prairie.

The wind was blowing in from the west; it set the low hushes to rattling. They both squinted against a sudden gust, and turned their backs to it. The wagon covers were flapping, sparks were dancing in the air above the fire. Hadley put his arm around her, and they walked to the fire together. From the open-topped Oates wagon, they could hear the Indian woman murmuring in her sleep.

Hadley took off his boots, and watched as Minerva delicately pulled back the hem of her skirt and began unlacing her shoes. Her legs were still as splendid as they'd been when first he viewed them on their wedding night, Minerva standing tall and still and radiantly expectant. Her slender ankles were revealed now as she dropped one shoe and then the other to the ground, and lowered her skirt again, raising her eyes to catch his glance. A thin, knowledgeable smile crossed her mouth. She unbuttoned the bodice over her bosom, still firm and ample. There were things on a woman never changed, Hadley thought: legs and hips and bosom; that was a fact. Well, maybe they changed just a mite.

Beneath the blanket together, she rested her head on his shoulder and her hand on his chest, the way she'd done for as long as he could remember. They were silent for a bit. Then she whispered, "What do you think of the carpenter's wife?"

"What about her?"

"She does go on nursin that child of hers," Minerva said. "Yankin out a teat ten, twelve times a day, never mind who's lookin."

"Ain't nobody lookin," Hadley said.

"Bobbo's looking. You ought to tell him to quit, Hadley."

"Hell, Min, she's just sucklin the babe, is all."

"Ain't a baby alive can take that much milk 'thout turnin into a calf," Minerva said, and Hadley burst out laughing.

She tried to shush him, but she was laughing herself now. In the night, they clung to each other and quaked with laughter while the wind howled in over the prairie. And at last, when they had both quieted down again, Minerva telling him to hush now before he waked the entire party, Hadley claiming it was *her* cackling like a hen, she whispered again to him about Bobbo, and he promised to warn the boy against spying on Mrs. Comyns. "Though she has got a fine pair of pumpkins there," Hadley said, and Minerva got to laughing again till someone from one of the wagons— they thought it was the Indian woman, but hushing sounded just the same in any language—*shh*ed at them to keep still.

They were adept at making love with others sleeping not a stone's throw away. Silently, they went about it. And as always, Hadley had to clap his hand over Minerva's mouth to stifle the scream that would have wakened living and dead alike and caused St. Peter at the pearlies to think for sure that sinners had taken over the earth and were reveling in the joys of the flesh.

In a little while, it began raining gently.

By two in the morning, the camp was a quagmire. What had started as the mildest of rainfalls became a blustery fearsome storm that woke the entire party and sent them scurrying for cover inside or under the wagons. Bobbo, standing guard with Timothy, walked from position to position around the perimeter, peering through the heavy rain, listening for sounds other than those he could readily recognize, not knowing what on earth an Indian might sound like in the dark. Probably wouldn't sound like nothing at all, wouldn't even make a whisper, just *zzzzzzzt*, and your throat'd be cut, and *zzzzzzzt*, your scalp'd be taken.

He passed the Comyns wagon, and thought of Sarah Comyns inside there, and wondered was she naked. Seemed to Bobbo she nursed her infant daughter far too often for the comfort of the men in the party, though suckling wasn't no sin and a breast nothing to hide. He'd caught himself stealing a glance at her more than once today, and was fearful the carpenter might have noticed. Had enormous hands, Comyns did, could just see them gripping a hammer and driving a nail home. Bobbo'd witnessed enough women suckling their babes back home; wasn't right to stare that way each time Sarah yanked herself out of her bodice and began squeezing. Blondy-haired she was, same as Rachel Lowery, who his brother Gideon had fucked. Freckles on the full sloping tops of her breasts. Bobbo guessed she was twenty-four or -five, the carpenter's second wife.

The rain kept falling.

Bobbo walked the perimeter with his pants bulging, thinking of Sarah Comyns, thinking of Rachel Lowery, even thinking of the Indian woman who was Timothy's wife, wondering what her quim might be like under that long elkskin skirt, Indian black and Indian tangled, he supposed, thick as the hair on her—

He heard something.

He stopped dead, raised the rifle.

There. Again.

The sound was coming from within the circle. He whirled, his finger on the trigger.

Timothy Oates was huddled under his wagon, a blanket tented over his head, his rifle in his lap. He was guzzling whiskey from a bottle. Bobbo stared at him in disbelief. Timothy had traveled with the military; he certainly knew better than to leave his post, rain or not! A man standing guard did not run under a wagon when a few raindrops fell. He did not cradle his rifle in his lap. He especially did not swill booze from a bottle.

Bobbo sprinted across the circle. Rain drilled the enclosure, sending up wet puffs of mud wherever it struck the ground. It rattled on twill covers, soaked the open wagon under which Timothy Oates crouched, with his wife beside him. Bobbo knelt and peered under the wagon.

"I know," Timothy said. "I drink too much."

"We've a watch to stand here," Bobbo said. "Come out from under the cart."

"It's raining," Timothy said.

"I know it's raining," Bobbo said. "Rain is what I'm standing in here. Now come on out of there before we're scalped in our sleep."

"We'll neither of us be scalped in our sleep," Timothy said, "since neither of us is asleep, you'll notice."

"I'm talking of the others. Come on now—get out from under that wagon."

"I prefer it here, I think, to there."

"Are you drunk, man?"

"Yes, I'm drunk," Timothy said, and nodded.

"Then a cold bath'll sober you," Bobbo said, and yanked him out from under the wagon while the Indian woman shrieked and howled to the night as though her husband were being dragged to a hanging tree. It was the most Bobbo had heard from her since they'd left Independence, but he was in no mood for her yelling, especially since he understood not a word of it. He told her to shut up, and was surprised when she obeyed. From inside the Comyns wagon, Sarah asked, "Is it Indians? Is it an attack?" and Timothy replied in his drunken stupor, "It is an Indian, madam, but not an attack," and Sarah said, "What? What did he say, Jonah?" and Comyns said, "Hush."

In the rain, Bobbo walked Timothy around the

perimeter from wagon to wagon, supporting him with one arm around his waist, his hand clutching the leather belt there, his other hand holding his rifle upside down so that rain wouldn't enter the barrel. Timothy began singing.

"Quiet," Bobbo said. "How'd you get so drunk, man?"

"By drinking," Timothy said, interrupting his song for just an instant and then bellowing into the rain again. He was singing in gibberish, it seemed at first, till Bobbo realized he was using an Indian tongue, more'n likely his wife's. "*An-pe tu wi,*" he sang, "*tan-yan hi-na pa nun . . .*"

"Shut up, man," Bobbo said. "You'll wake the camp."

"It's a fair-weather song," Timothy said, reeling, almost knocking Bobbo into the mud, and then bellowing again, "*We he a he, an-pe-tu . . .*"

"Be still."

"*Wi tan-yan . . .*"

"Shhh, shh."

"Learned it from the Sioux," Timothy said, and suddenly began singing it in English, bellowing it as before, but at least making sense now. "May the sun rise well," he sang, "may the earth appear, brightly shone upon," and was suddenly silent while the rain poured down as before. A lot of good his fair-weather song had done. Bobbo walked him around in the storm, hardly looking for Indians at all now, though half convinced that Timothy's song would have drawn raiding parties of whatever tribes were currently warring with the Sioux. Bobbo had no idea who those might be, nor even any idea whether this was Sioux country or Cheyenne or whatever; only Indians he'd ever seen were the handful of Cherokee, Creek, or Chickasaw in Virginia. Them and the woman silent now under Timothy's cart.

"Do you know why I drink?" Timothy asked.

"Why?"

"I drink, that's right, Bobbo."

"I can see that."

"You know why?"

"Why?"

"Catlin," Timothy said.

"Cattle?"

"Catlin, Catlin."

"What's catlin?"

"It's *who*," Timothy said.

"Make sense, man."

"George Catlin."

"Who's George Catlin?"

"An artist."

"What's he got to do with your drinking?"

"Never mind," Timothy said. "Let's go back under the wagon. It's wet out here, Bobbo."

"Timothy, you've put the party in danger, getting drunk this way."

"That's right, I'm a drunk."

"I don't know as you're a drunk, but you're drunk for sure tonight."

"It's Catlin."

"Sure, sure," Bobbo said.

"Who's better?" Timothy asked. "Catlin or me?"

"I don't know the man. Now hear me well, cause—"

"Bobbo, let's get out of the rain. It's cold out here, Bobbo. What are we doing marching around in these puddles?"

"We're sobering you up, is what we're doing. Now listen to me, Timothy. If we're to trust you to lead us west—"

"You can trust me. Do you know how many times I've traveled to the Rocky Mountains and back?"

"How many?"

"Ten times, that's right. With the military," Timothy said, and nodded. "But not a soldier, nossir. An artist!" he shouted, and raised his right hand, the forefinger extended as though proclaiming his profession to the night, and to the raging storm, and perhaps to God Almighty Himself. "*Better* than Catlin, you want to know. No matter what you may say or think, I'm the better artist. That's a fact, Bobbo."

They marched about in the rain from wagon to wagon, drenched to their bones now, boots and trousers thick with mud, clothes hanging sodden and limp, the normally stiff brim of Timothy's flat black hat flopping loose around his ears and his forehead and the back of his head, his rusty beard bedraggled.

"Know this trail like my own backside," he said, "can navigate it blindfolded, been back and forth ten times. Know Indians, too, better'n that fuckin Catlin, can draw and paint em better'n he can. But who gets all the glory, eh?"

"Catlin," Bobbo said.

"Catlin, right."

Catlin was his subject, his cause, and his passion. It was Catlin finally sobered him up, but it was Catlin'd no doubt cause him to drink himself drunk again. Bobbo now understood that Catlin was an artist who painted Indians, same as did Timothy. Practiced law in Philadelphia for a few years and then gave it up to study art. Became a portrait painter in New York before he headed west some twelve years back, to live with Indians and paint them. That was two years before Timothy himself got the idea of doing the very same thing.

"Too *late*," he said. "Got back to Philadelphia, dealers said it was divitive."

"Was what?"

"Drivitive."

"I don't know what that means."

"My *work!* Divitive. One publisher . . . Jesus! Said I'd copied Catlin's painting of Laramie! More mistakes in it . . . laughable. Said I'd copied it. Hadn't even met the man! Didn't know he existed! Ah, shit, Bobbo," he said, and began weeping.

His rage was exhausted before it was time to wake the next watch. Exhausted but not vanquished; it would never be that, Bobbo suspected, though drown it over and again Timothy might. He helped the man back to his wagon, where the Indian woman undressed him, and dried him, and put him to sleep. The rain had stopped, the wagon covers were sodden. The ground he and Timothy had traversed back and forth through half the night looked as though a herd of cattle had stampeded through it. Bobbo went to rouse his father and the Baltimore carpenter, and then went to sleep himself. When he wakened again at sunrise, the first thing he thought was that he'd have to look at Timothy's pictures one day.

The Comyns lads, whose task it was, led the animals outside the circle of wagons, hobbling them where they might graze till it was time to move on. The aroma of coffee filled the morning air, setting to rumble stomachs empty since the night before. In Independence, the party had pooled its resources to purchase the stores needed for the long journey. There would be game ahead, Timothy told them, and friendly Indians wanting to barter fresh vegetables and fruit. But they stocked the wagons with staples nonetheless, and were carrying in addition such luxuries as coffee, bacon, and eggs. The bacon was packed in barrels of bran to keep it from rotting in the mid-June heat. The eggs were similarly packed in meal, which would be used for baking bread once the eggs had been eaten. Coffee was the most expensive luxury, but Timothy told them it would disguise the bitter taste of water that had alkali in it. Bacon sizzled in the skillets now, and eggs were dropped into the pan, and soon were crackling in the bubbling grease. They finished breakfast by six-fifteen on that morning of the eleventh, and were on the trail again not ten minutes later.

Minerva hadn't realized how lonely she'd been for the companionship of another woman. They had left Independence only yesterday morning, but now with the new day stretching ahead as endlessly as the prairie itself, she turned eagerly to Sarah Comyns.

"I've never been to Baltimore," she said. "What sort of place is it?"

"Oh, it's very nice," Sarah said.

Silence.

They were sitting together inside the Comyns wagon, sunlight illuminating the cover so that everything within took on a golden glow. The wagon was packed even more tightly than the Chisholms' own. They sat on stools the carpenter himself had made, swaying with the roll of the wagon, bouncing whenever it hit a ridge or a rut. The baby was asleep on Sarah's lap. This morning she'd suckled the child in the privacy of her own wagon; Minerva guessed the carpenter had spoken to her about showing her teats to all and any.

"Big city, is it?" Minerva said.

"Oh, yes," Sarah said.

"About the size of Louisville?"

"I guess," Sarah said.

Silence.

"Did you live in the city itself?" Minerva asked. "Or outside of it?"

"Yes."

"In it?"

"Yes."

"Husband have a shop there?"

"Yes," Sarah said.

"Must be interestin being married to a man can fashion things with his own two hands."

"Yes, it is," Sarah said.

"Hadley puts his hand to making a table or chair, it comes out all catty-wampus."

"Oh, yes," Sarah said, and laughed.

"My Gideon's the one has a sure hand with a hammer and nail," Minerva said. "You haven't met him; he's off with his brother in Illinois. Man stole my eldest son's horse, big raindrop gelding, beauty of a horse. Just rode off with it one night. I miss him somethin fierce," she said, and found herself confiding to Sarah that Gideon was her favorite, had been from the minute the granny woman laid him puny and wet across her belly. Loved them *all* to death, she did, but for Gideon she felt something special, a kind of . . . *joy,* she supposed it was, every time she saw him. She knew it was wrong worrying about them the way she did; they were both grown men and knew how to take care of themselves. But they'd been gone more'n three weeks already. Last time she'd seen them was on the twentieth of May, Gideon waving from his saddle, big grin on his face.

"I guess that's the nature of it, though," Minerva said. "Worrying over your children even when they're all growed up."

"Oh, yes," Sarah said.

Minerva decided she was a twit.

When they stopped for their nooning that day, it seemed a break in the routine, though it was itself a part of it. The sky had been blown flawlessly clear by the storm the night before; they could see everywhere around them for miles and miles. A stream surprised the landscape here. They watered the animals and drank themselves, and then filled the barrels and kegs. Bobbo and the Comyns boys started the cooking fires, and the women fried the meat and boiled the vegetables they'd bought in Independence. There was the smell of coffee and of warmed corn bread. After the noonday meal, they dozed. The voices of Annabel and Willoughby's eldest girl broke the golden stillness.

"Do you get it now?"

"No, I don't."

She had stringy brown hair and eyes like a cat's, yellow with flecks of green. Must've been her mother's eyes; Willoughby's were as brown as Christmas pudding. Her name was Julia.

"It's a cipher, is all," Annabel said.

"But what use is it?"

"Say I want to send you a letter in Lancaster—"

"I don't live in Lancaster no more."

"Just say. And I wanted to tell you something secret."

"What would you want to tell me?"

"Well . . . I don't know," Annabel said. "Say I wanted to cuss or somethin."

"*Would* you?"

"Course not, we're just sayin. So I'd whip out the cipher here and write it all in code, and nobody but you or me'd be able to read it."

"Let me see it again," Julia said.

Annabel showed her the scrap of paper.

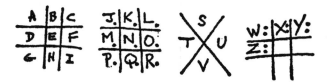

"Say you wanted to make an A," Annabel said.

"Yeah, how'd you do it?"

"You see those lines around the A there?"

"What lines?"

"The one under it, and the one comin down to meet it. You just draw them two lines instead of the A," Annabel said. "Them two lines take the *place* of the A— you get it?"

Julia studied the cipher again. "But then it'd be the same for J, wouldn't it?"

"No, the J's got a dot."

"Oh," Julia said. "Yeah."

"You get it now?"

"Yeah," Julia said, nodding.

"It's good, ain't it?"

"It's *real* good," Julia said. "Where'd you learn it?"

"Everybody back home knows it," Annabel said.

What had appeared dull in southern Illinois seemed exciting now in retrospect. There, at least, a ridge, a knoll, a hillock rose occasionally to startle the unexpecting eye. Here, there was a wide road trodden level, the land on either side of it as flat as the road itself, stretching toward a horizon visible wherever one turned.

The effect was stultifying.

The wagons moved at the center of a perfect circle, the circle unchanging, the landscape eternally the same, the mules and the oxen and the horses plodding ahead but succeeding only in moving the circle intact, center and circumference, so that there was a sense of standing still rather than progressing.

They came fourteen miles that second day. The day before, they'd come sixteen by the chart. They were bone-weary when they formed the circle again at sunset. They made their fires, they posted their guards. They ate. They slept. In the morning, they moved on again.

They were emigrants, they supposed.

You look forward to nooning, Bobbo thought.

Damnedest thing ever.

Get off your horse, stretch your bones, eat some good hot food. Sit around afterward doing nothing. Just looking all around. Dozing. Looking again. Over there in the back of the Oates cart was Timothy's

Indian wife. Never budged out of that cart. Sat there day and night, you'd think her backside was glued to it. Appeared every bit as sorrowful as the widower, staring out over the prairie. Always looked west. Bobbo followed her gaze one time. Thought maybe she was seeing something he couldn't make out. Wasn't nothing out there. Not a damn thing.

Timothy'd brought her some food, and now he was taking his sketch pad and a boxful of pencils from the cart. Way he talked about painting and drawing made it sound like it was *work*. Like plowing a field or shoeing a horse. Bobbo couldn't understand that. Friend of his, Roger Colby back home, was always drawing pictures, too, some of them pretty enough to frame. Bobbo himself couldn't draw a straight line, but he admired people who could do that sort of thing. Draw pictures, a dogwood tree or something. But work? Hell, it wasn't *work*. Still hadn't seen any of Timothy's pictures, didn't know whether the man could really draw or was just wasting his own good time and God's, too. He was sitting on a big rock now, watching every move the carpenter made. Trying to get a likeness, Bobbo supposed.

There was the widower Willoughby, sorrowful as could be. Never knew when he was going to break into tears. Last night just before supper, Annabel said something about the nice stitching on the pinafore his toddler was wearing. Willoughby put his face in his hands and started crying. Must've been his wife had made the pinafore. Went back to his wagon, climbed up on the seat, sat there with his face in his hands, weeping. Wouldn't touch a bite of food. His daughter Julia went over to him and touched him on the shoulder.

"Pa?" she said.

"Yes, darlin."

"Pa?"

"Yes, darlin, that's all right, darlin."

Timothy was still trying to draw a picture of the carpenter. Be a miracle if he got anything at all down on paper, way Comyns ran around like a man half his age. Maybe *had* to move fast to keep that titty young wife of his happy on her back. Bobbo got up from where he was sitting, and wandered over to Timothy. His head bent over his pad, he kept scribbling away with the pencil. Bobbo stood directly in front of him, trying to sneak a look around the edge of the pad. Didn't want the man to think he was nosy.

"How many miles you expect we'll cover today?" he asked.

"Oh, fourteen, fifteen," Timothy said, without looking up.

"Has Willoughby talked to you about maybe turning back?"

"He has."

"Do you think he will?"

"I'm hoping not," Timothy said.

"Seems a man *talking* about it so much is a man going to do it. Don't it appear that way to you?"

"Maybe," Timothy said. "What do you think of this?" he asked suddenly, and turned the pad so Bobbo could see it.

Jonah Comyns was there on paper exactly.

Quick sure pencil strokes delineated the long angular body with its massive chest and shoulders, the oversize hands and thick fingers. A thatch of hair sprouted from the head of the drawn image as wildly and as randomly as did Comyns's real hair. Here, too, were the

quirky eyebrows and fiercely burning eyes, the nose
that could split a log, the thickish lips, and something
more—Timothy had captured on paper the restless
energy of the man. Looking at the pencil sketch, Bobbo
was certain it would leap off the page at any moment,
run scurrying to tend to the animals or the fire, shout
an order to a son.

He did not know he could be so moved by pencil
marks on paper. Speechlessly, he stared at the drawing,
and realized that Timothy was waiting for his reaction.

"It's the most beautiful thing I ever seen," Bobbo
said.

There was an instant's silence. Timothy looked up
sharply into Bobbo's face, searching it for insincerity.
Then, so softly Bobbo almost couldn't hear him, he
said, "Thank you."

Sarah Comyns was nursing her baby when the Indian
appeared.

They'd camped the night of the thirteenth on the
bluffs overlooking the Kansas River, three to four miles
wide there, the river valley thick with timber, the hills
rising from a prairieland as green as Minerva's eyes. In
the morning, they moved on to a nooning place where
the river was boiling yellow. Their rest period seemed
in contrast more peaceful than it normally did, the stillness of the camp exaggerated by the incessant roar of
the river. The men were talking about how they
planned to get to the other side. Timothy suggested
that they take off the wheels and float the wagons
across like barges. But there were no hides to nail to the
bottoms, and Comyns was afraid they'd sink without
waterproofing. Hadley thought they should build

themselves a raft. There was plenty timber to cut, and fashioning a raft was a simple thing enough. The women had washed the dinnerware and put it up already; Minerva and the girls were resting now in the shade under the trees. Inside the Comyns wagon, Sarah briskly removed a breast from within the unbuttoned yoke of her bodice, reacquainted her baby's mouth with the oozing nipple, and then cupped breast in hand, kneading it, her eyes closed as the baby began to suck. When lazily she opened her eyes again, the Indian was staring in at her from the rear of the wagon.

He was at least five feet ten inches tall, his face an oval with prominent cheekbones, eyes almost the color of his skin, long black hair falling to his shoulders. He said something to her, Sarah didn't know what and didn't care. She yanked her squirting breasts loose from her baby's mouth and began screaming. The Indian turned and ran from the wagon. He got no more than ten feet toward the woods beyond when Jonah Comyns dragged him kicking to the ground. There was a pistol in Comyns's hand. He put it at once to the Indian's head. In that moment, Timothy came running around the corner of the wagon. "Hold your fire!" he yelled, and clamped both hands onto the carpenter's wrist.

"Let go!" Comyns shouted. "I'll shoot the bastard dead!"

Inside the wagon, the baby began shrieking. The Indian was babbling frantically now, the pistol flailing closer and closer to his head, Timothy desperately trying to hear his words over the baby's squawling and Comyns's shouting. The widower Willoughby came running toward the wagon with his suspenders hanging, a rifle in his hands, his face pale. The youngest

Comyns boy ran up and began dancing a frightened little jig.

"Let him be!" Timothy shouted. "He wants to ferry us across the river!"

From inside the wagon, Sarah said, "He spied me naked."

The Indian was a Delaware.

He had come as spokesman for his tribe, searching for someone with whom he might negotiate, and had peered into the nearest wagon only to find himself face to face with a crazed white woman. Now that everyone had calmed down, he explained that his tribe, together with their partners the Shawnee, had constructed a raft sturdy enough to transport the party across the river. This for a price the white man would surely recognize as reasonable. He said all this in Algonquian—which Timothy understood but incompletely. He gathered the Delaware's name was Ferocious Storm, but it might well have been Fearful Storm, or indeed Fear of Storms; the Indian spoke quite rapidly, never once deferring to Timothy, who was trying to converse in a tongue not his own.

Ferocious Storm asked a gallon jug of whiskey for each wagon his people carried across the river. In addition, he wanted four eggs for each. And three kegs of flour. And a dozen trinkets he would personally select from whatever jewelry the women had with them, plus thirteen yards of blue homespun.

They haggled for close to an hour.

By the end of that time, Ferocious Storm had reduced his total price to one gallon jug of whiskey, half a dozen eggs, two small kegs of flour, two calico bonnets he saw the women in the camp wearing, and in place of the jewelry and the thirteen yards of homespun, six slabs of bacon. Timothy said they would give the Indians all save the whiskey and the meat.

"Then I will have some sweets," Ferocious Storm said.

"Sweets as how?" Timothy asked.

"Preserves."

"In what amount?"

"Three jars of fruits."

"Nonsense."

"It is my price," Ferocious Storm said, and rose to leave.

"Two jars and we have a bargain."

"The river is high; we will have to work hard against it. Three jars."

"And if we lose livestock or property in the river?" Timothy asked.

"Then there is no price. You have made the crossing without it costing you a penny." Ferocious Storm grinned suddenly. His teeth were stained a brown darker than his skin, and some of them were missing, and the rest of them were crooked. But his smile was so contagiously mirthsome that it caused all the men standing around him to grin in return. "And if any of you should drown," he said, smiling, "*we* will pay *you* the agreed-upon price."

Timothy laughed. The others, not knowing what had been said, laughed too. The bargaining had been concluded.

The Indians had built their landing at a bend downstream, where a rock-strewn cove of silt and coarse

sand formed a small natural harbor. Their vessel was a
raft some fifteen feet wide and thirty long. It lay at the
landing now, its forward end lashed at each corner to
the makeshift dock, its stern—if one could so distin-
guish either end from the other—tossing and bobbing
in the restless current. The raft looked flimsy and
primitive, its lashings frayed, its logs of uneven length,
battered and skinned from collisions with river rocks
and floating timber.

Close by the landing, a white man crouched over a
small pit, striking sparks from his flint into a bed of tinder. He was brown and grizzled, the knuckles on his
hands oversized, the wrists bony; he seemed to be made
altogether of sinew. A woman probably his wife was
coming up from the river carrying meat dripping water.
She was as tall, as spare, and as brown as he was. Her
flowered dress and sunbonnet were both faded almost
white and one of her shoes was worn through at the little toe. A little way off, a covered wagon stood on a
grassy level patch of earth. A pair of hobbled oxen were
grazing alongside it. Two young boys with pale pinched
faces peered through the puckered opening of the
cover.

The woman put the meat into a skillet. Her husband
asked her to get some buffalo chips from the wagon,
and she went to it and returned a moment later carrying a handful of dried dung. Hadley knew there were
no buffalo this side of the Kansas nor even anywhere
nearby on the other side. So where'd the buffalo chips
come from?

"Good morning, sir," he said.

"How d'you do, sir?" the man said, and glanced up
briefly at Hadley, and then went back to the fire.

"Hadley Chisholm," Hadley said.

"Ralph Hutchinson." He did not introduce the woman. She stood waiting for the tinder to catch. When it did, she dropped the buffalo chips into it and fanned them to a blaze with her bonnet.

"Where are you bound, sir, may I ask?" Hadley said.

"East to Council Bluffs," Hutchinson said.

From the corner of his eye, Hadley saw Jonah Comyns walking up from the river landing, where he'd been inspecting the raft. "Are you traveling alone then?" he asked.

"Just me and mine," Hutchinson said. "Left a train of eleven wagons bound for Oregon."

Comyns was at the fire now. He nodded to Hutchinson in brief greeting. Hutchinson nodded back.

"How far ahead are they?" Hadley asked.

"Left them a week ago."

"Any reason?"

"Children took ill," Hutchinson said.

"Of what?" Comyns asked at once.

"We thought at first it was cholera, like swept the land in '32."

"What was it then?"

"Don't know," Hutchinson said, and shook his head. "Camp fever, I guess. More'n a dozen in our party came down with it."

Comyns's eyes looked troubled; they kept darting to where Sarah stood talking to Bonnie Sue, the baby in her arms. Hadley didn't like what was happening. He knew the Pennsylvania widower had been preaching turnabout to anyone who'd listen. Here now was a man telling of fever on the trail ahead, and Comyns was taking it all in. Willoughby came up to the fire and stood there like a spook, tall and mournful, his ears open as water jugs.

"Is there game ahead, though?" Comyns asked.

"Game aplenty," Hutchinson said. "You won't go hungry on the plains unless you're lazy. This is buffalo meat right here. Wife was just down the river cuttin out the maggots and givin it a rinse."

"Are there Indians beyond?" Willoughby asked.

"Yep," Hutchinson said. "That's what there is out there; that's Indian territory out there." He brought the skillet to the fire, leveled it on the rocks surrounding the pit and the flames. The meat began to sizzle at once. Its aroma was unlike anything Hadley had ever sniffed before. He'd eaten breakfast not an hour and a half before, yet the smell of the cooking meat set his stomach to growling again.

"But you can kill an Indian by putting a bullet in him," Hutchinson said. "I don't know any way to kill a thing I can't see, that's causin my sons to burn with fever. I fear disease," he said simply.

"And I," Comyns said.

"The trail back to Council Bluffs? Has there been rain to turn it soft?"

"We came from Independence," Comyns said. "There was rain Monday night, but only sunshine since."

"Ah, good then," Hutchinson said.

"I can't risk it," Comyns said abruptly. "I'm sorry, Chisholm, I cannot risk it. I'd brave the river, I'd shoot wild Indians, but I can't risk the infant coming down with a fever might consume her. I'm sorry," he said, and shook his head, and turned again to Hutchinson. "If

you want company the way back," he said, "there's me
and my family'll provide it, sir."

"Welcome then," Hutchinson said.

Hadley waited.

"I'll join you, too," Willoughby said, and nodded.

Bobbo watched wagon and raft whirling away from the
dock and was certain all their goods would be carried
clear back to Westport, where the river poured into the
Missouri at the center of the nation. The Indians were
wearing only breechclouts and moccasins, shouting
instructions to each other in the language common to
both their tribes, poling the raft across the river as if it
were a pony they'd each and separately ridden before.
By the time they returned again to the right bank to
collect the humans and the livestock, Bobbo was beginning to feel a bit more confident of their skill. But that
was before the raft lurched away from the landing and
the current caught at it and sent its forward end plunging below the surface for a heart-stopping thirty sec-
onds.

It was worse than the Falls of Ohio.

The mules began pawing at once, pulling against
the pickets driven into the logs, braying as they had on
the descent through the Kentucky chute. The raft
dove again, water coming up over its forward end to
engulf it, the river hitting Bobbo's face in a harsh cold
smack. He closed his eyes against it, and then opened
them again immediately, fearing he'd drown without
witnessing the cause of it. Muscles rippled like
whitleather along the brown backs of the Indians.
Biceps bulging, breechclouts slapping about their legs,
they stepped swiftly and constantly for balance, as if

dancing a jig across the river. When at last the raft reached the opposite shore, Bobbo looked back and marveled that he was still alive. Timothy haggled further with Ferocious Storm, who insisted that the agreed-upon price be honored even though the Indians had ferried across only two wagons rather than four. Timothy staunchly maintained that the price should be cut in half. They reached a compromise Ferocious Storm apparently did not enjoy. He muttered something in his native tongue and then carried the bartered merchandise onto the raft, lashed it down tightly, and crossed the river again with his partners, never once looking back at the white men standing wet and bedraggled on the shore.

They camped for the night on a bend of the river some ten or twelve miles upstream. The sunset was more vivid than any they had ever seen back home. The entire horizon glowed with orange and gold that turned a deeper red and then a purple like gerardia. Blue then. And black. The blackest night, not a single star showing.

There were only the two wagons now.

You rode the seat till your backside was sore and aching, sun beating down on you, mules shitting—you could find the damn trail west just by following the animal shit of the party ahead. There was always the stench of manure in your nostrils. You'd think out here in the open, the stink'd be blown away in a minute, but you was moving so slow all the time, just that damn steady pace of the mules, that whenever one of them let go, you always got a whiff could knock you off the wagon seat. Walked beside the wagon sometimes. Got off the seat and walked. You could keep up easy enough, wagon was going so slow. Walked awhile, then got back up on the seat again, swapped places with Pa maybe, handled the reins awhile. Or went back inside to sit with Ma and the girls. Got your brains jiggled all the time.

Kept moving.

Through a valley thick with grass high as your waist. Streams fanning out from the river like the veins on the backs of your hands. Clouds coming up over the timbered hills behind.

When you was driving the mules, you yelled "Ha-ya!"

Some fun, this moving on west.

"I'm afraid here," Annabel said.

"Ain't nothin to be afraid of."

"Yes, Indians," she said.

They came calling on the morning of the seventeenth.

There were six in all—four full-blooded Kansas braves, a woman who was squaw to one of them, and a half-breed trailing a cow. Timothy hid his wife inside the covered Chisholm wagon, and went out to greet them. Their language was Siouan, which Timothy could only sing. But the half-breed knew some English, and they were able to communicate. He wanted to trade the cow for a horse. He kept looking around for where they had hobbled their horses. "For cow, horse," he said.

"We have no horses," Timothy said.

The half-breed looked around.

"No horse," he said.

"Correct. No horse."

"Mule then. Two mules. For cow." He held up two fingers. "Two."

"We need the mules," Timothy said.

"Then what?" the half-breed asked.

The squaw spoke French. She said, *"Qu'est-ce que c'est? Il n'y a pas un cheval?"*

The half-breed blinked.

"Pas des cheveaux," Timothy said.

"Alors," she said, and clucked her tongue.

They had fresh vegetables to trade, butter and milk. They showed the produce—onions, beans, lettuce, pumpkins, corn—and invited tastes of the milk and butter to prove the one wasn't sour and the other churned to creamy smoothness. When they left the encampment, they were carrying with them a string of beads that had been Annabel's, and a pocket watch Timothy claimed he would not need once they reached the Platte. Minerva, too, had been willing to part with half her tin of coffee for the good fresh milk and the sweet butter. The squaw called back *"Au'voir,"* and the party rode off through the trees.

Timothy explained then why he'd hidden his wife.

"There're two tribes who've been at war with the Pawnee since last spring," he said. "One's the Dakota, beyond and to the north. The other's the Kansas, right here and now."

"You think they saw her?" Bobbo asked.

"I don't know," Hadley said.

"Cause, Pa, if they *did* . . ."

"I know what you're thinkin."

The wagons were drawn up on either side of the fire, thirty feet between them. One end of the camp was against the river; the sound of splashing water would serve as an alarm if anyone approached from that side. In the open end of the U formed by wagons and river, Bobbo and Hadley stood guard.

"They'll come *get* her, Pa," Bobbo said. "Them people are *enemies*."

"Same as us and the Cassadas."

"Worse'n that, Pa."

"I'm wonderin about the one spoke a little English," Hadley said. "He seemed to want them mules real bad. Kept eying them all the while we were tradin for butter and milk."

"I saw him," Bobbo said.

"Had to have seen how small a party we are."

"Blind man would've seen that," Bobbo said. "Pa, he might come back tonight with a whole damn *tribe!*"

Hadley didn't answer.

"Pa?"

"Yeah, he sure enough might," Hadley said.

At the fire, Timothy was reading to the women. In a voice deliberately hoarse, he whispered, " 'During the whole of a dull, dark, and soundless day in the autumn of the year, when the clouds hung oppressively low . . .' "

They left the river bottom on the morning of the nineteenth, following the trail to higher ground. In the distance, ten miles or more away, they could still see the Kansas flowing eastward to Missouri, blue against a lush surrounding green. The hills through which they traveled now were consistently verdant. Red sandstone boulders erupted from the vegetation like huge blood blisters. Thickets of willows filled the ravines. Even in creeks run dry there were natural springs. Antelope raced through the woods.

Each time one crossed the trail, Bobbo thought it was Indians.

They came upon the village by accident.

It had been burned to the ground.

The wilderness claimed whatever had been consumed by fire, weeds and grass encroaching to the doorsteps of blackened lodges.

"Kansas village," Timothy said.

On the ground there were shields marked with Pawnee symbols, broken Pawnee lances. Strewn everywhere about in scorched garments were the skeletons of Kansas women and children. The skies were gray. There were ghosts in this place. They moved through it and past it swiftly.

The temperature that night dropped to forty-nine degrees.

The road northwestward to the Platte took them through shaded forests and glittering shallow pools, crossed them over streams that rushed as swiftly as rivers or dribbled away to nothingness. Amorpha was in bloom everywhere on the sun-washed hillsides, purple clusters bursting against soil almost black . . . and now there were roses!

Roses blooming on the prairie in small bunches, like unexpected cries of welcome. Roses thicker yet, spreading wild across the meadows, wafting a thick sweet scent on the southerly winds. Hadley picked a bouquet for Minerva, and she blushed as pink as what she held in her trembling hands.

Roses.

But not a sign of an Indian anywhere.

Timothy said the Indians were busy with their own problems, but Bobbo still feared that the ones who'd come to trade had spied a glimpse of his wife in the wagon, and would eventually come get her. Either that or her *own* damn people'd think she was being held prisoner, come raiding to rescue her. This was Pawnee country, Timothy said, as if that would keep them safe from attack.

The landscape kept changing.

The soil was coarser, red rocks mixed with some a sick yellow color, others gray as death. Big black boulders in the creeks. Bobbo worried about Indians all the time, worried, too, about catching up with the Oregon train. If just they *could* catch up, he'd stop worrying about Indians altogether. But the train were always just ahead.

"They're just ahead," his father kept saying.

Just ahead. Find traces of their fires. Pair of spectacles in a creek run dry. But never *them*. Like chasing a dream, Bobbo thought. You reach out for it, all that happens is you wake yourself up.

On the twenty-fifth, they made camp near where a Pawnee party had been hunting sometime past. There were still buffalo bones on the ground. A broken knife. Wooden frames upon which the Indians had stretched their hides to dry. The river bottom was covered with thistle, and the scent of something sweetish filled the woods.

"Pa," Bobbo said, "I got to tell you what's troublin me."

"Same thing that's troublin me," Hadley said.

"We'll be reachin the Platte sometime tomorrow," Bobbo said.

"Aye."

"Timothy'll be leavin us."

"I know that."

"We'll be alone, Pa."

"We're just as near alone now," Hadley said.

"Pa, how we gonna stand guard just the two of us the livelong night?"

"Son," Hadley said, "what do you want me to say? You think I don't know we're out here in the middle of goddamn *nowhere*? You think I don't *know* that?"

"It's . . . Pa, I'm scared."

Hadley put his arm around him. "Bobbo," he said, "maybe Timothy's right—maybe they're too busy fightin each other to pay us any mind. What we'll do anyway, we'll start movin a little faster each day, how's that? Try to pick up a few miles each day, close the distance 'tween us and the party ahead. They're just ahead, son," he said. "We'll catch em, don't you worry."

Timothy's wife came up from the river. She was singing. It was the first time any of them had heard her sing. Her voice was small, the Pawnee tune scarcely melodic. She had picked milk plant below. She boiled the pods now and offered them to the rest of the party, moving from one to the other, smiling and saying over and again in English, "Taste, please."

Her face was radiant.

She was almost home.

Ahead was the Coast of Nebraska.

"It's from the French," Timothy said. "Trappers named it *la cote de la Nebraska*. The Nebraska's the river, also known as the Platte. Those bluffs mark the bank on this side—the French were saying 'the *hills* of the Nebraska.' "

There was cactus growing on the bluffs, a pale bristling green against the royal purple of the amorpha. The hills were perhaps fifty feet high, the grass upon them thick and luxuriant. An early morning rain had washed the skies clean. They moved through the wide level valley and came at last to the shore of the river, got out of the wagons.

"Well . . ." Timothy said.

"Well then," Hadley said, "you got us here. We thank you, Timothy."

"I've got something for you," Timothy said, and went to the wagon. His wife watched as he rummaged through his things. "I hope you like these," he said. "They're not worth much, I know."

Along the way, he had made drawings of them all.

He presented these almost formally, seemingly embarrassed, shaking hands with each immediately afterward. His wife followed him, clumsily imitating the white man's custom, nodding and smiling as she gripped each hand in turn. She hurried Timothy back into the wagon then, eager to move on.

From the wagon seat, Timothy waved.

"Goodbye!" he shouted. "Good luck!"

"And to you!" Hadley called.

"Didn't even know her name," Minerva said, almost to herself.

"Hope she finds them," Annabel said.

"She'll find them," Bobbo said. "This is Pawnee country both sides of the river here." He looked at his father.

"Better get moving," Hadley said.

They watched a moment longer. Then Hadley got up on the seat of the wagon, with Minerva beside him, and the girls and Bobbo in back. Minerva had a rifle across her lap, and Bobbo had the muzzle of one resting on the tailgate.

He was wishing Gideon and Will were there.

V

ANNABEL

The buffalo were on one of the islands in the middle of the river. When she saw them, she thought at first they were just some bushes clumped out there on the island, brown and standing six feet tall. Then one of them moved, and she recognized them from drawings she'd seen, and said to Bonnie Sue, "Hey, there's some buffalo."

Bonnie Sue just looked at them and said nothing.

Annabel didn't know what on earth was wrong with her. Maybe she missed home same as did all the others, or maybe just Sean Cassada, who used to kiss her in the cornfield fore the feud started. The buffalo weren't scary at all. They just stood there, five of them in all, chewing grass. Looked like big hairy cows, was all. One glanced up across the river, probably smelled humans or heard them, but went right on back to eating. All five of them paid no mind to the wagon as it went rumbling by.

"Like to shoot me one of those for supper," Bobbo said.

"How'd you get over to the island without spookin em?" his father asked.

"Don't know," Bobbo said. "Water's shallow here, no more'n two or three feet deep."

"I'll bet any splashin'd set em runnin," Hadley said.

"Yeah," Bobbo said, and kept watching the buffalo.

They stopped later to look at the chart again. Ever since leaving Timothy and his wife, they looked at that chart like it was the Bible. They were getting close to the South Fork, Annabel guessed, which was where Pa said they'd have to cross over. Be there in a day or so, he said, meanwhile we just keep following this old river. The chart was marked with the word PAWNEE on either side the river, but Annabel hadn't seen a one of them and didn't want to either. Further west, where the river branched, there was CHEYENNE on the South Fork, and ARAPAHO on the North Fork, and to the northeast there was DAKOTA. However you looked at it, seemed like a big mess of Indians out there. Every time they came across some buffalo bones, Bobbo and her father studied them real close, trying to figure from whatever meat the wolves had left just how fresh the kill was. Where there were buffalo, there were Indians hunting them. But aside from those five grazing midriver, they didn't see hide nor hair of *either* till the Fourth of July.

They all got near to drunk that Independence Day.

"You're too young to be partaking of hard liquor," her father said.

"She's a woman now, Hadley," Minerva said.

"Eh?"

"Give the child a sip."

"Woman or child, which is it, eh?" Hadley asked, and handed Annabel the jug. She drank from it, and then passed it on to Bonnie Sue, who sat there looking . . . Annabel didn't *know* what. Angry or something. Minerva began giggling.

"Way we're swillin the stuff," she said, "the Pawnees'll descend on us for sure. Find a drunken band of no-goods."

"We'll ask them in to share a nip," Hadley said, and winked.

"Ask them in *where?*" Minerva said.

"Why, here in the family circle," Hadley said, and slapped Bobbo on the back suddenly and hugely, almost knocking him into the fire.

"Thought we were just stoppin to noon," Minerva said, and again giggled. "Instead, here we are havin a party."

"That's right," Hadley said. "This is Independence Day, the birthday of this great nation of ours. . . ."

"Okay, Pa," Bobbo said, grinning.

"Be ashamed to call myself American, we didn't celebrate one way or another."

"Right, Pa."

"Where's my rifle?"

"What you want with your rifle?"

"Need to shoot it off in the air, make some noise around here."

"Hadley, don't you go shootin—"

"You know what I hate about bein out here? It's so damn *quiet* all the time."

"You go shootin your gun, you'll draw Indians," Bobbo said.

"Hell with it then."

"No reason to cuss, Had."

"Let's have another drink. Hell with it."

The sun hung a fuzzy ball in the sky, the landscape seemed to shimmer. Annabel looked off into the distance. There was only dust at first. A moving cloud of dust. Rising. As though the earth itself were ascending heavenward. And then what seemed to be the timber moving. Her mouth fell open. Those were buffalo out there.

Thousands and thousands of them.

They stretched from horizon to horizon. Where her first glimpse less than a week ago had been somewhat akin to looking at a drawing in a book—five of them grazing motionless—this now, this *population*, struck her dumb with terror and disbelief. She had never before seen so many living things in one place or under one sky, neither humans collected in a circus tent in Bristol, nor horses or cows in pasture, nor even bees swarming or ants skittering when she poked at a hill with a stick, nor anything on God's green earth as multitudinous as these buffalo now that darkened the plains.

They came galloping down from the hills and through the ravines toward the river, chattering among themselves to raise a din that sounded less than choirly, the thunder of their hoofs rolling like drumbeats to accompany their own disharmony. Brown they were, so brown as to be black, moving out of the shimmering haze so that it seemed their very motion caused the ground to quake and shift them out of focus, dust and haze and motion combining to create an ocean swell of furry humped flesh and flying hoofs. Minerva's eyes popped wide open soon as she heard that distant murmur like a crowd of people mumbling stead of what were only shaggy beasts nudging and nattering as they rushed for the bank of the river. Even Bonnie Sue, who Annabel was of a mind to ask, "Excuse me, are you dead?" stirred enough to look off toward where the entire universe was in rolling motion.

Bobbo raised his rifle. Its crack sounded thin and sharp on the air. Smoke rose from the barrel in a wisp darker than the moody sky, rushing away on the wind. A beast toppled and skidded into the dirt, and Bobbo's exultant cry carried away as swiftly as the dissipating smoke.

They ignored the parts Timothy had told them were relished by Indians, usually eaten while the beast was being butchered and the organs still fresh. Timothy had witnessed virtual orgies, he'd said, braves smashing in the skulls of slaughtered cows or bulls to get at the succulent brains inside, slashing open bellies to scoop out blood with their cupped hands. Kidneys, eyes, testicles, and snouts, hoofs of unborn calves, udders warm with milk, livers, tongues—all were delicacies. Said he'd once enjoyed a raw pudding of liver and brains, still steaming, offered to him by his father-in-law in a bowl made of ribs cut from the slain buffalo. Enough to have made Annabel want to throw up. Never told them how to skin one, though, so they just went about butchering it the same way they'd have butchered a deer back home.

Bobbo cut off the balls and then slit the jugular and let the blood drain out. He cut a ring all the way around each of the hind legs, and then sliced both legs up to the crotch and peeled off the hide and did the same with the front legs, where he made his cuts up to the massive chest. He was sweating long before he finished peeling all four legs, and was beginning to think there was an easier way of doing this. He'd have to ask somebody when they got to Fort Laramie, but meanwhile the carcass and the job were spread out there on the ground in front of him.

The shaggy beast must've weighed fifteen hundred pounds at least; took the whole family to roll him over so Bobbo could make his cut from belly to chest. He realized he'd never get the hide off in one piece, so they rolled the animal over again, and Bobbo made another cut from the neck over the hump to the tail. The bull was on the ground on his belly now, his legs spread and already peeled, looking like somebody'd taken off his black wool stockings but left on his black fur coat. Bobbo surmised by now that there'd been no need for peeling the legs at all, but he'd already done that, so there was no use fretting over it. With Hadley's help, he pulled and sliced and yanked both halves of the hide loose from the animal and then Hadley chopped off the head with an ax, just behind the ears, same as he would have a deer.

This was no dainty little deer they were carving up here, though. It was instead a beast could feed a regiment, and they became speculative butchers on the spot, chopping the animal up the middle with the ax and then quartering it, and seeking out what they thought were the choicest cuts, Minerva hovering and advising, telling them to save this or that organ till to all intents and purposes they were keeping for food all the Indians themselves might have kept, save the eyeballs and the other balls Bobbo'd cut off first. Minerva

even had them keep for marrow the leg bones Bobbo
had meticulously exposed when he'd still thought he
was dealing with a doe or a buck, and she asked him
now to rescue whatever blood he could from spilling
onto the ground; said it would make a good rich gravy
later on.

There were buffalo chips everywhere, scattered
among the bright yellow sunflowers. They made their
fire, and fed it with the dried and weathered dung, and
then put up steaks to fry, three inches thick. Hadley
lifted his cup and said, "God bless this land of ours,
God bless it."

On a hill some three hundred feet above where they
sat around the fire and raised their cups and echoed
Hadley's toast, partially hidden by a conical peak
sculpted by wind and rain, an Indian watched them.

The scout was called Otaktay.

He was one of the braves in a Dakota war party of
four. The organizer and leader of the party was an
eighteen-year-old named Teetonkah. He was the oldest
of the four; the youngest was only sixteen. Teetonkah
had still been a small boy many years before when during the Moon of the Duck Eggs, a Pawnee war party
attacked his village and captured half a dozen Dakota
women, who, it was rumored, later caused the smallpox
epidemic in the Pawnee nation, killing countless numbers of their children. Teetonkah had been on many
war parties since that time; raids were constant, the war
between the tribes was incessant.

When he decided to organize *this* war party, he did
so because he wished to gain more honor for himself by
capturing Pawnee horses. And Pawnee women. He

liked Pawnee women. His first experience had been
with a Pawnee woman captured by his uncle.
Teetonkah had taken her fiercely and proudly. She had
whimpered beneath his assault. There were now four
Pawnee women in the village, and he found all of them
more comely than any of the women in his own tribe.
He wished to own a Pawnee woman of his own.
Perhaps two. Horses as well. A dozen horses perhaps,
and three or four Pawnee women.

He sat at the fire now and listened in astonishment
to Otaktay's report. Otaktay had removed the white
scouting cloths from his head and shoulders, and was
sitting on his haunches to the right of Teetonkah, who
was his cousin. In the first quarter of the Moon of
Moulting Feathers, Teetonkah had invited him and two
others to his tipi. He told them first that he knew them
all to be courageous and venturesome and that he
trusted each of them well. He then went on to explain
that at the time of the Wood-Cracking Moon last year,
a band of Pawnee raiders had stolen from his older sister Talutah a pony she had dearly loved, and she had
been crying over the theft since that winter past, and
this made Teetonkah's heart very bad. He wished now
to ride out against the Pawnee and find their horses
where they were and take them away as they had taken
Talutah's.

He said this was an auspicious time for such a raid
since it was at this very moon a year before that the
tribe had attacked the Pawnee in vast numbers and
taken many scalps and many horses. Teetonkah asked
his cousin and his friends to join him now in this quest
that would heal his sister's broken heart. He wished as
well to capture some Pawnee women, whose skills were

surely being wasted planting seeds when there were strong Dakota braves eager to plant within them seeds of quite another sort. All the young men laughed. They had all sampled the treasures of Teetonkah's uncle's captured Pawnee maid.

The young men talked long into the night about the route they would take to the Pawnee village, though the route was familiar to all of them. Teetonkah, as organizer and leader, scratched a map into the earthen floor and promised to leave his uncle a drawing on buckskin of their exact route, indicating which rivers and hills they expected to cross or climb, so that they could be found at any time by others in the tribe. In acceptance of Teetonkah's plan, they smoked the pipe he proffered, and left the village on horseback early the next morning. There was no grand farewell as they rode out south. There would be time for celebration if and when they returned victorious. With horses. With women.

Teetonkah was carrying several pairs of moccasins, and a wooden bowl attached to his belt with a leather thong; on the warpath each man ate and drank from his own dish. He carried, too, a leather pouch of vermilion paint and grease, with which to decorate himself and his horse before he rode into battle. A wolfskin was draped over his left shoulder, the animal's nostrils threaded with the leather thong at the end of Teetonkah's war whistle. A medicine bag was tied to his horse's bridle. There were herbs in this leather pouch that could be ingested by horse and man alike to cure toothache or lameness, stomach trouble or pains of the heart. None of the four who rode out that morning had any intention of meeting with the white man or engaging him in battle. They were off to steal Pawnee horses and Pawnee women; this was the only war they expected to make.

"A wagon alone," Otaktay said.

The others looked at him.

"Alone," he repeated.

"It is a trick," Teetonkah said.

"I saw nothing else wherever I looked. If there are others, they are hidden better than I can find them."

"Yes but it is a trick," Teetonkah said, and then immediately asked, "How many are there in the party?"

"Five that I could see."

"And how divided?"

"Two men and three women."

"Horses?"

"None. But two mules drawing the wagon."

"We are far from home," one of the others said. His name was Enapay, and he had been named for his courage. "Were we to attack the white man, we would have to abandon our plan against the Pawnee."

"Why do you say that?" Teetonkah asked.

"We would have captives," Enapay said. "We would take the women captive, would we not?"

"Yes," Teetonkah said.

"Then we would have them with us when we rode against the Pawnee."

"No," Teetonkah said. "We would ride home with them first. Then later—"

"While others in the village—"

"—ride against the Pawnee."

"While others in the village enjoy what we have risked our lives for," Enapay said.

"There are those we trust," Teetonkah said.

"I trust no one where it comes to a woman's belly," Enapay said. "White women secrete a musk that can be smelled even by horses. I have seen horses pawing at lodges where white women were kept bound within."

Teetonkah laughed.

"It is true," Enapay said.

"It will be safe to take them to the village. My uncle will guard them."

"The way he guarded his own Pawnee woman," Enapay said sourly. "If there is one in the village who has not had her, I will gift him with however many horses I capture from the Pawnee." He scowled into the fire, and then said, "If ever we ride out again."

"We will do this with the white man first. And when we have taken the three women home, we will ride out again."

"That was not our plan," Enapay said. "I do not like changing plans."

"But the wagon is alone," Teetonkah said simply.

"There are two men," Enapay said.

"Who do not know we are here."

Enapay considered this. It was true that four surprising a smaller number of men could be thought of as eight or even ten. But the white men had rifles, and in this war party there were none. He mentioned this now. "There are rifles," he said. "Otaktay, are there not rifles?"

"Yes, there are rifles."

"And we have none."

"We will have rifles later this night," Teetonkah said.

"The women, all three, have hair of a yellow color," Otaktay said.

"The women are sometimes fierce," Enapay said darkly.

"More the reason to take them," Teetonkah said, and grinned.

On the ground near the fire, the wolfskin he had earlier worn on his shoulder was spread with the head pointing toward what had been their destination: the Pawnee village. He lifted the skin now, and placed it on the ground again so that the wolf's nose was pointed toward where Otaktay said he had seen the solitary wagon.

"Is there any here who has dreamed of a wolf?" he asked.

Howahkan, who had been silent till now, said, "I." He was the youngest among them. His face looked troubled. Two of his brothers had been slain in encounters with the white man, and though he was eager to avenge their murders, he was also somewhat afraid. He accepted from Teetonkah the pipe he offered, and holding the bowl in his left hand, the stem in his right, said in the strange rasping voice for which he had been named, "Wakang'tangka, behold this pipe, behold it. I ask you to smoke it. We want to get horses. I ask you to help us. That is why I speak to you with this pipe." He reversed the position of the pipe now, holding the bowl in his right hand and the stem in his left, pointing up toward his left shoulder. "Now, wolf," he said, "behold this pipe. Smoke it and bring us horses."

"There are no horses," Otaktay said.

"I know that," Howahkan replied.

"Then do not pray for horses when we know there are only mules."

"Pray for help in capturing the women, too," Teetonkah said.

"I would have you do the pipe," Howahkan said,

insulted, and started to hand the pipe back to Teetonkah.

"It is you who dreamt of the wolf," Teetonkah said.

Howahkan nodded sullenly, put the unlighted pipe in his mouth, and said, "Wakang'tangka, I will now smoke this pipe in your honor. I ask that no harm come to us in battle. I ask that we may get many horses."

"*Again* the horses!" Otaktay said. "He *knows* there are only mules."

"And many women," Howahkan said, looking to Teetonkah for approval. He lit the pipe and puffed on it then, holding the bowl in both hands. "Behold this pipe," he said, "and behold us. We have shed much blood. We have lost brothers and friends in battle. I ask you to protect us from shedding more blood, and to give us long lives." He puffed on the pipe again, and then passed it to Teetonkah. Teetonkah smoked the pipe solemnly and silently, and then passed it to Otaktay, who puffed on it and handed it to Enapay, who still seemed doubtful. He accepted the pipe, but before he smoked it, he said again, "I do not like changing plans. The plan was for the Pawnee." He put the stem between his teeth then, and drew on the pipe and let out a puff of smoke.

There was no medicine man among them, who would have sprinkled water on the wolfskin and sung a song and prayed to Wakang'tangka for rain to hide them when they attacked. But Howahkan had dreamt the night before of the warrior wolf, and they asked him now to sing a song for rain. He was not a medicine man; he knew no songs for rain. So he sang a song he thought applied to the attack they would make as soon as it was dark. They stood about him as he sang hoarsely in the gathering dusk; beside him, Enapay imitated the sound of an owl.

"Someone like this," Howahkan sang,

"Is not likely to reach anywhere,

"You are saying.

"Horses

"I am coming after."

Enapay reached into the leather pouch at his waist and daubed his fingers with vermilion paint. He painted a crescent on his mouth so that it appeared a grinning red wound curling upward to his cheekbones. He painted his hands and his feet red. From a rawhide case he took a single feather and fastened it at the back of his head, standing upright, for he had earned it by killing an enemy without himself having been harmed. Below that single erect feather he fastened two others horizontally, to signify that he had counted coup on two fallen enemies in the same battle. The others were fastening feathers now and applying paint. Otaktay was putting on a decorated war shirt. Howahkan, expecting they would be attacking the Pawnee on the morrow, had searched all that day for earth a mole had worked up, and he mixed that now with blue paint and a pow-dered herb, and rubbed the war medicine on his body and on that of his horse. He offered some of the medi-cine to the others, and they all accepted, rubbing it on their chests and their limbs, Teetonkah mixing his with vermilion paint, which he daubed in a wide band across his forehead and across his horse's chest.

Otaktay complained that they had done and were *still* doing everything wrong—starting with Howahkan praying for horses while doing the pipe, and again just now when he'd sung "Horses I am coming after," though he had been told repeatedly there were only mules. And now each was painting his horse and face in colors and designs different one from the other when surely they had been on war parties where a medicine man was in attendance and the horses and faces had been painted uniformly. On such a party recently, a man named Wambleeskah had made medicine, and had painted Otaktay's horse and those of the others with white clay lightning flashes from the mouth over the chest and down the front legs and on the hind legs as well. He had then painted a blue band across the forehead of each horse and had painted blue spots on their flanks. There had been six braves in the party, and he had painted each of their faces blue and had then painted white lines across their foreheads and trailing down their cheeks.

Otaktay insisted that those in *this* party at least mount their horses facing east and then walk them single file in a circle before riding out against the wagon. Teetonkah told him he was an old woman. Howahkan, his face blue and smelling of earth and medicine, laughed—but only because he was nervous.

It was close to seven-thirty now. The night air was cool. The afternoon haze had burned off before suppertime, and there were stars and a moon, lazy cloud traces occasionally crossing its face to cast drifting shadows on the ground. The fire blazed not thirty feet from where the wagon stood. The mules were picketed between the wagon and the fire. Everyone in the family was still awake, but a guard had been posted nonetheless—Bobbo on the side of the wagon exposed to the prairie. Marauding wolves ventured closer and closer to the fire, drawn by the scent of the slain buffalo, eager to get at the carcass. In the darkness, they howled their intention, circling restlessly. Annabel didn't think they'd come clear into camp, but she wasn't sure.

"Can I take a shot at them, Pa?" Bobbo yelled.

"No, leave them be," Hadley yelled back.

"Raise the dead, way they're yammering," Bobbo said.

Standing just this side of the wagon, between it and the fire, Minerva was brushing her hair, counting the strokes.

"Drive a man crazy with that countin out loud," Hadley said.

"Thirty-three, thirty-four, thirty-five . . ."

"You've had too much to drink, Min."

"Thirty-six, *hush*, thirty-seven . . ."

The wolves were still howling.

"Let me take a shot at them, Pa," Bobbo called.

"Leave em be, son," Hadley said.

Bonnie Sue had already crawled under her blanket. "Does anyone in this family have any notion of sleeping tonight?" she asked.

Annabel giggled. She'd taken off her bodice and skirt, and was walking barefooted in her petticoat, toward the dark side of the wagon. "Whyn't you let him shoot one of the critters?" she said. "Otherwise, they'll be at it all night long."

"Ain't there *nobody* planning to sleep tonight?" Bonnie Sue asked.

Annabel giggled again.

"Forty-seven, forty-eight, forty-nine," Minerva said.

A little distance from the fire and the wagon both, not so far from either so that the wolves would get her,

Annabel lifted her petticoat and let down her drawers
and was preparing to pee when she heard what sounded
like a whistle or a pipe, one of them wooden pipes the
mountain people back home were all the time whittling. She peered into the darkness and could see nothing. It occured to her that not a moment before she'd
seen the moving shadows of the wolves, had even been
able to make out their eyes gleaming in the darkness.
She couldn't see nary a wolf now, nor did she hear them
howling anymore.

"Bobbo?" she called.

"Yeah, Sis?"

"You hear something just—"

Somebody grabbed her from behind. She screamed,
and urine ran down the inside of her leg and then
stopped abruptly. He pulled her over by the hair, flat on
her back, her underdrawers bunched around her ankles.
She saw him only upside down. His face was painted
with a grinning red mouth, feathers were in his hair. He
had a tomahawk in his hand. She screamed again, and
tried to scramble away, but he pinned her to the ground
and straddled her as he would a pony, and then put the
tomahawk down and reached for something at his belt.

She grabbed for the tomahawk at once.

Her fingers closed on the leather-encased haft and
she swung the thing like the simple hatchet it was. His
hand was coming up from his belt; there were leather
thongs in it. He dropped the thongs and, tried to protect his face, the fingers of his hand widespread. The
sharp flint edge of the tomahawk cut through two fingers and struck him clean between the eyebrows, splitting open his forehead. Blood spurted out of him like a
fountain. Annabel screamed and let go the hatchet.

She was still screaming when she came around the wagon tongue, pulling up her underdrawers. There were three more of them, one of them painted blood red like the one she'd just split open, another blue, the last a color seemed brown or black. Her father lay on the ground just near the back of the wagon, blood pouring from the side of his head. Bonnie Sue was on the bottom of an Indian straddling her same as she'd just been, only this one was wearing a beaded shirt. Bonnie Sue kicked and punched at him, but he had his forearm pressed hard against her throat and she was choking. Annabel ran to the fire, pulled a flaming stick from it, and ran back to where the Indian was on top of Bonnie Sue. He had a knife in his hand, he'd pulled a knife from his belt, Jesus, he was going to kill her!

She pushed the burning stick at his naked arm where the shirt ended, and the Indian let out a yell and jumped off Bonnie Sue. Annabel threw away the stick and started running. She could hear horses out there someplace; there'd be more Indians on them in a minute. The one she'd just poked with the stick grabbed her arm, swung her around, and punched her full in the face. She heard something snap inside her nose, and fell to her knees in pain, her hands covering her face. Blood was pouring from her nose. Where was the Indian, where'd he . . . ? She turned, saw him running back to where he'd dropped his knife. He picked up the knife. It was a metal knife, the firelight glittered on its edge, he was coming back to where she sat with her petticoat tented over her knees.

Almost without looking at her, he stuck the knife in her and pulled it out again.

She felt only pain like she'd been burned, and then

saw blood spreading into the white petticoat, and clutched for the wound. Blood welled up between her fingers. He pulled her hair away from her face, and brought the knife to her forehead. She thought: *Please, no*, and tried to scream but could not find the strength, and could not raise her hand to stop him. He slit the flesh across her forehead, just below the hairline, and was beginning to peel back her scalp when Bobbo shot him in the back. Feathers and beads exploded between his shoulder blades. He fell forward onto Annabel, his hand releasing the knife, the blade still caught between the scalp he'd been lifting and the skull beneath it.

The other two Indians had hold of Minerva, the one of them wearing the wolfskin and the other with his face painted entirely blue. Bobbo couldn't reload, they gave him no time to reload. He ran to where his mother was trying to fight them off, and swung the stock of his rifle at the back of the one with the wolf-skin, but the Indian was strong and fierce and shrugged off the blows like they were flies annoying him. Minerva was holding to the wagon wheel with one hand, and with the other she was hitting them with her hairbrush. The Indians kept talking to themselves all the while they tried to pry her loose from the wagon wheel, and finally the one with the wolfskin began punching her repeatedly in the chest, and the one with the blue face turned on Bobbo with a knife and came at him with the blade extended toward his gut.

Bobbo reached for the Indian's thrusting hand instinctively, ignoring for the moment the knife that was clutched in it, grabbing for the wrist the way he'd grabbed for Will's or Gideon's when they were rassling, pulling the Indian toward him, using the force of his own momentum, and at the same time bringing his knee up into the Indian's groin. The Indian's eyes opened wide in the painted face. Bobbo saw the face an instant before he dropped the knife. As Bobbo stooped to pick it up, he thought: *He's no older'n me.* His hand closed around the bone handle. *Maybe younger,* he thought. The Indian was doubled in pain on the ground, his hands clutching his balls. Bobbo plunged the knife blade deep into his chest. He raised the knife and plunged it again. And then another time. Then he turned away and vomited into his hands.

Behind him, the Indian with the wolfskin pulled Minerva off the wagon wheel, looped one arm around her waist, and began dragging her toward where she could hear horses whinnying and pawing the earth. They had torn her petticoat up the front during the struggle and her breasts were exposed; she was embarrassed that her son would see her this way. Oddly, she felt neither fear nor anger. She knew only that this Indian painted red was trying to take her someplace she didn't want to go. Stubbornly, she resisted. Kicking, striking with her closed fists wherever she could reach him, she resisted with every ounce of strength she possessed. She could still feel the pain where he had struck her between the breasts, but she struggled fiercely until he hit her again full in the mouth, splitting her lip and causing it to bleed, knocking loose two teeth, which she spat with blood into her hand. He knocked her hand away from her mouth, and the teeth went flying. He caught hold of her wrist, dragged her into the darkness. She could see four painted horses. He unhobbled one of them and threw her over a blanket stinking of sweat and piss, and then swung himself up over the horse's back and made a clucking sound to the animal. She knew then that unless she did something at once, unless she found the will and the strength to stop him, he would take her wherever he wished. She thought suddenly of the patroon Jimmy Jackson. The horse was in motion.

She rolled back against him and eased herself upright so that she was riding as she might have sidesaddle. He must have thought she was preparing to leap from the horse; he immediately put his left arm around her, twisting his hand into the torn petticoat, his right hand clinging to the reins, the wolfskin on his shoulder stinking as bad as had the blanket. It was then that she clawed for his face, reaching for his eyes. He screamed aloud, the horse veering as he yanked at the reins. Her spread right hand found something soft and jellylike, her fingers were closing on his right eye, she would pluck the eyeball from its socket like a hard-boiled egg, in an instant she would blind him.

He threw her from the horse. He flung her away from him as though she were a curse. He did not look back. He kept galloping away from her while behind him she lay trembling on the ground with the thought of what she had almost done.

By their reckoning, they were still two hundred miles from Fort Laramie.

They feared Annabel would die before they got there. They had made poultices of spirit turpentine and sugar, and they applied one of these to the head wound, and wrapped it tight with a clean cotton petticoat torn into bandages. The second poultice was larger; they put it over the jagged gash in her side, but the blood wouldn't stop, it kept seeping up through the poultice. They changed the poultice three, four times that night, and each time the blood worked its way through, and they didn't know what else to do to get it to stop. They had no recourse to remedies they knew: chimney soot mixed with lard, pine resin. All they could do was change the poultice each time it got drenched again with blood.

They kept expecting the Indians to come back.

They figured the one who'd got away, the one wearing the wolfskin, would return with a passel of them this time, if only to retrieve the horses. There were angry black and blue marks on Minerva's breasts where the Indian had struck her, and she ached with each breath she took. Hadley had pulled the stumps of her broken teeth, and she'd stuffed a rag into her mouth to stop the bleeding. But her jaw and lip were swollen, the lip split besides from the force of the Indian's blow. She swore to Hadley she'd have blinded him like Samson given just another moment. He said, "No, you wouldn't have, Min."

The horses were fine animals, a stallion and a pair of mares, looked like the Chickasaw running woods horses they were familiar with back home, Spanish breeds crossed with those the colonists brought from England. Bobbo wanted to ride one of them ahead, try to catch up with the wagon train. If there was a doctor in the party . . .

"No," Minerva said.

"Ma," he said, "I could fetch him back with me."

"I'd fear for your life," Minerva said softly.

By morning, Annabel's bleeding had stopped. They put a fresh poultice on the wound below, and bandaged it tightly, and changed, too, the poultice and bandage on her head. At six o'clock, they broke camp and began moving toward the South Fork of the Platte.

She was burning with fever when they crossed the river on the morning of the seventh. The weather had turned sticky and hot, adding to her discomfort. She lay on a quilt in the wagon bed, covered with a linen bed sheet had been part of Grandmother Chisholm's dower. There had been little rain in this part of the country, and the river was low and the bottom firm. For this much they were grateful; they could not have coped with anything the likes of the Kansas.

"Have I been scalped, Pa?" she asked.

He smiled and patted her hand. "No, darlin," he said. "You've still got all your beautiful hair on your head, where it's sposed to be."

"What happened to your ear that's all bandaged?"

"An Injun figgered I'd look best with but a single ear."

He'd seen the Indian an instant before the blow struck, saw the rounded stone head of the weapon in his hand and knew it was not a hatchet. There'd been the whistle first, and then the sound behind him, and he'd turned to see the Indian with his face painted blue, the same one Bobbo later stabbed, and the maul coming for the back of his head. He'd turned, trying to duck away, but the blow caught him full on the ear, and that was the last he knew of anything till he felt Minerva's gentle hands upon him, washing away the blood and dressing the wound. He had a headache now the likes of which he'd never had in his life.

"Did he take it from your head then, Pa?" Annabel asked.

"No, darlin, it's still there," Hadley said, and they both laughed.

"Is my nose broke? It feels broke."

"Yes, darlin," he said.

He knew she was going to die.

The earliest they could hope to find a doctor was at Fort Laramie, unless there was one in the Oregon train ahead. But with Annabel sick this way, Hadley couldn't push too hard, and their rest periods were longer and more frequent. He was afraid as well that too much jostling would start her wounds to bleeding more heavily. They were seeping blood again, and Minerva was worried they'd soon begin to fester. On the high plateau between the two forks, they found a pine forest and slashed the trees for resin and made poultices to keep in readiness should the bleeding get worse. When they moved out of the narrow crotch where the river forked, they could for miles still see both forks, the one to the south angling ever wider, the other constantly on their right. They stopped often to wet the cloths they put to Annabel's burning forehead. Were they home, they'd have made snakeroot tea, or boiled wild ginger roots or pennyroyal leaves to bring the fever down. But they were not home.

The pine forest was the last real timber they saw for several days. Here and there a solitary tree stood specterlike on the riverbank, but for the most part the plains were unwooded. The thick luxurious grass that had earlier covered the prairie was all but gone now. The animals seemed not to notice the difference, and ate the yellow grass as heartily. But to the family the entire countryside had of a sudden become barren and dry, and they began to think of this as the true landscape of the west, and wondered if it would remain this way till they reached the Rockies. Already the rock out-croppings seemed to promise distant mountains.

More and more often, they found discarded items from the party ahead. It was as though the parched and empty land discouraged the trappings of civilization, made butter churns and spinning wheels seem super-fluous and perhaps foolish. There *was* no milk to churn or yarn to spin in this sandy land of limestone, granite, and marl. The discarded household items made the Oregon train more real, almost tangible. If only they could travel a mite faster, if only those ahead would rest a bit longer, why then they would meet. And, God will-ing, there'd be a doctor with the party who could min-ister to Annabel and relieve her pain and make her well and whole again.

The two Indian mares were tied to the wagon on short halters behind. On the wagon's right, Bobbo rode the stallion; he'd washed the paint off it last time they'd stopped to water. He was having difficulty staying on the frame saddle, and swore at the animal as if it under-stood English. On the seat up front, Hadley clucked to the mules, and Minerva scanned the horizon for Indians. A rifle was on her lap. Inside the wagon, she heard Annabel ask again had she been scalped, heard Bonnie Sue answer, "No, you've still got your scalp right there where it should be."

Minerva turned her face away from Hadley's lest he see she was on the edge of tears.

The valley of the North Platte was ahead of them now.

This was the sixteenth day of July, and they hoped to reach Fort Laramie by the eighteenth or nineteenth. It no longer mattered whether or not they overtook the Oregon-bound wagon train. They had given up hope of doing so, as easily as a pauper gave up hope of one day becoming rich. Now Fort Laramie was their salvation; at Fort Laramie there would be a doctor; at Fort Laramie there would be medicine. The fort signified civilization; without whatever help awaited them there, they knew Annabel would die.

They marvelled that she was not dead already, and praised God for his mercy.

The touch of her flesh was blistering. Neither the gaping wound in her side nor the gash where she'd near been scalped had even begun to heal. Instead, both were festering with pus. Her eyes were luminous and round, glowing with the fever that ignited her. She spoke of playmates none of them had ever met, and once she screamed aloud that the top of her head was gone and begged Bobbo, who was sitting by her side, to please, sir, find her head as was missing, sir, not recognizing him as her brother though she stared full into his face, her green eyes wide and wet.

They passed without interest landmarks they might normally have greeted with enthusiasm. Ash Hollow, where after miles of shadeless travel, they found the forest of magnificent trees that had given the bottom of the valley its name, undergrown with roses and other wildflowers, running with a spring of icy cold water. Court House Rock, which was said to resemble an actual courthouse in St. Louis, though they'd been there and could remember none like it, four hundred feet or more of clay and volcanic ash rising in tiers beside the trail. Close by it stood the rock called Jailhouse, which did not look like a jail to them, nor did they care. Fourteen miles past that was famous Chimney Rock, about which they'd heard so much in Independence.

Annabel did not see it when they passed it now. She was babbling in delirium of a red devil with brighter red spots, and Bonnie Sue recalled that the Indian who'd stabbed her had his arms painted that way.

"There's the rock resembles a smokestack," Hadley said.

"Aye," Minerva said, and touched her daughter's forehead.

She died just as they were crossing the plain beyond.

The ground here was covered with cedar driftwood. They could not bury her on this wood-strewn plain, where all seemed rotted debris. Bobbo remembered hearing in Independence that there'd been a flood years back, carrying timber down from the Black Hills. Hadley said that seemed likely. They stood with their hands in their pockets. Inside the wagon, Minerva was keening.

They crossed the cedar plain to the place marked Scotts' Bluff on their chart, and near the river escarpment they found a patch of level land sparsely covered with browning grass. There were no flowers in abundance, as they'd seen the month before, but Bonnie Sue found growing by the river some wildflowers she could not identify, and she wove these into a garland they placed on Annabel's head, over the bandage covering her wound. There was no sawed lumber with which to build a coffin. They wrapped her in blankets as though she were a babe in swaddling clothes, and then they lowered her gently into the earth. Hadley spoke over his dead daughter. He did not read from the Bible, he knew the words by heart; nor could he have seen them anyway with his eyes brimming. Minerva stood beside him, clinging tightly to his hand.

" 'The harvest is past,' " he said, " 'the summer is ended, and we are not saved. For the hurt of the daughter of my people am I hurt; I am black; astonishment hath taken hold on me. Is there no balm in Gilead?' " he asked softly. " 'Is there no physician there? why then is not the health of the daughter of my people recovered? Oh that my head were waters, and mine eyes a fountain of tears, that I might weep day and night for the slain—' " His voice broke. He began crying openly. " '—of the daughter of my people,' " he said, and then said, "Amen."

"Amen," the others said.

They stood with heads bent as Bobbo shoveled earth into the grave. Then they replaced the browned sod, and drove the wagon back and forth over the grave so that Indians would not find it and dig it up. They camped that night a little way from where they had buried her, not wanting to leave her alone so soon in the wilderness.

In the distance, they could see the snow-covered peaks of the Laramie Mountains.

They reached Fort Laramie on the twentieth day of July.

Minerva's swollen jaw had subsided by then, her split lip had healed. Beneath the bandage still on Hadley's head, his ear was crusted and scabby where the Indian maul had struck it. But the ear was covered, and there was nothing about the physical appearance of any of them to indicate they'd been attacked by Indians two weeks before. Unless you looked into their eyes.

A dozen or more tipis formed a virtual Indian village on the level stretch of ground behind one wall of the fort, and more were scattered everywhere on the surrounding terrain. The Chisholms passed through them on their approach, Bobbo riding the Indian stallion, the mares trailing on halters behind the wagon. There was still war paint on the chest of one mare, where they could not scrub it clean this morning at the river above the fort. Indian dogs barked and nipped at the wagon wheels and the hoofs of the horses. Indian children ran half-naked in front of the mules, taunting them with sticks. Tall Indian men in white buffalo robes eyed the horses and noticed well the painted chest of the one mare. Squaws stood over simmering kettles, stirring, watching silently as the wagon went through.

At the main entrance to the fort, they left Bobbo to watch the animals and the wagon, and went through first a gate and then an arched passage. A second gate beyond opened into a courtyard that looked to be a hundred feet square. There were as many Indians inside the fort as there were out, squatting on the ground or in the doorways of rooms built against the walls. The walls were at least fifteen feet high, topped with a stockade fence shorter and flimsier than pictures they'd seen of the old fort back home, before the pickets were torn down. There were Indian squaws and children inside here yapping and yammering, food cooking, Indian men stopping at one or another kettle to pluck a piece of greasy meat from it. At the end of the fort opposite the main gate, there was a postern gate and a railing where half a dozen mules and as many horses were hitched. A flight of steps rose to a gallery above. As they approached, a man came down those stairs, his hand extended.

"My name is Lucien Orliac," he said. His voice was tinged with the faintest French accent. "I am in charge of the fort."

"Hadley Chisholm," Hadley said, and took his hand. "My family."

"How do you do?" Orliac said. He shook Hadley's hand briefly and then said, "Ladies," and nodded to Minerva and Bonnie Sue in welcome. He was wearing a broad-brimmed black hat, a sleeveless buckskin jacket over a homespun blue shirt banded at the wrists. His trousers were brown, and he wore leather leggings and beaded Indian moccasins. He had a thick black beard and black eyebrows, and black hair spilled in ringlets from beneath the flat black hat. From the neck up, he looked like a charcoal drawing Timothy might have made.

"You are traveling alone?" he asked, surprised.

"Yes, sir," Hadley said.

"You are lucky to have come this far unharmed."

Hadley said nothing.

"The apartments in the fort are completely occupied at the moment—"

"We want only a place to—"

"Company personnel," Orliac said. "Their wives, their children. You understand."

"We need to rest," Hadley said.

Orliac looked into his eyes. "You are welcome to stay within the walls," he said.

"Thank you," Hadley said. "I'll go fetch my son."

He began walking toward the main gate. Orliac fell into step beside him. Minerva seemed uncertain as to whether she should follow or not. She took Bonnie Sue's hand, and together they stood close by the interior wall, watching the Indians, listening to their alien babble.

"The factor is in Winnipeg just now," Orliac said. "I would have offered you his apartment, but it is occupied."

"That's all right," Hadley said.

"A wagon train was here ten days ago; they've departed now for Oregon. All but some with lingering fever. It is they who are in the factor's apartment."

"Thank you anyway," Hadley said.

"You'll be safe here inside the fort," Orliac said. "Or indeed anywhere near it."

"Are there soldiers then?" Hadley asked.

"Soldiers? No, no," Orliac said, shaking his head. "This is the American Fur Company, eh? We are here for trade, that's all. No, no, this is not an army outpost."

They had reached the main gate now. Outside, Bobbo still sat on the wagon seat, looking apprehensively at the Indians all around. Orliac saw the horses at once.

"You have met Indians?" he asked.

"Yes," Hadley said.

"I would bring the horses inside," Orliac said. "I do not think any of the Indians here would steal a horse belonging to a white man, eh? But these . . ." He shrugged elaborately. "The saddles, the bridles, the paint . . ." He shrugged again. "They are without question Indian horses. I would bring everything inside. The wagon, the mules, the horses especially. Yes," he said, and nodded, and extended his hand to Bobbo. "How do you do, young man. I am Lucien Orliac."

"Bobbo Chisholm."

"Come, come inside. Where did you meet these Indians?" he asked Hadley. "Bobby, bring them in. Come."

Bobbo put the rifle on the seat beside him, and then picked up the reins. He shouted to the mules, and the wagon moved forward through the gate, the horses behind it. Orliac stepped aside to let them past.

"You said where?" he asked Hadley.

"Thirty, forty miles before we crossed the Platte."

"Ah? They were Pawnee?"

"I don't know," Hadley said.

"No matter, you are safe now," Orliac said, and smiled. "Here the Indians are interested only in trade, eh? They bring us furs, we give them in return guns, powder and lead . . ."

Hadley looked at him.

". . . blankets," Orliac went on, "cloth, looking glasses, beads, tobacco—never whiskey. It is company policy never to trade whiskey to the Indians. Come. Ah, there's Gracieuse," he said. "My wife."

The woman was an Indian. Buxom, barefooted, her face long and slender, eagle nose, prominent cheekbones decorated with bright red circles of paint. She struggled across the courtyard with a pile of buffalo robes in her arms. A spotted dog trailed her, sniffing at the backs of her legs. She kicked at the dog, almost stumbled, and then kicked at it again. The dog went yelping away across the courtyard.

"Her name in the Sioux language is Mahgahskahwee," Orliac said, and laughed. "It means Swan Maiden. I call her Gracieuse. . . . Do you speak French?"

"No," Hadley said.

"That means 'graceful.' It could be a second meaning, don't you think? Gracieuse!" he called, and his wife dropped the robes against the wall and hurried to him. He spoke to her rapidly in what Hadley supposed was a mixture of Indian and French, and the woman rushed off again.

"I've asked her to prepare some tubs, eh?"

Orliac said. "You will want to bathe, I am sure."

"Thank you," Hadley said.

"We'll find food for you as well. You are not to be frightened by any of the Indians inside the fort. The women are either married to our people, or else are sisters or cousins of the wives. The men are also relatives of one sort or another. *C'est comme une grande famille*— fathers, cousins, uncles. There is nothing to worry about, truly."

"Where do you want us to . . . ?"

"Near the wall there. Where Gracieuse has put the robes. That will be all right?"

"Yes, fine."

"I know it is not very private . . ."

"It's fine," Hadley said.

"If you wish, we can unload the wagon and find someplace to store your belongings. Then perhaps the women could sleep in the wagon. If that is what you prefer."

"We're used to sleeping on the ground," Hadley said.

"There has been very little rain; maybe we will be lucky still, eh?" Orliac said, and smiled apologetically, and hunched his shoulders, and held out his hands, the palms showing. "She is heating the water. It will be in the kitchen that you will bathe. I shall ask the cook to go somewhere," Orliac said, and took a watch from his pocket and looked at it. "Yes, there is time before he starts the meal."

"Thank you," Hadley said again.

"I have put you there near the offices and storerooms, where there is not much traffic at night. It is away from the corral, too." He glanced across the courtyard to where Bobbo was taking the harness off the mules. Five or six Indians had gathered around the wagon and were studying the horses. "Ah, Bobby!" he called. "You found where to put them, good!" He turned again to Hadley. "How many were there? The Indians."

"Four," Hadley said.

"Pawnee?"

"I don't know."

"But you took three horses from them, eh? Good."

"They killed my daughter," Hadley said.

Orliac looked into his face.

"I am so sorry," he said, and took his hand at once.

A party of white men arrived the next day.

They were dusty and bearded, wearing blue army uniforms. They arrived in a convoy of two mule-drawn wagons and eight horses. Minerva watched them as they crossed the courtyard toward the stairs at the far end. They were carrying leather cases that seemed heavy from the way the men were bent under them. Probably valuable, too, otherwise they'd have left them in the wagons outside the main gate. They were on the gallery now. One of them knocked on Orliac's door. Behind her Minerva heard the shuffle of feet. She turned.

The Indian was wearing a white buffalo robe.

He was tall and straight and his face was painted black. There were shells in his ears and strung around his neck.

"*Un-p'tee-plez,*" he said to her.

"What do you want?" she said.

"*Un-p'tee-plez,*" he said, and thrust out his hand.

"Get away from me," she said, and whirled toward the wall, and picked up the rifle leaning against it. "Get *away!*" she said sharply, and thrust the muzzle at him. Her finger was inside the trigger guard and wrapped around the trigger. The Indian scowled at her. Then he took his nose between thumb and forefinger, and blew snot into the dirt at her feet. Turning, he stalked regally across the courtyard again.

Minerva was trembling.

The men were government surveyors returning from South Pass, where they'd spent the summer. The leader of the expedition was a major named Abner Duggan, burly man with a browned, wrinkled face, white mustache under his bulbous nose. Must've been about Hadley's age, Minerva figured, but looked a lot older. Drank too much wine. Was pouring for Hadley now, and leaning over, and talking straight into his face. Wasn't drunk, but his tongue was loose enough to make him sound a trifle disrespectful. They were in the Orliac apartment, six of them sitting around a big wooden table. Orliac and his wife, Gracieuse, Hadley and Minerva, Duggan and his aide. The invitation had not included Bonnie Sue and Bobbo. This had seemed strange to Minerva, who was used to everybody in a family eating at the same time. The two of them were in the fort's kitchen now, but she'd have preferred them here beside her. She'd almost turned down the invitation, in fact, but Hadley'd convinced her they could learn things from the two surveyors about the trail ahead.

"When did you plan to leave?" Duggan asked.

"As soon as my sons catch up," Hadley said.

"Where are they now?"

"I don't know. We left them outside St. Louis near the end of May."

"The twentieth of May," Minerva said.

"It's my hope they've done what they had to do, and are already on their way here," Hadley said.

"Just the two of them alone?" Duggan asked.

"Yes."

"Well," Duggan said, "the Pawnee've got troubles of their own right now; maybe your sons won't be bothered."

Orliac glanced swiftly at Minerva and immediately said, "Major Duggan, the Chisholm family has recently—"

"Let me tell you what you'll find west of here," Duggan said, and lifted his glass and drank, and smacked his lips. In what sounded like surprise, he said, "Very *nice*, Orliac," and then wiped the back of his hand across the wine-stained white mustache and turned to Hadley. "What you'll find—beside *Indians*, that is—"

"Cheyenne, Sioux, and Gros Ventres," Duggan's aide said. He was a man named Howard Kelsey, a captain. Very thin, with pale white skin, delicate as a woman's. Had a mustache, too, but his was narrow and black. He offered the information about the Indians as if Duggan had called for it. Duggan acknowledged it with a tap of his forefinger on the air.

"Right," he said, and *tap* went the forefinger. "Roaming out there in parties a thousand strong, some of them."

"Major Duggan," Orliac said, "I feel I should tell you—"

"Four thousand, one party," Kelsey said.

"Right," Duggan said, and tapped the air. "You ever see four thousand Sioux or Dakota or whatever they choose to call themselves—"

"Dakota," Kelsey said.

"—riding across the prairie in war paint?"

"Scary," Kelsey said.

"But that's not all you've got to worry about, Chisholm. There hasn't been rain out there for the past two months—"

"Serious drought," Kelsey said.

"Indians cutting down cottonwood boughs to feed their horses."

"No grass at all."

"Or burned yellow where you find a patch of it."

"Plague of grasshoppers, too," Kelsey said.

"What the drought didn't finish off, the grasshoppers did," Duggan said, and laughed and poured himself another glass of wine. "Orliac," he said, "this is really very nice wine."

"*Comment?*" Gracieuse asked.

"*Le vin. Il trouve bon, le vin.* She speaks no English," he said. He seemed to be explaining this more to himself than to anyone sitting at the table.

"No water, no grass," Kelsey said.

"And no game," Duggan said. "The Indians are eating their own horses out there. That's what's out there, Chisholm," he said, and nodded for emphasis.

"Were you thinking of heading for Fort Hall?" Kelsey asked.

"Fort Hall's five hundred *miles* from here," Duggan said.

"You couldn't get much beyond there," Kelsey said. "There'd be snow in the Rockies."

"You'd be stuck at Fort Hall for the winter," Duggan said.

"Some picnic, that," Kelsey said, and rolled his eyes. "It's a smaller trading post than this, you know."

"You want wilderness," Duggan said, "that's wilderness."

"Snow-filled Rockies ahead of you."

"Behind you hostile Indians."

"That's wilderness," Kelsey said.

Duggan tapped the air.

"What do you say, Bobby?" Orliac asked. "You want to be in the fur business? We expect to trade this year alone more than fifty thousand robes. I have room for another clerk here, eh?"

"I don't think so," Bobbo said.

The robes were piled high in the center of the courtyard, the fur on them thick and black. They all looked alike to Bobbo, but Orliac was sorting them for quality. Everywhere around them, there was teeming activity. Women bickering and children scampering, babies shrieking. Company men bawling orders in French. Trappers striding through the fort in leggings and leathers. Through the main gate, Bobbo could see tipis being taken down, travois being packed with goods acquired in trade. In the distance, more Indians moved slowly toward the fort, laden with robes to barter. Like the robes, the Indians all looked the same to him.

"Do you know how they treat these hides?" Orliac asked.

"No, sir."

Whenever he thought of his sister, whenever he tried to remember her as she'd been, he could only visualize the Indian with the blue face, and the Indian writhing in pain as Bobbo plunged the knife again and again and . . .

"They take the brains of the animal, eh? And they mix it with ashes. That's after the hide is scraped clean of flesh. The women do the work. It's why they have so many wives. A man can shoot a dozen buffalo in as many minutes, eh? But to dress the hides? That is quite another matter. It takes all spring and half the summer." He lowered his voice. "I have heard of a tribe that dresses the hides with piss. *Piss!* Do you think that's true?"

"I'm sorry," Bobbo said. "What did you say?"

He had been thinking again of Annabel.

And had seen again the Indian with the blue face.

The river here was cold and clear and running swift. It reminded Bonnie Sue of the Clinch back home. Except that in Virginia, she had gone to the river to write in her diary or to try to think of stories. Here, she came to the river to cry.

She cried for Annabel, and she cried for herself.

She cried for her baby sister because she could remember her when she was still in her wooden cradle with her eyes searching all over and her thumb in her mouth and her pillow wet with drool. You leaned over the cradle and a toothless smile came on that round little face, made you want to bust out laughing. She could remember holding Annabel's plump sticky hand and taking her for walks in the woods, showing her where there was a rabbit hole and here was a wasps' nest, and little Annabel nodding, like she knew just what was being said about this or that, but probably not understanding a thing. Looked so cute that Bonnie Sue would just scoop her up in her arms and hug her to death. She could remember Annabel being a pest, too, asking questions all the time about what was it made a cat meow and a pig oink and a dog bark instead of talking like people did. Or wanting to know how you danced a jig, or knitted and purled, or baked cookies, or wrote the letter M, which she always had trouble with, making it look more like an N all the time. Bonnie Sue kept telling her to just add another loop, and whenever Annabel did, it came out looking like a worm crawling along, loop after loop after loop.

She loved that child.

Alone by the river, she cried for her.

And knew—ah, God—knew that if her sister hadn't come at that Indian with a burning stick in her hand, poked it at his arm and made him jump off Bonnie Sue, where he was straddling her and choking her . . .

She squeezed her eyes shut.

She could hear the river rushing swiftly.

She could feel the beat of her own pulse.

She began to cry again. For her sister, for herself.

On the twenty-seventh of July, a week after the Chisholms arrived at the fort, the family from the Oregon-bound train emerged at last from the absent factor's apartment. There were six of them. A man and woman who looked to be about Hadley's age, three daughters in their teens, and a strapping son who reminded Minerva of Gideon. Pale and thin, blinking at the sun, they came down the gallery stairs. A gaggle of squalling Indian brats followed them across the courtyard to where Minerva and Bonnie Sue were sitting on robes against the wall. The wall, and the wagon close by it, had become their home. The robes were their beds and their coverlets, the wall was their protection from whatever dangers lay outside the fort, the wagon contained the clothing, the tools and utensils they needed to get through the day and then the day following it. Minerva watched as the woman turned abruptly and flapped her hands at the Indian children, who scurried away laughing. She came to Minerva then and extended her hand.

"How do," she said, "I'm Martha Hasty. I've heard of your misfortune, ma'am, and me and mine wish to offer our condolences."

"Thank you," Minerva said softly, and took Martha's hand. "I'm Minerva Chisholm, this's my daughter Bonnie Sue. I'm glad to see you up and about."

"This here's my husband Jeb . . ."

"Ma'am," he said, and took off his hat.

"My daughters Mary Louise, Ellie Jean, and Josie . . ."

The girls curtsied.

"And my son Tom here."

"Ma'am," he said. Hair the color of Gideon's, curly like his, too. Not as big. Grinning. Didn't know what to do with his hands. Stuck them in his pockets at last.

"Mrs. Chisholm, might you care for some tea?" Martha said.

The two women sat in the kitchen of the fort, on

stools at the huge table the cook used for chopping vegetables and carving meat. It was eight in the morning. He had long since finished with breakfast, and would not be starting the midday meal for hours yet. He listened as the women talked and sipped the tea they'd brewed on his stove. He could not understand a word they said, but he liked the lilt of their voices. He liked American women. They were skinny. He liked skinny women. *Mais belles poitrines aussi.* Skinny but soft. He liked that.

"We shouldn't have come *this* far," Martha said, and laughed. She had a laugh that jingled like silver, twinkled clear up into her blue eyes. There were freckles across her nose and on her cheeks; Minerva'd never before seen a woman her age with freckles. Always thought freckles were for young people. Liked this woman Martha Hasty. Liked her from the minute they shook hands, offering her sympathy, husband taking off his hat like a gent, little girls well-mannered, boy the image of Gideon. Pale, so pale, the lot of them. "Should've turned back when Mary Hutchison did . . ."

Hutchison's wife. The tall spare woman in the sun-faded bonnet and dress. Minerva nodded.

". . . just after her children took sick. But Jeb said we'd gone *that* far already, and we *was* with a big party, he figured it was safer. It was my thinkin if a party's takin sick all around you, then best to leave the party, wouldn't you say?"

"I'd have left in a minute," Minerva said.

"Cause when you get right to it, we're headin back anyway, ain't we?" Martha said. "Them surveyors are leavin day after tomorrow, and we're going with em, hell or high water. It's six hundred miles to

Independence, which ain't just a walk in the park, but they's eight armed men on horses, and another two drivin the army wagons, not countin Jeb and Tommy. That's an even dozen men with guns; that ought to be enough t'discourage any Injuns between here and Independence, don't you—"

Minerva burst into tears.

Martha blinked at her. The cook looked up at the sound of the weeping.

"*Qu'est-ce que c'est?*" he asked. "*Pourquoi pleut-elle?*"

"Oh my God, I'm sorry," Martha said. "Mrs. Chisholm? Are you all right?"

She blamed herself.

She should have been firmer with Hadley, should have insisted back there in Louisville, forced him to turn around right then and there. Or certainly at the Kansas, Ralph Hutchison telling them there was fever ahead, his own two children looking frail from the ordeal, the river raging besides. Should have told him there was no sense continuing, didn't *want* to go on, just them and the Oateses, with her not speaking a word of English. Should have said, Hadley, let's turn around with the others. Hadley, let's go home. Kept her mouth shut instead. Knew there was no use saying another word. Stubborn as a mule once he made up his mind. Knew there was nothing she could say to get him to give up.

She blamed him.

Blamed him for whatever it was made him decide to quit Virginia. Wasn't nothing wrong with Virginia. Had a good home there, a *life*. Wasn't a life anymore, the minute they left. Blamed him for not telling his sons and daughters alike to just keep their mouths shut

that time in Louisville. He was the father here, he was
the head of this family; if he wanted to sell his whiskey
dear and head back home, why then that was his business and never mind voting. That's what he should've
done right *then*, taken a stand, told the young'uns they
didn't like the way this family was being run, why then
they could just go find theirselves a better one. But no,
he got himself bullied into continuing on. Blamed him
for what happened at the river, too, when they were
waiting to be ferried across and anybody with a grain of
sense was turning around for home. Should've realized
that once they missed the chance there at the Kansas,
why there'd be no heading back ever again. They'd be
left alone at the Coast of Nebraska, and Indians would
find them sure as rain.

Blamed Bobbo, too.

Supposed to be standing guard that night, yelling
instead all the time about wanting to kill the wolves,
like he was on a *hunting* expedition instead of out in
the wilderness with Indians creeping up. Yelling back
and forth to his father, Hadley still drunk. Both of
them probably drunk, the one supposed to be watching for trouble, and the one supposed to be his father.
Pair of worthless . . . Why didn't he shoot sooner?
Why'd he shoot *after* the man had . . . Oh, Jesus.
Couldn't he see the man was . . . God, God. Should've
shot him, killed him, killed him before he could,
before he . . . Dear, dear God. Blamed Bobbo, and
blamed Bonnie Sue for being so homesick and moody
all the time; hadn't been so involved with her own mis-
ery and with pining for Sean Cassada, she would've
maybe been able to do something that night, help
Bobbo, help her sister.

She blamed them all.

She blamed herself.

In their corner of the courtyard, with a buffalo robe beneath them and a light comforter covering them, they whispered in the coolness of the night.

"The Hastys are leaving for Independence in the morning," Minerva said.

"I know that," he said.

"Be going with Major Duggan and his people. . . . What do you think of him, Hadley?"

"Loudmouth."

"Aye, but of what he said."

"He seemed to know."

"Hadley, I want to go with them," she said, and caught her breath, and waited. "We could be back in Independence before summer's end," she said, and again waited. "And if we chose to go all the way to Virginia—"

"Min, it's—"

"—we could be through the Gap by November."

Hadley was silent.

"I want an answer," she said.

"Min," he said, "it's six hundred miles to Independence."

"Aye, and five to Fort Hall."

"We're halfway between nothin and nowhere," he said. "I'm scared, Min. I don't want to go ahead, and I don't want to go back where my little girl . . ." He fell silent again. Then he said, "Forgive me, Min, I thought I was doin right. I wanted to find us land we could plant and harvest, I wanted to make a better life than we had back home. Instead, I—I seem to have done everything all wrong. Sent my two sons off to God knows where, took my family into a wilderness where—where my daughter . . ." He could not utter the words, he choked them back. "Min," he said, "I'm a man can't move for fear and for sorrow. I don't know what to do, Min. I never been scared of nothing in my life, I never grieved for nobody this way before. I miss her so much, I miss her to death."

"What do you want to do, Had? Whatever you want to do . . ."

"I want to stay here, Min. At least through the winter and maybe longer. Maybe always."

She said nothing. He waited, but she said nothing.

"There's land up by the river, timber enough to build us a fine cabin. We could clear a field for planting; the soil's rich, Min, we could grow things here."

"Aye," she said.

"Min, do you not long for a floor to sweep?"

"I do, Hadley."

"Min, I don't know who owns the land up there. If it's American Fur does, then I'll talk to Orliac about a fair price for what we'd need. If it's public land, then we'd have to write the government, I reckon, tell them our intentions, ask what the price would be. I'm guessing a dollar, a dollar twenty-five an acre, and I think there's a minimum you *got* to buy, a quarter section I think it is. We could squat, meanwhile, if it's government-owned. Ain't nobody going to come chase us off it. Min?"

"Yes, Hadley?"

"Would that suit you, Min?"

"If it would help you to mend again, it would suit me."

"I only know I can't leave here now," he said.

"Then we'll stay, Hadley."

"I'll talk to Orliac."

"Yes," she said.

"Min," he said, "I love you, Min."

"And I love you, too," she answered.

The surveyors had packed their instruments into the wagons, and now they stood in the morning sunshine, waiting for the Hastys to say their farewells. The day was clear and hot. Captain Kelsey had taken off his hat and was wearing a blue bandanna around his forehead. It gave him a devil-may-care look entirely out of keeping with his prissy nature. Major Duggan stood with one hand on his horse's bridle, chatting idly with Orliac. A dozen or more Indians were standing against the adobe wall, watching the leave-taking.

Minerva recognized among them the one who'd accosted her shortly after their arrival at the fort. Despite the heat, he was still wearing the white buffalo robe. His face was painted black; it glistened greasily in the bright sunshine. His eyes found hers. He grinned toothily, and then shoved himself off the wall and came toward where she and Martha were talking. Minerva was already starting to back away. But the Indian thrust out his hand to Martha instead. "*Un-p'tee-plez,*" he said, his voice demanding and somewhat threatening. Martha giggled nervously, and then shrugged. Orliac turned from the major.

"*Allez! Allez!*" he shouted, and shooed the Indian away with his hands. The Indian grasped his nose between thumb and forefinger. Apparently thinking better of what he was about to do, he turned away sullenly and went to stand against the wall of the fort again.

"He wants a favor, *un petit plaisir,*" Orliac said, and shrugged. "They are spoiled by emigrants all the time, eh? They want only a biscuit or two, a cup of coffee—but they are nuisances. You must never show you are in the slightest afraid. They can read faces; I sometimes think they can read minds."

"Minerva, will you be all right?" Martha asked, and took her hand between both her own.

"I think so, yes."

"We've scarcely met," Martha said.

"I shall miss you," Minerva said.

The women embraced. Jeb Hasty shook hands with Hadley, and then climbed up onto the wagon seat. "Tommy?" he said.

"Yes, Pa."

How much like Gideon he looked. She was about to weep again; she wished she could learn to control these sudden fits of weeping that came upon her. She bit her lip. Kelsey wheeled his horse about; the crowd of Indians backed away.

"Let's *move* it then!" Major Duggan said, and pointed sharply eastward with the same forefinger he'd used to tap the air.

They watched the wagons and horses departing. Martha waved from the seat. Surprisingly and unexpectedly, the Indian with the painted black face stepped out from the others and waved back. He kept waving. The wagons moved into the distance. Far out on the horizon, Minerva saw dust rising, moving. She watched. Horses and riders coming from the east, closing the gap between themselves and the wagons. The horses stopped alongside the lead wagon. The dust settled. And now again the horses were in motion. A pair of riders. One of them astride a piebald. The other on a black . . .

Gideon, she thought.

Will, she thought.

Aloud, she shouted, "It's them, Hadley, they're here!"

Arms wide, skirts flying, she ran to greet her sons.

VI

———◆•◆———

WILL

The night had turned cool.

Outside the fort, the open tops of the Indian tipis glowed with fires from within, triangular patches of light on the rolling hillside. Occasionally a dog barked, and was answered by another, and yet another, the final bark sounding before the echo of the first had died.

Will was drunk.

He sat against the outside wall of the fort, the baked clay bricks still warm from the day's sun. There was a bottle of wine in his hand, the third one tonight, most of it already gone. He lifted the bottle to his mouth, and drank from it, and tried to make sense of what had happened, and could make no sense of it. *Hell with it*, he thought, and drank again, and shook his head, and said, "Shut up," when a baby down below began crying. He listened to the baby crying.

Cried like a baby himself when they told him. Didn't suspicion nothing at first. Him and Gideon riding up this morning, Ma running down from the fort, looking like a girl half her age, didn't even recognize her. Grabbing Gideon to her, and then stretching out her hand: "Will, Will, darlin!" All of them up at the fort later. Pa looking a bit strange. Bobbo sort of standing off to one side. Bonnie Sue hugging them both. It was Gideon who said, "Where's Annabel?"

He lifted the bottle to his lips again.

He could remember Annabel asking him how was the fighting in Texas. He had been planing a door out back. Had taken it down cause it was sticking in the August heat. Had it set up between two big rocks and was planing it. Curls of white wood coming up from it.

"Well, it wasn't much good," he'd said.

"What'd you do there?"

"Just yelled and hollered and shot at people."

"That don't sound fun, Will."

"It wasn't," he said. "Much rather go catfishin in the Clinch."

"Then why don't we?" Annabel asked.

Big grin.

"Why don't we just?" he said, and put down the plane.

Shit.

You . . .

You get here and they tell you your baby sister . . .

The Indian woman came out of the night silently, startling him. His hand jerked. Wine spilled from the bottle tilted to his mouth, dribbled over his chin, splashed onto his shirt. He brushed at the shirt, and looked up at her. "What do you want?" he said . . .

She was tall and slender, wearing an elkskin dress, the sleeves open and hanging, no beads or quills or ornamentation of any kind, fringed at the bottom where it came to just below her knees. She wore unbeaded moccasins, soft upper flaps turned back like cuffs. Black cotton stockings showed above them, one pulled to her shin, the other falling to her ankle, bunched there above the moccasin cuff. Her hair was black and plaited on either side of her head, the braids held fast with leather thongs. She had high cheekbones painted with solid circles of vermilion. In the moonlight, her eyes were luminous and black.

Approaching him silently, she stood before him and grinned, head tilted to one side, teeth flashing. She put her hands on her thighs as if to dry the palms on the treated hide, but then bent slightly at the knees and grasped the fringed bottom of the skirt in both hands. Standing erect again, she pulled the skirt up over her waist. She was naked under it; he saw the tangled blackness of her crotch an instant before she lowered the skirt again. She smiled in invitation, her brows rising in silent inquiry. Then she extended her hand to him, the fingers curled into a beggar's bowl.

"Why the hell not?" he said.

There were dogs barking outside the tipi. He watched them warily. Shouldn't never show your teeth to a dog. Nor any wild animal. Think you were going to attack. Never smile at them. There's a nice boy, but no smile. She'd been in there four, five minutes already. He'd give her just till he finished the wine, then he'd leave. Chilly out here; no sense waiting in the cold for a whore. No sense to *nothing*, you wanted to know.

She was coming out of the tipi now. Fat squaw with

her. Squaw looked annoyed, like she didn't want to be chased out here in the cold while the whore entertained a customer. *Too bad about you*, Will thought, and almost grinned, and remembered the dogs. The dogs were still yapping. Squaw said something to them, didn't bother them a jot; they just kept at it. She slapped one across the snout. He began whimpering and then shut up. She said something in Indian to the whore then, and the whore nodded. Fat squaw pulled her robe around her, called to the dogs, and went walking over to another tipi. She said something else in Indian and then went inside. The whore was holding open the flap of the tipi here. Will nodded, finished the wine in the bottle, and then crouched and went on in.

There was a fire in the middle; he went to it and held out his hands to the flames. Smoke going up through the hole there in the ceiling or whatever they called it. Painted shield hanging there from one of the poles. Couple of lances. Buffalo robes all over the dirt floor.

"How much's this gonna cost me?" Will asked.

The woman held up a finger.

"Shit," he said. "I can get a *white* woman for that."

Wasn't half bad-looking here in the light, though. Wasn't half *good*-looking neither. Brown like any other Indian he'd ever seen, lips parched and cracked, sore in the corner of her mouth. Looked like good tits under the elkskin dress.

"I'll give you half a dollar," he said.

She shook her head.

"Hell with it then," he said, and turned to go, and couldn't find the flap he'd come in by. "Now where . . ." he said, and realized he was still holding the empty wine bottle, and tossed it aside angrily. Feeling his way around the tipi hand over hand, touching the warm hide walls, he found the opening at last and was crouching to go out when he felt her hand on his shoulder. He looked up. She nodded. "Yeah," he said, and let the flap fall again. He staggered to his feet and clutched one of the lodge poles for support. "Half a dollar, right?" he said.

She nodded again.

"You understand English, huh?" he said. "How many white men you fucked in your life, huh? You get that sore from a white man?"

She touched her lip, shook her head.

"What *is* that sore there?"

She held up her hands, the fingers widespread, and shook them back and forth, shaking her head at the same time.

"I don't have to worry, right?" he said. "Never met a whore *yet* I didn't have to worry. Where'd I put that goddamn . . . ?" He was digging in his pocket for a fifty-cent piece, couldn't find one by just the feel of it, and pulled out a handful of coins. Opening his palm, he held out the coins to her and said, "Take a half dollar, go ahead."

She lifted a coin from his palm.

"That's right," he said, and put the other coins back in his pocket. "What's your name?" he asked.

She shook her head.

"If you don't know it in English, say it in Indian."

She shook her head again.

He shrugged. First time he'd ever in his life asked a whore her name, and she wouldn't tell him. He shrugged again. Hell with her, he thought.

"I'm Will Chisholm," he said. "Hell with you. You

happen to see a man ridin through here on an Appaloosa?" He burst out laughing, and fell onto one of the buffalo robes near the fire. "Ahh," he said, "nice," and closed his eyes. "Chased him all over creation," he said. "Carthage alone three times in June. *Three* times," he said, and opened his eyes and held up three fingers to her. She was standing by the fire. She had taken off the dress. Her face and throat, her arms where the sleeves ended seemed darker than the rest of her body. Her belly, breasts, and legs looked almost white there in the firelight. "Man who stole my horse," he said.

She raised her eyebrows, puzzled.

"Looking for him," he said.

She nodded and came to the robe. There were bruises on her legs, dried scabs. She was a filthy Indian whore; what the hell was he doing in a tent stank of dog shit and Indian grease? Smell of the fat squaw here on the robe, smell of *this* one too, whore's smile on her face, fixed, frozen; he'd never known a whore didn't have that same smile on her face.

"You don't even *know* me," he said.

She looked at him curiously.

"What're you wearin *paint* for?" he said. "Jesus!"

She got to her feet instantly, and walked across the tent to a pile of rags near an upended travois. Vigorously, she began rubbing at the paint. Will fell back on the robe, sighed heavily, put the back of his hand over his closed eyes. "Always gone," he said. "Told his mother we had money to give him, owed him money. She knew we was lying. Gideon's got a face like an angel, but he couldn't fool the widder Hackett, nossir. Said, 'We owe him money, ma'am,' blue eyes open wide, good ole Gideon, that ole liar," he said, and burst out laughing. "My brother Gideon. What're you *doin* there? You takin off that paint there? What the hell . . . ?"

He raised himself on one elbow and looked across the tent to where she was scrubbing at her face with one of the dry rags. "Takin off the paint," he said in surprise, and fell back on the robe again. "Canny as a weasel, that old lady. You just missed him, boys. Was here a day or so ago, and's plumb gone now. Canny. We followed him that first time deep in Iowa territory— you know where that is? Iowa? Hey, you! Hey, beautiful!" he called, and laughed. "You know where Iowa territory is?"

She turned to him, puzzled. The rag in her hand was covered with paint as bright as blood.

"Yeah, sure you do," he said, and laughed again. "Lost him there, too, went back to Carthage again. There's old mother Hubbard—*Hackett*," he said, and laughed, "old mother Hackett standing on the porch, hands on her hips. Why, boys, I *do* declare, you just missed him again. He's *been* and is gone. Whyn't you just let me have that cash you owes him, I'll see he gets it. Sure. Oh, sure. Left *again*—gettin to be a reglar thing we did, like going to church on Sunday. Leave Carthage, go *back* to Carthage. Went west this time. You know the Mississippi? River. You know *river?* Water? *Canoe*—you know canoe? Shit, you don't know nothin. . . ."

Weeks of rain there along the Mississippi, insides of cabins thick with mud, others completely washed away, furniture smashed, river clogged with floating tangles of logs. Couldn't find him on the Illinois side nohow, crossed the river into Iowa again, searched for him there. Spent weeks traveling through towns looked like they was thrown up in ten minutes. Oh, yeah, man on an Appaloosa passed this way, sure enough. Yep, black hair and brown eyes, dressed entire in blue, that's the fella. Too late. Been and was gone. Gideon wanted to try Carthage again, rode back up there through towns looked all alike; one thing about this here America is you can't fault it for being different one place from another. This time she's waitin' on the porch with a shotgun in her hands. Your son been back, ma'm? I ask her, and she says *Git*, and shakes the gun at us. . . .

The Indian woman was beside him.

She had scrubbed the paint from her cheeks, and she stretched beside him now, and he took her in his arms. He wouldn't kiss her, the sore on her mouth; he'd never kissed a whore. He touched her face. Stroked her face. Her eyes were closed. The sore was just at the corner of her mouth on the right side of her face. Said he didn't have to worry about it. Wouldn't kiss her, though. Touched her nipples, touched her below. Bed of fuckin straw, dry as any whore's. No feeling, whores. Did it for money, that was all. Touched her jaw again. Ran his hands over her back. Felt—

Touched her back again, puzzled.

Moved her away from him, rolled her on her belly.

Her back was covered with healed welts thick as ropes. The scars were twisted and brown. The skin around them was as white as his own.

In the morning, he looked for Orliac and could find him nowhere in the fort or around it. He talked instead to Orliac's first clerk, a man named Schwarzenbacher, little blond man with a twitchy blond mustache, blue eyes constantly roaming, alert, watching as if he expected Indians to attack the fort any minute. Will guessed he was about Gideon's age, twenty-three, maybe a bit older. He was at his desk putting figures in a ledger, and he looked up when Will approached.

"Don't want to bother you," Will said.

"No bother," Schwarzenbacher said, and smiled.

"Just wanted to know if there was somebody here spoke both English and Indian."

"What *kind* of Indian did you have in mind?" Schwarzenbacher asked, still smiling.

"Well . . . what do you mean?"

"There are different languages."

"Oh," Will said. The thought had never occurred to him. He'd figured Indian was Indian and *all* of them understood it. "What are they talking out *there?*" he asked. "The ones outside the fort."

"Different tribes out there," Schwarzenbacher said. "Was there someone in particular you wanted to talk to?"

"Well . . . yes."

"I speak some Algonquian and Siouan; perhaps I can help. Is this person . . . ?"

"I don't know *what* she is."

"A woman. Ah."

"In fact, I think she's *white*," Will said. "She's dressed like an Indian, and her face and arms are brown, but underneath she's . . ."

"Catherine, do you mean?" Schwarzenbacher asked.

"Is that her name?"

"The whore?"

"Well . . . yes."

"Catherine's her name."

"*Is* she white?"

"She's white, yes."

"I thought so, but . . ." He gestured vaguely. He'd woke up this morning, nobody in the tipi but the fat squaw poking him off the buffalo robe. Mean old yellow dog growling at him while he put on his boots. Couldn't remember whether he'd even *fucked* the whore, but began worrying right off about that sore on her lip. That's why he was here now talking to this twitchy Schwarzenbacher, mustache going a mile a minute, eyes looking all around, sunlight hitting his head like God was singling him out for a miracle. *Thought* she was white, but hadn't even been sure of his own *name* last night, no less the whore's color. If she *was* white, though . . . if she understood what he was *saying* . . .

"Didn't answer me," he said, puzzled. "Didn't say a word." He looked into Schwarzenbacher's face. "Why's that?"

"She has no tongue," Schwarzenbacher said. "They cut out her tongue."

"Who did?"

"I have no idea. Perhaps the Ojibwa. She's supposed to have lived with them for a while. I know she understands Algonquian. Why are you interested?"

"I ain't," Will said. "I just wanted to find out about that sore on her lip. She's got a sore on her lip."

"Probably the Spanish disease," Schwarzenbacher said.

"You think so?" Will said.

"She sleeps with Indians, you know."

"Yeah."

"She's a common whore."

"Yeah. You see . . . I was thinkin if I could *talk* to her, I could ask her about the sore."

"Well, she understands hands. I've seen her conversing with—"

"Cause I sure would like to find out if she's *got* anything."

"I understand."

"I have some medicine I bought in Texas . . ."

"I'd suggest you use it," Schwarzenbacher said.

"Well, it ain't to be used lightly," Will said. "Burns like hell, worse'n the disease, you want to know. So I thought if I could *talk* to her, she'd be able . . ."

"You'll find out soon enough anyway, won't you?" Schwarzenbacher said.

"Well . . . sure. Sure I will. If . . . sure."

"When you begin dripping," Schwarzenbacher said.

"Sure. I just thought . . ." Will shrugged.

"Of course, if it would set your mind at ease . . . '

"Yeah?"

"I *do* understand the gestures that are common linguistic currency among the various tribes on the plains. . . ."

"Yeah?"

"And if you'd like me to . . ."

"I would," Will said. "Yes. Yes, I would. Thank you. I would."

They found her squatting cross-legged outside the tipi. The fat squaw was tossing scraps of meat to half a dozen dogs, who leaped into the air each time another morsel was thrown. The squaw spotted Will first. She called something to Catherine, who looked up immediately and smiled. Looked more like an Indian than the goddamn squaw did. Hair shiny and black, eyes almost as black as the hair. Red paint on her cheeks again; was she going out to war someplace? Black stockings hanging down around her knees; probably hadn't washed them or herself in months. Jesus, had he really stuck his pecker into *that*?

"I need to talk to you," he said.

The squaw put down the empty bucket. Hands on her hips, she watched. All around them, the dogs were eating, growling when another came too close. Flies buzzed about the bucket. Catherine was still smiling the fixed smile. The squaw nodded encouragement to her. Will suddenly wondered how much of that fifty cents Catherine had got to keep last night.

"I want to know about the sore on your lip," he said. "Is it . . . ?"

She shook her head.

"This man here knows how to read hands. I'd appreciate it if you told him just where you got it and how long it's been there."

Catherine nodded. The squaw was still watching, hands on her hips. Catherine's hands began moving.

"That's the sign for fire," Schwarzenbacher said. "Ah," he said, nodding. "Ah. She says it's a burn."

Uninvited, the squaw began explaining to Schwarzenbacher in a language he presumably understood. Catherine's hands were still moving. Schwarzenbacher kept watching her hands and listening to the squaw at the same time.

"Yes, it seems to be true," he said. "Hot grease from a kettle. That's a burn on her lip."

"Well, that's good," Will said. "I'm sure glad to—"

"Of course, the squaw may be lying," Schwarzenbacher said at once.

"Yeah, but—"

"They lie a great deal."

"Yeah."

"But perhaps she's telling the truth."

"Yeah," Will said, and sighed heavily.

"I suppose she's telling the truth," Schwarzenbacher said.

Catherine nodded. She nodded at Will, she nodded at Schwarzenbacher. The squaw nodded, too. They were both nodding now. Catherine smiled her whore's smile. The squaw looked to Will for his approval.

"Ask her what's her last name," Will said.

"She can hear perfectly well, you know," Schwarzenbacher said.

"What's your last name?"

There was no word for it in her hands. She raised them, and then realized this, and looked at Schwarzenbacher helplessly.

"Where are you from?" Will asked.

Her hands began moving. Fingertips together to form a triangle . . .

"Tipi," Schwarzenbacher said.

A circle of her arms . . .

"No, *camp*. Ah, village. Yes, village."

Watching her hands. A village in the north. The squaw said something. Schwarzenbacher turned his head momentarily. "An Ojibwa village in the north," he said to Will, and nodded, and looked back to Catherine's hands again. She was making the sign for springtime now, literally "little grass," hands out with the palms up, right hand moving in front of her body, fingers closing slowly till only the index finger was slightly higher than the others.

"She's saying she left there in the spring, which I suppose is true enough," Schwarzenbacher said. "She arrived here sometime in May." He looked at her hands again. She crossed her arms over her breasts, the sign for love. She clasped her hands in front of her body, the sign for peace. She made the combination of gestures meaning sunshine in the heart.

"She was very happy there," Schwarzenbacher said.

"Why'd you leave then?" Will asked.

Her hands moved.

"Her husband died," Schwarzenbacher said.

It was close to midnight when he went down to the camp again. Tiptoed through it like he was in a cemetery. Damn tipis all looked alike in the dark, finally found the one he guessed was Catherine's. No door to knock on, how in hell did you let anybody know you were standing out here in the cold? He'd had a lot to drink again. Not Orliac's wine this time, but his father's good corn liquor. *Had* to be drunk even to *consider* fuckin a pig like this one.

"Hey, anybody home?" he yelled.

A dog began barking.

Will pulled his Mexican knife from the sheath at his belt.

Damn dog came out here, he'd slit its throat. Down the line, somebody started yelling in Indian. "Shut up," Will muttered. The fat squaw poked her head outside, frowning. She saw it was Will then, saw the knife, too. "Come on out here," he said, and she nodded and came out at once, smiling. She was half naked, wearing only a pair of leather breeches resembled bloomers, had to have once belonged to some fat old Indian brave. That's all she had on. The breeches and a beaded band around her forehead. Tits hanging clear down to her waist, a true beauty, a prize.

"Where's Catherine?" he asked.

She nodded and went back inside. He could hear her saying something inside there, could hear her voice getting louder and then a bit irritated. Catherine came out yawning, wrapped in what looked like an army blanket.

"Hey, how you doin?" Will said, and grinned.

She grinned back. Whore's frozen smile. Paint still on her cheeks. Even slept with the fuckin paint on her cheeks. She held out her hand.

"No more money," he said. "Uh-uh."

The squaw came through the flap again. She'd thrown on a robe over the breeches, all dressed up to go next door.

"Tell your friend here," Will said. "No more money. I've got food for you."

Catherine turned to the squaw, talked to her with her hands. The squaw turned to look at Will. She was frowning again.

"That's right, Fatty," Will said. "Here, look." He reached into a pocket of his coat. "Dried buffalo meat. Very good." He reached into another pocket. "Turnips. Raw turnips."

They were waiting.

"That's it," he said. "That's all there is."

The squaw was still frowning. She took Catherine aside and began whispering to her. Catherine nodded. The squaw nodded. "Big business deal goin on there,"

Will said. The squaw came to him then and took the meat and turnips from his hands. Catherine pulled hack the flap of the tent and Will went inside. The fire was still burning, but just barely. He took a log from a stacked pile, dropped it on the dying embers, fanned the fire to brighter flame with his hat.

"Come on over here," he said.

She came to the fire.

"Let me see that sore again," he said.

She knelt by the fire. He cupped her chin in his hand and studied her lip.

"Yeah, I reckon," he said dubiously. He let go of her chin, went to the buffalo robe, dropped down on it, and began taking off his boots. She was still standing by the fire, the army blanket around her. He wondered how many soldiers she'd had to fuck for that blanket. "Who's the squaw?" he asked. "Your business manager?"

Her hands came from under the blanket. The blanket hung from her shoulders, open over her naked breasts. Her hands moved in the firelight, shadows danced. He couldn't understand a fuckin word she was saying.

"You know how to write?" he asked.

She nodded.

"I'll fetch you what to write with," he said. "Tomorrow."

The cottonwood was huge. It had probably been here on the riverbank for a century or more. They sat beneath it side by side, shaded from the hot July sun. The river was dry; it had not rained since the beginning of the month. Will had borrowed a carving board from the kitchen, and this was propped on her knees. Her left hand kept a dozen sheets of foolscap in place on top of it. In her right hand she held a mechanical pencil he'd borrowed from Schwarzenbacher.

"You just write down the answers, okay?" he said.

She nodded.

"Okay, what's your full name?"

She wrote *Catherine Parrish.*

Under that she wrote *Kewedinok.*

And under that, *Wumin of the Wind.*

"Woman of the Wind?" he asked.

She nodded.

"Is that what this . . . Kewe . . . Ke . . . however you say it? Is that Woman of the Wind?"

She nodded again.

"Well . . ." he said, and looked again at what she'd written. "Where were you born, Catherine?"

Boston, she wrote.

"How'd you get out here?"

I came west with my father and brother.

"When?"

1837.

"How old were you?"

14.

"That makes you . . . you're twenty-one, is that it?"

In Octowber, she wrote.

"So . . . uh . . . you had an Indian husband, huh? How'd that happen? I mean, where'd you meet a . . . an Indian to marry? You know what I'm saying?"

After, she wrote.

"After what?" he asked.

Trapers.

"Trappers?" he said. "I don't follow. Was your father and brother trappers?"

She shook her head.

Alown, she wrote. *Leff me alown. Trapers came.*

They had gone off hunting, expecting to find game in the woods nearby. But instead the afternoon shadows lengthened, and she was still alone in the wagon, becoming frightened. She heard the sound of horses' hoofs, thought at first it was her father and brother returning. Voices. Men riding out of the woods. Six of them. The one riding the lead horse had a patch over his right eye. Black leather patch. Took them only a minute to realize she was alone in the wilderness. The one with the patch dragged her from the wagon. She pleaded with him to stop, begged him, but he just kept hugging her and kissing her, talking to her in French, saying over and again, "*Je t'adore.*" She would remember those words always though she understood no French. He forced her open, she screamed in pain. The others laughed. They took her then in turn, the other five, and then the one with the patch again. She lay on the ground bleeding. She could hear them talking to each other in French. Their voices sounded worried. The one with the patch came to her, and squeezed her chin hard in his hand and said something to her. She knew it was a warning. She nodded. Yes. Please. Yes. Go. Leave. Please. He took a knife from his belt. He forced her mouth open.

An cut out my tung.

Her hand did not waver when she wrote this. Her eyes were dry. She sat stiffly beneath the cottonwood tree, and the pencil scratched into the stillness. In the river, a fish splashed.

The warriors who found her wandering later in the woods, half-crazed and starved, were a party of eight Ojibwa braves, far from home in search of horses and scalps. They'd apparently got both, though not of the "lesser enemy" variety they were seeking; these were no Dakota horses they trailed, six of them with leather saddles. She recognized them at once as having belonged to the trappers who'd raped her. Dangling from the warriors' belts were fresh bloody scalps. She almost fainted at the sight of them, though she herself was still bleeding—from her mouth where the tongue had been taken from it, and from below where the trappers had brutally torn her. The leader of the war party threw her over his saddle and carried her north with him to his village, where she became the second wife in his tipi. She was happy there until he was later killed in battle. Then his brother took for his own not only Catherine but the other wife as well.

"Is that the squaw you're living with now?" Will asked.

She nodded.

"Who put those scars on your back? Who beat you, Catherine?"

Brother, she wrote.

"Your brother? I thought—"

She shook her head.

Husbin brother.

"Your brother-in-law, you mean? The one who . . ."

She nodded.

"And you left in the spring, is that it? You and the squaw both. The son of a bitch let you go?"

Killed. Big batil, she wrote. *Dakotah.*

"And so you came here."

She nodded.

On the paper she wrote: *It is a bern, you need not wurry.*

"I wish I could do like you," Gideon said. "Get myself drunk, push it out of my head that way."

"It don't help none," Will said.

They were sitting high above the fort, the river at their backs, the Indian village below. This was the first of August. They had been at the fort for three days and three nights, but had not yet talked together about what had been waiting here when they arrived. There was a surprising chill on the early morning air now, and Will sat hunched inside his coat, his arms folded across his chest, his back against the rock ledge behind him.

"Just don't seem like *us* no more," Gideon said.

"I know."

"Without her, I mean. It don't seem like the *family,* Will,"

"Won't never *be* the family no more, Gid," he said. "Not the *same* family anyway."

"I wish we could get them to move on," Gideon said. "I have the feelin it ain't good for them here. Too many damn Indians here. Remind them all the time of what happened. Don't you think, Will?"

"I don't know," Will said.

"We could make it to Fort Hall before winter, couldn't we?"

"I reckon. Be hard to get them goin, though. Pa's already wrote to the government about buyin a quarter section on the river. He's plannin to squat there till he hears. Be a cabin goin up before you know it, Gid."

"Will . . ." Gideon said, and hesitated. "I wouldn't even mention this if I didn't think they'd be safe here.

But they've moved into that empty apartment now, and they'll be comfortable there till a cabin gets built. Will, I don't see no earthly purpose you and me could serve here, do you?"

"Pa'll need help raisin the cabin."

"Bobbo's a man now."

"Still and all . . ."

"Will, I don't rightly know how to put this. But I think you and me has come to this late, and are apt to grieve longer. I know that ain't the right way to say it. I cry all the time at night, Will. I lay on that buffalo robe and just cry into it. Cause I loved her a lot."

"Yes," Will said, and nodded.

"And I think we're going to be hind'rin the others. I think they've made some kind of peace toward livin with it, Will. I ain't done that yet, and I don't think you have either."

"I haven't, no."

"What I'm suggestin is that we ride on out ahead of them. Meet them next year in California, if they're of a mind to come on after us."

"I think once that cabin's up, they'll be staying here."

"All the more reason for us to move on now. Do *you* want to stay here?"

"No, not particularly," Will said, and thought immediately of Catherine and wondered why he was worrying about a whore. Seemed to him when you started doing that, why then it really *was* time to move on. He had to keep telling himself it was true she was a whore. He *knew* it was true, damn it, but he had to keep reminding himself anyway. Catherine Parrish—Woman of the Wind—*whoever* the hell—was a whore who'd lay down with anybody had the price. Sailor, soldier, Indian chief, throw her a few scraps of meat, she'd roll right over on her back for you. She was a whore, there were no two ways of looking at it. It was time to get out of here, move on west like Gideon was saying.

"Seems to me the Indians out there've got enough trouble finding what to eat, never mind botherin anybody on the way to Fort Hall."

"Well, according to Orliac—"

"You been talking to him, too, huh?" Gideon said.

"I been asking him some questions."

"What'd he say?"

"About what?"

"About whether—"

"Whether the Indians 'tween here and Fort Hall be bad? He said yeah, they would."

"He told me the same thing. You believe that?"

"Well, the ones here at Laramie seem all right, and lots of *them* are Sioux, ain't they?"

"I don't understand this whole damn Indian shit anyway," Gideon said. "Do you understand it?"

"No, I don't understand it," Will said.

Didn't understand the Indian shit, nor the white man shit either. Sons of bitches, served them right to get theirselves scalped afterward. Would've scalped them himself, he'd come across them. Bad enough they raped her, but then to cut out her tongue—Jesus! Fourteen years old, you'd think her father and brother'd have *known* better'n to leave her alone, think at least one of them would've stayed behind. Hadn't been the trappers got her, would've been the Indians. Got her *anyway*, an Indian did, threw her on his horse, took her home to where he already had another wife. Shit, a goddamn *squaw* was what she'd been, never mind that Woman of the Wind shit.

From a distance he saw the rider approaching. Came out of the east, the sun behind him, rode out of it in a shimmer of haze. He was wearing a coonskin hat like Davy Crockett in pictures of him getting killed at the Alamo, buckskins like Dan'l Boone. He had long black hair and a black beard. Will wouldn't have recognized him but for the Appaloosa he was riding, an altogether distinctive raindrop gelding, sixteen hands high, black leopard spots on . . .

He shoved himself off the rock ledge and began running down the slope of the hill, sliding, digging in his heels, arms flapping like he was a big bird. Gideon was right behind him. His hat fell off, but he didn't stop to pick it up, kept racing along behind Will, helter-skelter through the Indian camp, dogs chasing them, nipping at their heels. On the Appaloosa, unaware, Lester Hackett rode leisurely toward the main gate of the fort.

They came puffing up behind the gelding, and he heard the yapping dogs an instant too late. Will was coming around one side of the horse, Gideon around the other. He tried to whip the horse forward, but Will grabbed him from the saddle and pulled him to the ground. The horse reared, wheeled in fright toward the wall of the fort. Crouched in the dust, Lester pulled a dagger from a legging sheath. He was coming out of his crouch to thrust it at Will when Gideon kicked him in the head from behind.

He sprawled flat into the dirt.

Gideon stepped on his hand, grinding his heel into the back of it. Lester screamed and let go of the knife. Will was coming at him. He scrambled to his feet and ran for the horse. He almost had the rifle when Will grabbed him from behind, hand in the collar of the buckskin shirt. He fell over on his back in the dirt, and Gideon kicked him again, in the rib cage this time. He felt another kick; son of a bitch knew nothing but to fight with his feet. Will twisted a hand into the front of the buckskin shirt, pulled him off the ground. They both had him now, one on either side, and were running him toward the wall of the fort. Jesus, they were going to—Jesus—bang his head against the clay bricks like a battering ram. "Hey, listen," he said, and suddenly they turned him, and stood him against the wall, and began punching him in the face and in the chest.

He was unconscious when they dragged him inside and told Orliac he was a horse thief.

They locked him in a storeroom on the gallery. It was there she went to talk to him the next day. There were kegs and barrels in the room, stacked wooden crates, bulging hempen sacks, buffalo robes. A single window opened onto the courtyard, and a man with a rifle stood outside that window all the while they talked. Bonnie Sue expected he heard every word they said.

Lester said, "Ah, it's good to see you, Bonnie Sue," and opened his arms to receive her, but she stood where she was, just inside the door locked from the outside, looking at him and trying to see through the beard to the face she knew and loved. He seemed older than she remembered. She herself had turned sixteen since last she saw him, her birthday having fallen on the twelfth day of July, with Annabel close to dying and no one dreaming of celebration. She thought to tell him she was sixteen now, tell him too the secret that was surely his to share. She told him neither.

"You left of a sudden," she said.

"I did," he answered.

"And took Will's horse with you."

"Aye," he said.

"They'll hang you for that, you know."

"I didn't steal that horse, you know," he said.

"Ah, didn't you? They seem to think you did."

"I was off after highwaymen."

"And did you find them?" she asked.

"I've missed you, Bonnie Sue," he said, and again opened his arms to her. She did not go into them. "I've thought of you often these past two months. I knew your brothers were behind me; my mother told me of their visits. And I knew they were thinking I'd stolen the Appaloosa, but there was no way of telling them—"

"You stole it, Lester," she said flatly.

Their eyes met.

"I stole it for sure," he said.

"Why?"

"Cause I was bound for Carthage and needed a horse to get there."

"You said you had friends in St. Louis who'd—"

"I have friends nowhere," he said. "Not even here, though I hoped someone here might love me."

"Not me," she said.

"I guess not," he answered.

"They'll hang you," she said. "The horse is branded and earmarked both. You were a fool to come this way."

"I thought you'd be long since gone. I knew I'd lost your brothers. . . ."

"Where are you bound then?"

"California," he said, and grinned. "To make my fortune there."

"Your fortune, aye," she said. "They'll hang you here for sure."

"Then they'll hang me," he said, and she almost went to him in that moment, but still she delayed. "Would you care, Bonnie Sue? Would it matter to you?"

"Why'd you run from me?" she asked.

"I was afraid."

"Of what?"

"Of loving you," he said. "I'm twice your age or more."

"I'm sixteen now," she told him. And almost told him the other as well. But did not. Could not. Could not bring herself to do it.

"Sixteen," he said. "Ahh."

"Lester," she said, "did you plan to steal Will's horse all along?"

"It was sounds I heard in the night. I jumped on the horse's back and rode off to investigate, taking with me a rifle as well, in case the noise I'd heard—"

"You told me a minute ago you'd stole the horse for sure."

"Yes," he said. "But that's a lovers' secret, and not for the ears of those who'd hang me."

"We're not lovers now," she said. "We're man and woman standing here with nothin between us except what happened a long time ago."

"Are you sure of that, Bonnie Sue?"

"As sure as I am of my own name."

"Then there's little to say but goodbye. Will you kiss me farewell, love? Will you let me hold you in my arms just once again before—"

"Stop it," she said. "I'm no longer the fool I was."

"I'll no longer be the man I was, come sundown. You'll find me hanging by the river, swinging in the wind. The Indians'll wonder at it all. They'll ask what crime I've committed, and when told I stole a horse, they'll marvel at the ways of the white man. The Indians, you see, believe that capturing horses from the enemy is an honor. Yet hanging from a tree will be a man who—"

"My brother wasn't your enemy. You needn't have took his horse. You wanted it so bad, he might even have *given* it to you."

"Ah, sure."

"You don't know Will."

"I know his sister, and she's refusing me now the last chance I have to live beyond this day."

"I'm refusing you nothing."

"You're refusing to tell them what you saw and heard the night I fled—or *seemed* to flee."

"You fled indeed."

"I was chasing voices I'd heard."

"There *were* no voices. . . ."

"Unless you swear there were."

"No voices but yours and mine."

"You heard that *I* heard, Bonnie Sue. Voices that could've been highway robbers. You heard them."

"I heard only a liar telling me he loved me."

"That was true."

"Aye. Loved me so dearly he left by morning. True love indeed."

"Let me kiss you, Bonnie Sue."

"I'd sooner kiss a snake."

"Let me touch you."

"No," she said, but she allowed him to take her in his arms. He drew her close and kissed her face, and she remembered that night in June and fell suddenly limp against him. His lips brushed hers lightly, his hands moved immediately to her waist, the fingers spread to frame her belly. She drew her mouth away from his, and whispered, "Lester . . ." as he lowered her to one of the buffalo robes, and then turned her head sharply toward the window of the room, fearful the sentry outside might be watching. But the buffalo robe was in a quarter of the room beyond his field of vision; he could not have seen them unless he thrust his head full inside the narrow opening. Lester had already raised her skirt above her waist and was unfastening her underdrawers, lowering them familiarly over her rounded belly. She wondered if he would place them on the floor here as delicately as he had on the floor of the forest that night.

"Lie for me," he whispered.

"No," she answered, but was hardly sure the word found voice in the raggedness of her own sharp breathing. She tried to close herself against him, squeezing her thighs together so he could not take off her drawers completely. He tore them instead, ripped them raggedly up the middle so that now she wore a part of them around each thigh and across each buttock, but nothing at all between. He said what he'd said that night outside St. Louis, "Open," and she replied, "*No*, damn it!" for if she opened she was lost. He seized her where the fabric of her underdrawers still encased each thigh, and spread them forcibly apart. She felt his hand upon her nakedness between, his fingers gently spreading her lips below. He said again, "Lie for me," and she shook her head, and he said, "Lie for me, Bonnie Sue," and she felt the rounded hugeness of him urging entrance, and spread herself wide to receive him and said "Yes," and thought she heard the sentry cough, or laugh, but didn't care by then.

It was Orliac's idea to hold the trial in the courtyard of the fort, where everyone—Indians included—could see and hear the proceedings. "A court in a courtyard," he said, and winked at Will, who found nothing at all amusing about the matter. Lester Hackett was an accused horse thief. Seventy years ago perhaps, before independence, a man convicted of such a crime might have been treated as leniently as though he were still living in the mother country. His ears would have been nailed to a board, the letter H branded on one cheek, the letter T on another. There was no such gentle consideration for horse thieves now.

The judges in the courtyard trial were three—Orliac himself, Schwarzenbacher the clerk, and a trapper named Sebilleau, who could neither read nor write. A long table had been brought out from one of the lower apartments, and the three presiding officials sat behind it now, the prisoner and his accuser sitting side by side on a puncheon bench before them. The courtyard and the balcony running around the upper level of the fort were thronged with company men, eager for whatever mild diversion the trial might provide, and Indians curious to witness the white man's method of dispensing justice.

The trial started with Orliac explaining to everyone present that the man Hackett was accused of stealing a horse, and these judges were assembled to determine his guilt or innocence. The punishment for stealing a horse, he further explained, was to be hanged by the neck till dead. The Indians wondered about this. Suicides by hanging were common in their tribes, but they did not know of hanging as a punishment for theft. Or was this to be a ceremony of sorts? In the Sun Watching Dance, warriors fulfilling vows suspended themselves voluntarily from a sacred pole, by means of cords fastened to painted sticks and passed through the flesh on their chests. But the white man's hanging was a hanging to the death. The Indians had never seen a ceremony of this sort. Would the white man first pierce the neck through with a blue stick and then attach a cord to it?

"Mr. Chisholm," Orliac said, "would you tell this court why you believe the Appaloosa now in the company corral was stolen by the accused?"

Embarrassed, Will got to his feet, cleared his throat, and looked out at the Indians and white men standing in the courtyard and on the gallery above.

"Well," he said, "Hackett here was guiding us to St. Louis, been with us since we met in Louisville. Just outside St. Louis he disappeared, and so did the gelding. So I rightly believe he was the one went off with it, since there was only the horse's tracks leading north, and the land was all so flat there you could see for miles if a man was out there on foot, which Hackett wasn't. Anyway, he's the one came riding up on the horse yesterday, so he's the one had to have rode off with it in the first place."

"How do you know the horse is yours?" Orliac asked.

"The animal's earmarked and branded," Will said.

"How?"

"There's a pothook brand on the left thigh, about eight inches above the stifle joint. And the right ear is marked with two cuts downward on either side of the point. The earmark, and the brand both, are registered with the county clerk back home," Will said.

"Emile," Orliac said to a man standing just alongside the table, "would you bring the horse for us to see, please?"

The horse was led from the corral. Nervous and skittish, it kept trying to pull away as the judges made their examination. There was a pothook brand on the left thigh, just as Will had claimed. The right ear was marked with a pair of downward slits, one on each side of the point.

"It would seem to be your horse," Orliac said, and went back to sit behind the long table again.

"It's my horse, all right," Will said.

"Mr. Hackett?" Orliac said, and Lester rose. "Mr. Hackett, is this the horse you were riding yesterday morning when you approached the fort?"

"It is," Hackett said. "But let me tell you this minute I *know* the horse is Will Chisholm's, and yes, I *did* ride off with it just outside St. Louis, as Will claims I did. But I didn't steal that horse."

"You rode off with the horse," Orliac said.

"That's right, sir."

"But you didn't steal it."

"No, sir."

"What then do you call riding off with another man's horse, eh?"

"I was guiding the Chisholms to St. Louis, as I'd promised, and I think I took the job seriously and did it well; I don't think anyone in the family'll dispute that.

The night I rode off with Will's horse, I heard voices and I didn't know who was out there in the darkness, so I rode off to investigate, as was my duty. I didn't have a horse of my own. I had to mount whatever was available, and it was Will's Appaloosa that was closest to hand. There were five men out there, it turned out, and they ambushed me and forced me to go along with them. I finally got away from them in Illinois, and've been searching for the Chisholms since. That's the truth of the matter."

"Mr. Orliac," Will said, "me and my brother went to Illinois looking for this man; we talked to his mother—"

"She told me about that," Lester said. "That's why I kept going back to Carthage, trying to locate you. But each time I got there, you'd be gone a day or so, and I'd traveled in a circle for no reason. You've got your horse back, Will. Would you hang me besides for riding off after men I thought were threatening the family?"

"There *were* no damn men, and you know it," Will said. "You're a horse thief, plain and simple."

"No, he's tellin the truth," a voice said, and all in the courtyard turned to locate the source of the voice, and could not find it till Bonnie Sue rose from where she was sitting with Minerva on a buffalo robe against the wall. The Indians watched her as she approached the long table at which sat Orliac and the other judges. Even Sebilleau, the illiterate Orliac had elected to the tribunal, seemed to have come at least half awake upon hearing her declaration. She stood before the table now, and looked directly into Orliac's face as though challenging him to challenge what she had just said. Instead, he asked for repetition, which was unnecessary since everyone had heard her clearly.

"What did you say?" he said.

"I said Lester Hackett's tellin the truth. There *were* voices that night."

"Bonnie Sue . . ."

"It's the *truth*, Will!" she said, whirling on him. "It's the truth," she said more softly, and turned again to face Orliac and the others. In the same low voice, she said, "I was awake. Lester and me were both awake. We heard the voices together. He said he'd find out what it was, and he climbed on Will's horse and rode off."

Will got off the bench, walked to where his sister was standing, looked her straight in the eye, and asked, "Why didn't you say any of this before?"

"I was afraid you'd ask me what I was doing awake," Bonnie Sue said.

"What *were* you doing awake?" Orliac asked.

"I was kissin Lester. Me and Lester were sittin by the fire, kissin," she said.

Schwarzenbacher looked at Hackett where he sat attentively on the puncheon bench, and tried to visualize Bonnie Sue kissing this man who was easily twice her age. He found the thought disturbing, found it even *more* disturbing that she'd admitted it before this assembly. Everywhere around, he could hear murmurs in French, *"Elle faisait l'amour,"* could see Indians making the plains gesture for fornication, the extended middle finger of the right hand plunging into a circle formed by the thumb and curled fingers of the opposite hand. He knew that everyone here, save perhaps the Chisholms themselves, believed as he did—that the "kissing" to which Bonnie Sue had just admitted was a pleasant euphemism for what she and Lester Hackett had actually been doing. Why else hadn't she revealed this crucial information to her family the next morning?

"These men on horseback," Orliac said. "How many did you say there were?"

"Are you talking to me, sir?" Lester said.

"Yes, I am looking at you, eh?" Orliac said, and smiled and said, "Thank you," and dismissed Bonnie Sue with a wave of his hand. It seemed to Schwarzenbacher that the gesture was entirely French and probably decadent, the equivalent of a sophisticated Gallic shrug. Orliac was effectively indicating that they were here not to determine what had transpired between a man and a woman by a fire, but only to decide whether or not a horse had been stolen. Either Lester *had* stolen the horse or else he had taken it to give chase to men who themselves were intending mischief.

"There were five of them, sir," Lester said, rising from the bench. There was a puzzled look on his face. He watched Bonnie Sue as she walked back to where her mother was sitting, and then he looked at Orliac again.

"What did these men want?" Orliac asked.

"Sir?"

"What were they doing out there in the dark?"

"Well, sir, I don't know," Lester said. "They never took me into their confidence. I assume they were there to steal horses. Or . . . well, I really don't know."

"Were they riding away from the camp when you gave chase?"

"Well, yes."

"Then why did you give chase?"

"Well, we heard their voices—"

"Yes, yes," Orliac said. "You were kissing by the fire

and you heard voices, so you got on Mr. Chisholm's horse—"

"Yes, sir, I did."

"And gave chase."

"Yes, sir."

"Why?"

"Why?" Lester asked.

"That is my question."

"Well, because . . . because I wanted to see what they were doing."

"They were riding away. Isn't that what you said they were doing?"

"Yes, sir."

"Did you think they were armed?"

"Possibly."

"Yet you gave chase. You went after five armed men who were already departing."

"Well, at first I didn't know there were five of them."

"You only discovered that later on."

"Yes."

"But even in the beginning, you knew there were at least *two*, isn't that so?"

"Sir?"

"Because you heard *voices*. You heard more than one voice."

"Yes, sir. Right," Lester said.

"So you knew there were at least two men out there."

"Yes."

"Or possibly more."

"Well, I . . ."

"And possibly armed."

"Well, I took a rifle with me, sir, just in case."

"Mm," Orliac said. "Are you following all this, Henri?" he asked Sebilleau, who seemed to be dozing again now that Bonnie Sue had gone back to sit against the wall.

"I am listening," Sebilleau said, and nodded gravely.

"You say these men later captured you, eh?" Orliac asked.

"Yes, they were waiting up ahead. They ambushed me."

"And took you with them?"

"Yes, sir."

"To Illinois?"

"Yes, sir."

"Where later they released you."

"No, I escaped."

"Mr. Hackett, why did these men take you with them?"

"I'm not sure. I suppose—"

"Mr. Hackett, why didn't they simply shoot you?"

"Well, as I said before, I never really learned much about them. I don't know why they—"

"I think they should have shot you," Orliac said.

"Sir?"

"It would have saved us the trouble of hanging you. Mr. Hackett," he said, "I think you stole the horse, eh? I would like to recommend now—"

"Now wait just a minute," Lester said.

"—that you be hanged by the neck till dead. Mr. Schwarzenbacher—"

"The goddamn girl just *told* you—"

"What is your opinion?"

"I think he's guilty and should be hanged," Schwarzenbacher said.

"Mr. Sebilleau?"

"Oui," Sebilleau said. *"Pendez-lui."*

There was stout timber by the river above the fort, but Sebilleau suggested justice might best be served by hanging Hackett in the courtyard. The other judges agreed this might be a good idea, and together they marched about trying to find a beam suitable to the purpose. They were followed by a dozen or more Indians who murmured among themselves, more curious as to *how* the hanging would take place than *where*. In the end, it was decided that a tree would do better than any of the beams supporting the gallery around the court. Besides, if a man could not be hanged in the center of the court for all to see, what purpose would it serve to hang him inside the fort at all? Convinced, Sebilleau and the others withdrew for their noonday meal, ordering Hackett to be bound and locked in the factor's empty apartment till 2 p.m., at which time he would be taken to the river and hanged. At ten minutes to two, the judges, a half-dozen other company men, and a large contingent of Indians dragged Hackett out of the apartment to lead him to his execution.

Sebilleau, who could neither read nor write, seemed possessed nonetheless of a fine sense of poetic justice, and suggested that Hackett be set astride the horse he'd been convicted of stealing. Will refused them the use of the raindrop gelding. His attitude about the hanging was pretty much akin to what all the family save Bonnie Sue felt. Lester Hacket had stolen a horse, and had to be punished for the crime as prescribed by law. They went down to the river to witness the hanging not because they were curious—they'd seen hangings aplenty in Virginia—and not because they felt vengeful or angry or indeed anything but dutiful; it was a Chisholm horse had been stolen, and a man was now to be hanged for the theft, and they felt it was their responsibility to be there.

A company man named Bertaut knew how to fashion a hangman's noose, having learned the intricacies of it as a boy, when someone taught him how to do it as a sort of game. The Indians lining the river and surrounding the huge cottonwood that had been selected as the hanging tree watched as Bertaut coiled the heavy rope around itself. He explained that the purpose of the noose was not to choke off the man's breath and therefore kill him by strangulation. Instead, when the condemned was jerked off the horse upon which he was sitting—a gray stallion belonging to the company cook—the huge knot behind his head would snap upward and break his neck, killing him instantly. Or so Bertaut hoped. He had never made a hangman's noose for use in a *real* hanging. An Indian who'd been listening to this explanation in French now turned to several other Indians and began explaining it in the Siouan tongue. The others nodded gravely. They understood completely the solemnity of this occasion by the river, and they watched now in awed silence.

The stallion would not stand still, foiling their efforts to loop the noose over Lester's head. Each time another horse came alongside, the stallion tried to rear away from the man holding its bridle. They finally put Lester on a more docile horse, and got the noose around his neck. Somebody asked him would he like to say a prayer, and he said, "Go to hell, man," not knowing to whom he was addressing the words because they'd blindfolded him as an act of mercy. Sebilleau somewhat gleefully brought the whip down on the horse's left buttock, shouting "*Allez!*" at the moment of contact. The horse leaped forward and Lester was jerked from the saddle—only to begin choking.

The Indians, who'd understood Lester would be killed instantly, now thought they'd heard incorrectly and turned for explanation to the one among them who spoke French. Schwarzenbacher recognized the trouble at once; Bertaut's damn knot hadn't worked and Hackett was choking to death. "The man's choking!" he shouted, more to himself in realization than to anyone else present. Leaping upon the back of the gray stallion that had earlier balked, he drew a dagger from a sheath at his belt and rode to where Lester was kicking and coughing and twisting at the end of the rope. Standing in the stirrups, he hacked at the thick hemp, virtually fiber by fiber, till at last it began to unravel and finally tore asunder, dropping Lester to the ground.

Orliac asked Schwarzenbacher why he had interrupted the hanging, and Schwarzenbacher replied somewhat testily, "The man stole a horse, he didn't murder a sleeping babe!" Orliac then ordered Bertaut to fashion another noose, a better one this time, a noose that would break the condemned man's neck as it was supposed to. Bertaut suggested that he was not equal to such an awesome responsibility, but then changed his mind at once, perhaps sensing the impatience and the mounting anger of his superior. He ran up to the fort to fetch a new hanging rope, and soon they were ready to try it another time.

•   •   •

Will didn't know what she was saying at first.

Sounded like she was babbling. Came rushing out of the woods to where he was sitting apart from the others on the knoll above the river. Tears were streaming down her cheeks, her nose was red and running, she said something about hiding, watching, couldn't bear to see it, prayers answered, God answered her prayers. "You've got to save him for good now, Will, please." She was on her knees, squeezing both his hands between her own. He shook one gently loose, and brushed wet hair back from her cheeks.

"It's your horse, Will," she said. "You could stop em if you wanted. They've put the rope on him again, Will. You got to go down there and stop em."

"Bonnie Sue . . ."

"Will, I love him. Please do what I ask. I beg you."

"I can't," he said, and shook his head. "The man stole—"

"I'm carryin his child," Bonnie Sue said.

"No," Will said.

"Will, I'm pregnant by him. I'm two months—"

"No," he said. "You ain't, Bonnie Sue."

"Will . . ."

"You *aint*, goddamn it!"

They stared at each other in silence. Tears streamed down her cheeks. She knelt before him and he looked down at her, and then turned his face away, refusing to meet her eyes lest he find there the eyes of a woman. "No," he said again, and in the next instant was sorry. He heard the shouted *"Allez!"* from below, and turned to look, and realized he was too late, he could no longer stop it if he tried.

The horse was running off along the riverbank.

Lester's body hung in the air, his boots some four feet above the ground, his head twisted at a peculiar angle, his tongue protruding grotesquely from his mouth. His hat had fallen from his head when the knot struck him violently from behind, and it lay now in the dirt below his swinging boots. Bertaut looked up at him and nodded in brief satisfaction. Wiping perspiration from his forehead, he went to stand with his Indian wife, who asked him something in French. Bertaut nodded. Beside Will, Bonnie Sue screamed. She got to her feet and, still screaming, ran to where Lester's body slowly twisted on the end of the rope. And clutched for his knees, and hugged his legs close, wailing, wailing as the Indians watched in wonder.

He went down to the tipi again that night. He was sober this time. Lifted the flap, went right on in. He had food with him, which he gave to Catherine and the squaw. The air had turned chilly outside; they still had the fire going. He asked them whether they'd already had supper, and Catherine nodded that they had and then talked to the squaw with her hands. The squaw sighed and made ready to go, draping the army blanket over her shoulders.

"You can stay, you want to," Will said. Catherine looked at him. "Tell her she can stay. Makes no difference," he said, and shrugged again.

The women held a conference, Catherine explaining with her hands, the squaw listening and then turning in surprise to Will. He nodded. She took off the blanket then, and went to the robe near the fire. Kneeling on it, she began unbraiding her hair, preparing for sleep.

"Take off the paint, too," he said.

The squaw turned to Catherine for translation. Catherine's hands moved. The squaw nodded and went silently to rub the paint from her face. She undressed without embarrassment, and then came back to the robe naked, and lay down on it, and pulled a second robe over her. In a little while, Catherine and Will got under the robe with her, Will between the two women. The squaw was almost asleep. Her hand found his pecker. She let it rest there lightly, fell asleep that way. Snored gently. Catherine made sounds. Little frightened sounds. All night long. He lay awake between them.

He kept thinking about Lester Hackett.

Kept thinking he could've stopped the hanging if he'd moved an instant sooner. Should've jumped right up when Bonnie Sue told him she was pregnant. Never mind Lester was a horse thief *deserved* hanging. This was his sister here telling him the man's child was inside her, and there he was with a noose around his neck. Should've done what Schwarzenbacher'd already done once, run on down there and cut the man loose. Shake his hand. Congratulations, Lester, you stole a horse and got away with it. Now about this other matter, Lester, this matter of having *also* stole my sister's honor. I reckon we had best start discussing a wedding, wouldn't you say, before my pa shoots you dead? Sat there looking at her instead. Didn't know *what* to say or do, his little sister telling him all at once she'd behaved like any whore. . . .

Catherine stirred beside him on the robe.

"You awake?" he asked.

She grunted and rolled over, her back to him. The squaw still had her hand on his pecker. Pair of whores, he thought. I'm here with a pair of whores, one looks like a cow and can't talk English, the other mute as any stone. Was a time . . . hell, he couldn't *remember* a time he hadn't loved Elizabeth. Four years old when he first spied her in her cradle. Fell in love right that minute. Asked his ma who the young'un was there in the cradle by the fire. Minerva said it was Mrs. Donnely's new daughter as lived down the ridge. Was minding her while they were in town. "She's a real *sun*flower," Will said. He was four. Loved her to death first time he saw her. He was thirty-one now—no, thirty-two already, layin here between two whores, gettin hard in spite of himself, the squaw's hand twitching in her sleep.

Thirty-two, he thought.

Don't know where I am or what I'm about.

Figured if we left Virginia . . .

Should've saved Lester, damn it! Cause when you thought about it . . . well, he got killed for a *horse*, wasn't that the long and the short of it? Man stole a fuckin horse, you strung him up. Them Indians who'd killed Annabel . . . oh, Lord, he thought, oh, dearest God, and lay motionless, eyes wide open. He could see stars above, through the hole in the top of the tent. Smoke rose from the smoldering fire. Way Bobbo described it, they'd come in there ready to kill. Maybe not *wanting* to, but ready to. Must've been following the wagon, saw the womenfolk, saw just Bobbo and Pa all alone, thought to have taken the women and the mules. Kill Bobbo and Pa, take the women and mules. Thirteen years old, saw Annabel as a woman, same as Ma and Bonnie Sue. Came in there ready to kill for what they wanted, ready to kill even the very *thing* they wanted. Made no fuckin sense. None of it. Not the

Indians killing Annabel, and not the white men today killing Lester. Cause that's what they'd done, they'd killed him, hanged him by law, but killed him dead however you looked at it. Wasn't what Bonnie Sue wanted, wasn't even what *Will* wanted when you got right down to it. What he would've rathered was for Lester to still be alive and kicking and marrying his damn dumb sister who'd let a horse thief . . .

He was losing the thought, he was letting it slip from his grasp.

It had to do with horses.

The horse Lester stole, and the horses Bobbo and Pa took from them Indians, two fine mares and a stallion. If you hanged a white man who'd stolen from you, and if you killed Indians were *trying* to steal from you . . .

And . . .

And if you claimed as your own the horses had belonged to the Indians, then what was to stop the one who'd run off from coming back to claim *all* the fuckin horses—the ones had belonged to him and his, and the ones rightfully belonging to you and yours, earmarked and branded? What was to stop anybody in this whole fuckin *world* from taking anything he wanted from anybody else? Take it or try to take it. Kill for it or be killed for it. White man or Indian, what difference did it make? There were only so many horses, only so many buffalo, only so much land. . . .

Trembling in the night, troubled, he moved closer to the squaw for warmth, and finally fell asleep.

By morning, he'd forgotten what he'd almost understood.

VII

---◆●◆---

GIDEON

Will was sitting there with his two women, one on either side of him. Fire in the middle of the tent. Place smelled awful, made Gideon want to retch. Some kind of food cooking there in the pot. Some kind of animal. Lots of Indians ate dog meat. He looked at his brother and wondered if he'd taken to eating dog meat now that he was sleeping with Indians. The squaw looked like the hog Gideon'd carried in the house that time. The other one was supposed to be white. She was wearing an old calico Will had bought from a trapper coming through. Hem had been let out cause she was so tall; you could see plain as day where the faded dress'd been made longer. Wore it with black cotton stockings to her shins. Moccasins, too. *Still* looked like an Indian; Gideon couldn't believe she was white.

"Will," he said, "you remember we were talkin about Fort Hall. . . ."

"I remember," Will said.

"If we're to go," Gideon said, "we'd best do it soon. This is now the middle of August. We—"

"I'm thinkin of waitin till spring," Will said.

"We could still make it before—"

"No, I'm thinkin we're late. The snow'd catch us. Anyway, Orliac's prob'ly right about the Indians out there. I don't want to chance it, Gideon."

Had nothing to *do* with snow. Nor Indians, neither, except for the two Indians right here—if she was white, then Gideon was Chinee. The fat one leaned over, said something to the other one. Her hands began moving. Will watched like he understood. Gideon said, "Well then . . ." and shrugged, and left the tent. Outside, he could still smell whatever was cooking in the pot. Up above the fort, he saw his father and Bobbo working on the cabin. The trees were already losing their leaves. He thought: *I'm trapped here for sure*, and then sighed and went on up to help them.

It took them less than two weeks to raise the cabin. Beginning of September, they moved into it lock, stock, and barrel, made it a twin to the one back home. Minerva's cherrywood dresser there against the wall, split-bottomed chairs on the same wall and the one opposite, benches either side the table. On shelves in all the corners, the family's pewter plates and utensils, tin cups and water pails, wooden bowls. Hanging on pegs all over the room was clothing and guns, cotton cards, handsaws and bridles. Same as back home. Even to the clock on the mantel. Its crystal had been smashed that time the mules bolted with Bonnie Sue, but otherwise it ticked off minutes just the same. Ticked. And ticked.

He sat by the fire and puffed on his pipe. He'd taken to smoking a pipe; kept him from getting too fidgety. There was an Indian at the fort always had tobacco to trade. Gideon figured he'd buried a cache of it in the hills someplace. Whenever he saw Gideon, he made a pipe bowl of his fist and pretended to be filling it with tobacco.

"*Tabac?*" he asked, grinning like he was selling a woman. "*Voulez?*"

"*Tabac*, aye," Gideon said.

He sat before the fireplace, rocking. Bonnie Sue was just the other side of it, a shawl on her lap. Gideon puffed on his pipe and looked into the flames. On the mantel, the clock ticked.

And ticked.

"Yep," Gideon said.

Across the room, behind the blanket, Minerva was preparing for bed. He could hear her bustling about.

"Yep," he said again.

Bonnie Sue looked at him, annoyed, and then went back to writing in her diary, or whatever it was she called it. Her pencil scratched into the stillness. The fire crackled. The clock ticked. Gideon sighed.

"Person could get fat and lazy around here," he said.

Bonnie Sue jumped up out of her chair. His jaw fell open. The pipe slipped from his mouth and spilled glowing little tobacco cinders onto the front of his shirt. He caught for the pipe and missed it, and it went crashing to the floor. Brushing at his shirt, he jumped up and started stamping at cinders on the floor, wondering what had got into her.

"You mind your own damn business," she said.

"What?" he said.

"You heard me! It ain't none of your business how fat I am or how lazy neither. You just keep your nose—"

"What?" Gideon said. "*What?*"

"You just—you just *shut* up!" Bonnie Sue said, and burst into tears.

His mother poked her head around the blanket. There was a peculiar look on her face. She walked past Gideon to where Bonnie Sue was sitting at the table, her head on her arms, bawling. Gideon stood there feeling like a dummy. He picked up his pipe. His mother was stroking Bonnie Sue's hair.

"I didn't say nothin, Ma," he said.

"You go take a walk outside."

"Ma, I really didn't . . ."

"I know, son. Go on take a walk."

There were times he didn't know what in hell was going on.

Next day, she sent him down to where the Indian tents were, told him to go fetch his brother Will. Wasn't but a handful of tents down there now. Most of the Indians who'd come to trade had already moved on again in search of more buffalo. Will came out in a buckskin shirt and leggings, moccasins, beaded band across his forehead. He'd started growing a beard, and it was coming in scraggly and patchy. He asked Gideon what Ma wanted. Gideon said he didn't rightly know.

It was a bright windy day. Leaves darted on the air, rattled underfoot. She was sitting on the porch with a shawl around her, seemed lost in thought as they came up. She motioned for Will to take a chair, and then told Gideon to go on inside. He went in the cabin, but he could hear every word they said.

"Had a long talk with Bonnie Sue last night," his mother said. "Told me she's carrying Hackett's child, said you've known about it since the day he was hanged."

"That's right," Will said.

"Whyn't you tell somebody?"

"I figured you'd have noticed by now, Ma."

"She ain't but in her fourth month, and carryin small as a walnut."

"Anyway, Ma, it's Bonnie Sue's own business, ain't it?"

There was a note of warning in his voice. Gideon heard it and supposed his mother had, too. She was quiet for a minute, maybe trying to figure whether or not to let the challenge pass. Instead, she said, "Seems everybody in this family got his own business anymore."

"Meanin what?" Will said.

"Meanin you go figure it out, son," she said. Gideon heard her chair scraping back. Next thing he knew, she was in the cabin, walking straight to the fire. She picked up the poker, seemed not to know what she'd intended doing with it, and set it right down again. Will came in, stood just beside the door.

"You got somethin to say to me, Ma, I'd appreciate your—"

"I got nothing more to say to you," she said. "Go on back to your squaws down there, go on."

Will looked at her. "Ma . . ." he said.

"Just go on," she said.

"I'm a grown man."

"I know you are."

"If I choose to care for—"

"Your sister was killed by an Indian," she said flatly.

"Catherine ain't no Indian."

"She's as Indian as the other one; I see scant difference."

"Anyway, that ain't even the point. They'd die without me to care for them. There's just the two of them alone. . . ."

"They seemed to be doin fine before you got here."

"Ma, they're people same as you and me."

"They're people same as who killed your sister! Will," she said, "you'd best go, fore we say things there's no turnin back from."

"Let's get them said then."

"I said all I got to say. Your sister was killed by an Indian, and you're livin with a pair of them."

"One thing's got nothin to do with the other," Will said. "My grandpa was killed by an Indian, too. What's—"

"*Yes!*"

"What the hell's one thing—"

"You cuss in this house!"

"*Shit*, Ma!"

"Go cuss with your squaws!" Minerva said. "Go cuss with them. . . ." She clamped her mouth shut, folded her arms across her waist, turned her back to him.

Will stood inside the door just a moment longer.

"I miss Annabel as much as you do," he said. "I loved her, too," he said, and went out of the house.

She was still standing at the fireplace, her back to the door. Gideon went swiftly to the window. His brother was walking down toward the tents again. His hands were in his pockets. His shoulders were hunched against the wind. Winter was coming.

•   •   •

The first snow fell early in November.

The woods were still and white. Gideon worked in them silently all morning, and by noon had chopped enough wood to last through Christmas anyway. He was bone weary when he finished. Slung his ax over his shoulder, started down through the cleared field toward the cabin. His father was there in the middle of the field, talking to Schwarzenbacher, the snow falling all around them. Schwarzenbacher was swathed in fur from head to toe, a fur hat and a fur coat and fur boots and fur mittens. He looked more like an animal of the forest than the living animals the hides had been taken from. He waved, and Gideon waved back, and walked to where they were standing.

"I brought you some tobacco," Schwarzenbacher said.

"Thank you," Gideon said.

Schwarzenbacher took off one of his mittens, began digging into the huge pocket of his coat. Hadley watched impatiently; Gideon figured he'd been in the middle of something. "It's supposed to be very good," Schwarzenbacher said, and handed him a folded oil-skin. Gideon rested the ax against his leg, unwrapped the oilskin, sniffed the tobacco inside.

"Ahhhh," he said, and nodded appreciatively.

"Yes?" Schwarzenbacher asked, eyebrows raised.

"Yes," Gideon said. "Thank you very much." He shivered suddenly. "Sweat's turnin to chill," he said. "You'll have to pardon me." He nodded to Schwarzenbacher and then to his father, and walked up to the cabin. His mother was at the table, kneading dough.

"You'll be wantin a hot tub," she said.

"Aye."

"I've heated water; it's ready behind the blanket."

"Thank you," he said, and went to take off his clothes. Cabin felt toasty warm, firelight flickering from around the edges of the blanket, steam rising from the water in the wooden tub. He climbed in, sloshing half of it all over the floor—nobody ever *could* get it in their heads just how big he was. Made him feel like a dunce sometimes, being so big. *"When you gonna quit growin, Gideon?"* Har-har-har, nudge in the ribs. *"Gideon, you're lookin more like an oak forest every day."* Har-har-har. He hoped the men out west were big, he ever *got* there. Felt comfortable with big men. Loved to rassle with his brothers. Will especially, even though he was a mite shorter than Bobbo. Knew more tricks, Will did. Grab your head, you'd think you was caught in a bear trap. Wasn't *Will* about to go west, though. Wasn't none of them, you wanted to know. They'd settled in for sure. They'd be here come spring and beyond, and forever. Wasn't no moving any of them out of here. On the other side of the blanket, Minerva was humming, slapping dough on the table-top, Gideon sighed, savoring the steam that rose around him. He heard the front door opening, heard Hadley and Schwarzenbacher coming in, stamping snow from their boots.

"Whooooo!" Hadley said.

"Whooo-*eeeee!*" Schwarzenbacher said.

"What you doin there, Min?" Hadley said. "Fetch us some whiskey."

"Fetch your *own* whiskey," Minerva said.

"You want some whiskey, Schwarzenbacher?"

"Yes, thank you," Schwarzenbacher said.

"Made it myself. Plan to do the same here, once I get my corn planted and picked."

Gideon heard the tin cups being set down on the table, heard the cork being pulled from the jug, the whiskey being poured.

"To your health," Hadley said.

"Your health, sir."

"Pour some for me, too, Pa," Gideon called from behind the blanket.

"What's that, eh? You hear something, Min? Must be a critter in the house."

Gideon laughed.

"You hear it, Schwarzenbacher?"

"Yes, sir," Schwarzenbacher said.

"No matter how you chink a place, they get in anyhow," Hadley said.

"Come *on*, Pa," Gideon said, laughing.

"There it is again!" Hadley said. "My, my, my. Schwarzenbacher," he said, "when I was a lad, the Indians'd steal the corn soon as it was ready to pick. Will they do the same here?"

"I don't know, sir."

"There's patterns, don't you think?"

"Pa?"

"Come get your *own* damn whiskey, son! What're you doin behind that blanket anyway?"

"Havin a tub," Gideon said.

"Well, dry yourself off and come have a drop of whiskey. I find it cold here, Schwarzenbacher. This time of year, it wasn't so cold back home. Makes me wonder will the plantin season be different? Do you know anything about that?"

"No, sir; I'm sorry."

"Where are you from anyway?"

"Yonkers, New York."

"Here you go, you lummox," Hadley said, and handed a cupful of whiskey around the blanket.

"Ah, thank you, Pa," Gideon said.

The whiskey was good. It ran fiery hot down his gullet to the pit of his stomach. The steam rose, drifting. Outside, the snow was thick enough to churn.

"You'd best go fetch your daughter," Minerva said.

"Where is she then?"

"To the fort, tryin to trade what you and your sons shot yesterday."

"I'll need a sled, this weather."

"You'll have to build one then," Minerva said, and laughed.

"I'll go with you, sir," Schwarzenbacher said.

"Stay, finish your whiskey. The chimney'll be out of his tub soon. Ain't that right, Chimney?"

Gideon grinned, and sipped at his whiskey. In a moment, he heard the front door opening and closing. A cold wind swept across the cabin floor and into the space behind the blanket. He hunkered down lower into the tub.

". . . in Yonkers this time of year," Schwarzenbacher was saying.

"Yes. Now you'll just have to get out of my way," Minerva said, "if I'm to get this bread baked."

"Sorry, ma'm," he said. "I was saying how different it is in Yonkers. This time of year."

"Aye, it is, I'm sure," Minerva said.

"Not that I miss it," Schwarzenbacher said. "Do you miss Virginia, ma'am?"

"I miss it still," she said. "Aye."

"I was glad to leave Yonkers, in fact," he said. "I came here to learn a trade, ma'am. There's a brisk market in furs back east, you know. My father's a lawyer, he wanted me to study for the bar. I told him I'd prefer going into business. He was very decent about it, contacted a client in Winnipeg. . . ."

Gideon got out of the tub. He felt warm and lazy and mellow and relaxed. He dried himself, and then put on the clean clothes his mother had set out for him. When he came around the blanket, she was carrying her oven to the hearth. The coals she'd raked onto it were glowing red.

"Now just move away from the fire entirely," she said to Schwarzenbacher. "You, too," she said to Gideon, though he was nowhere near it.

"My fiancée's still there, you know. In Yonkers."

"I didn't know you was betrothed," Minerva said, kneeling.

"Yes, I am."

"Well, that's nice," Minerva said, and set oven and lid on the coals.

"Miss Loretta Hazlitt."

"Eh?"

"My fiancée."

"How was your tub, Gideon?"

"Nice, Ma."

"You're not going to light that pipe again, are you?" she asked, and shook her head.

"Schwarzenbacher brought tobacco."

"Did you now?" she said.

"Yes, ma'am," he said. "She's twenty-one."

"Who is?"

"Loretta. Closer to my age than . . . well . . . Bonnie Sue, for example."

"Yes, that's true."

"I think your daughter's very courageous," Schwarzenbacher said, and cleared his throat. "Very courageous, ma'am."

"Do you think so?"

"Yes, ma'am. To have defended him that way. It couldn't have been easy for her, ma'am. I admire her for—for what she did, ma'am. I do."

Minerva looked up at him.

"I do, ma'am."

She was still looking at him.

"She's only sixteen, you know," Schwarzenbacher said.

"Yes, I know that."

There was something in her voice, something . . . Gideon couldn't fathom what. He shrugged and lit his pipe.

Kind of liked Schwarzenbacher. The man was totally ignorant of anything a body needed to know, but he liked him anyway. Sort of took pleasure teaching him little things.

"You never ate squirrel, huh?" Gideon said.

"No, never. And don't intend to either."

"You're missin something fine, Schwarzenbacher."

The dead squirrel was resting on a flat rock out back. Gideon had dusted the rock free of snow, and was now skinning and dressing the animal. Schwarzenbacher watched as he ringed the back legs with his knife and then cut around the base of the tail.

"You ought to learn how to do this," Gideon said.

"Why?" Schwarzenbacher asked.

"Well . . . out here," Gideon said, rolling the animal onto its back.

"I don't plan to *be* out here much longer," Schwarzenbacher said, and immediately lowered his voice. "This is confidential, Gideon."

Gideon nodded. There was nothing he liked better than a secret. He stepped on the squirrel's tail with his foot, and then yanked on the back legs. The animal came almost free of the hide. He cut off the paws and sliced the rest of the skin loose at the throat.

"I've been thinking of moving on to California," Schwarzenbacher said. "I feel there'd be more opportunity for me there."

"I'll be heading there myself come spring," Gideon said, and cut off the head. "When do you think the wagon trains'll start coming through again?"

"Sometime in June."

"Be lots of them?"

"Enough."

"You think they'd be partial to company?"

"You'd make a welcome addition to any party, I'm sure."

"As late as June, huh?" Gideon said, and cut off the back feet, and then began gutting the animal. Schwarzenbacher turned his head away. "I was hoping to leave earlier."

"June is when they arrive."

"Mm," Gideon said. "What you do, you cut it in little pieces and dip em in flour and salt and a little pepper. They fry up just delicious."

"Do you think Bonnie Sue might like California?" Schwarzenbacher asked.

"Bonnie Sue?"

"Yes, your sister."

"Well, what . . . ?"

"After the baby is born, I mean. Do you think she might consider moving west?"

Gideon looked at him.

"Well, I don't rightly know," he said.

"I thought to start a hardware store there," Schwarzenbacher said.

"Hardware's good business," Gideon said, and wondered what in hell hardware had to do with Bonnie Sue. Why was . . . ?

Oh, he thought.

They had cut a pine tree in the forest and decorated it with berries and candles. The scent of it filled the cabin. Beneath the tree there were presents wrapped in colored cloth and tied with ribbons. A fire burned brightly in the fireplace. There was the aroma of baking bread; it suddenly caused Schwarzenbacher to feel heartsick for the house in Yonkers. Bonnie Sue bustled about the cabin, the baby huge within her, and Minerva shouted to her to see to the grouse and the sage hen Gideon had shot the day before.

They'd fashioned the gifts themselves, or else acquired them in trade from the Indians. Schwarzenbacher was laden with presents he'd been hoarding like a squirrel, and he doled them out like a blond Santa Claus, beaming at each recipient. When he handed Bonnie Sue her gift, he said, "It isn't much," and she answered, "But I have none for you, Schwarzenbacher."

"It doesn't matter," he said. "Please open it," and

watched as she unwrapped the gift. It was a seventeenth-century toadstone ring that had belonged to his mother before her death. "I hope it fits," he said.

"Thank you," she said, and did not look up from the carved frog on the face of the ring, and did not try the ring on.

"It was my mother's," he said.

"It's beautiful," she said. And still did not put the ring on her finger.

Minerva was unwrapping her gift from Hadley. He had purchased it from the Indians, a necklace made entirely of shells. She thanked him, and kissed him, and slipped it over her head. There was a beaded jacket for Bobbo and a pipe Bonnie Sue had paid an Indian to carve for Gideon. There were leather vests and belts and buckles and bonnets and dresses hand-sewn, and a rattle Bobbo had fashioned from a gourd and given to Bonnie Sue for the baby that was coming.

Schwarzenbacher could not take his eyes from her. She still had not put the ring on her finger. He thought for a panicky moment that she would return it to him, but he saw her put it in the pocket of her skirt and remembered her ancestry, and knew she'd convince herself it was rude to turn back a gift. She was at the fire now, tending to the birds, the flames flickering on her golden hair.

"Won't you open your gift from the Chisholms then?" Hadley asked.

"Sir?"

"Sitting there on the mantel, Schwarzenbacher. If it were a snake, it'd bite you."

"Thank you," Schwarzenbacher said, and went to where a small package stood on the fireplace mantel alongside a pewter candlestick. The package was wrapped in green cloth, tied with a red ribbon. His name was on it, *Schwarzenbacher*, and beneath that, *Merry Christmas*. From the heft of it and the shape of it, he suspected it was a pocket watch, and was fearful they'd given him something too valuable, an heirloom perhaps, something he did not deserve, something that would embarrass him. His hands trembling, he slipped the ribbon off the package without disturbing the bow, and then unwrapped the cloth from it. In a small oval brass frame that had undoubtedly been carried all the way from Virginia, they had placed a delicate pencil drawing of Bonnie Sue.

"Fellow guided us to the Platte drew that," Hadley said. "Name was Timothy Oates."

"A better artist than George Catlin," Bobbo said knowledgeably.

Schwarzenbacher's heart leaped with elation; they were telling him they approved of him. And suddenly he began to quake inside. Acceptance was still forthcoming from Bonnie Sue. His rehearsed proposal all but vanished from his head. He wanted to blurt it to her now and at once, before it disappeared entirely—"Marry me, I love you!" But instead he turned to her where she was setting the table with pewter, and said, "Have you seen this, Bonnie Sue?" and she looked at the framed pencil drawing and said, "Aye. It favors me, don't you think?"

"Yes," he said. "Bonnie Sue," he said, "I wonder if I might have a word in private with you."

"What about?"

"Well," he said, "could we sit there in the corner? I don't want you puttering around while I make my speech."

"Is it to be a speech?" she said.

"Sort of," he said.

"Then by all means let's sit," she said, and put down the pewter plates and led him to where a puncheon bench rested against the wall. Sitting, smoothing her skirt, she turned to face him. Schwarzenbacher sat beside her. He cleared his throat.

"Bonnie Sue," he said, or thought he said, and then cleared his throat again, and said it too loudly this time, "Bonnie Sue," and lowered his voice and said, "I want to tell you a little bit about myself first."

"All right," she said.

"You may or may not know," he said, beginning the rehearsed speech, "and perhaps may not even *care* to know that my plan in coming here to Fort Laramie was to learn the fur trade, starting at the basest level, the acquiring of hides from trappers and hunters. I've changed my mind about furs, for to tell the truth there's nothing too stimulating about the skins of dead animals, and I'd as soon they kept their hides as parted with them." He nodded, rather pleased with what he'd just said. He looked into her eyes. Wide and green, intelligent and alert, they were studying his face. He suspected she was far ahead of him already, and cursed the cumbersome speech he'd memorized, but plunged ahead with it nonetheless. "I plan to leave for California in the spring," he said, "when my contract with the American Fur Company expires. I plan to seek my fortune in the west. I've talked with Gideon, your brother Gideon . . ."

"Yes," Bonnie Sue said.

"Yes, and I know something of his own plan to leave for California, and I thought we might make the journey together. I thought to convince Bobbo to come along as well, leaving the cabin here to your parents. . . ." He had departed from the planned speech; he was rambling. "Orliac is correct on that one matter, Bonnie Sue. . . ."

"What matter is that?" she asked.

"Of there being little danger of Indian attack here since the fort is a place of business, and Indians are as smart as any other men when it comes to trading. I'm saying your parents would be safe here should both your brothers decide to leave and—and you and the baby with them. The baby's coming in March—"

"In February, I reckon," Bonnie Sue said.

"That's better yet," he said, "which means by June you'd be strong enough to travel, you and the baby both. I'm asking you to go with me when I leave, Bonnie Sue. As my wife, Bonnie Sue."

He went back to the prepared speech again, picking it up not quite where he had lost it, but raveling up the yarn nonetheless, telling her how much he admired her, and of how his admiration had started that day of the courtyard trial when she'd nobly come to the defense of Lester Hackett, all of which he'd thoroughly rehearsed, and which he told her now with practiced ease and studied sincerity even though he meant every word of it. He told her, too, that he loved her more than he'd ever loved anyone in his life, loved her more than life itself—why, he would lay down his life for her in a minute if she asked that of him, without hesitation and without remorse. He told her he'd broken his engagement to Miss Loretta Hazlitt in Yonkers, New York, had dispatched a letter to her via some trappers who'd been at the fort, perhaps she recalled having seen the trappers, one with but a single ear, the other constantly drunk, he was sure Loretta had received it by now. He had, in short, performed his gentlemanly duty by releasing her from her vows, and he was free now to ask Bonnie Sue for her hand in marriage, which he was now doing. He wished to assure her that he would accept the baby as his own and love it as his own, be it boy or girl, it made no matter, he would love the child as deeply as he now loved its mother.

"If you'll have me," he said, "we could marry at once and move into my apartment at the fort, which is neither sumptuous nor grand, but which will serve us well till we leave for California in June. Will you marry me, Bonnie Sue?"

"I don't love you," she said.

"That will come," he said. "In time."

"No," she said.

The night was cold and sharp. Clouds of vapor puffed from their mouths as they came down the hill toward the fort, their arms laden with gifts for Will. Bobbo was drunk and singing. Gideon kept trying to shush him. There were only two tents outside the fort now, both of them sending up smoke to the crystal night. Will heard them coming, poked his head out, and then stepped into the cold.

"Hey, how you doin?" he said. "Merry Christmas!"

"Merry Christmas, Will," Gideon said, and took his hand.

"Hey there!" Bobbo shouted, and hugged his brother close. "Merry Christmas there, Will!"

"Come on in, you two! Hey, Catherine!" he yelled, and threw back the flap to the tent. "Look who's here!"

There was a fire burning inside. The two women were sitting near it. They got to their feet at once, both of them smiling welcome. Catherine gestured to one of the robes, and Gideon said, "Thank you," and put down the gifts he was carrying. Bobbo sat cross-legged. There was a strained moment of silence, and then Gideon said, "Hey, Will, we missed you today."

"Yeah, I missed y'all, too. Hey, wait'll you see what we got for you. How's Ma, is she okay?"

"She's fine," Gideon said. "Pa sent you this gallon of whiskey; it's most the last of it, Will. He's doling it out like it was gold these days."

"Hey now," Will said. "Hey, let's all have some whiskey. Sister, have some whiskey. Tell her whiskey, Catherine."

"Is that her name?" Gideon asked. "Sister?"

"Well, that's what Catherine calls her," Will said. "She's her sister-in-law actually. They used t'be married to the same fella. Here we go—ah, good," Will said, and picked up one of the hollow gourds Catherine put on the ground beside him. "Made some nice things for you," he said, and then said to Catherine, who was starting across the tent again, "No, honey, let it wait, have some whiskey first. Ask Sister if she wants some. Whiskey," he said to Sister, and nodded. Catherine's hands moved. Will passed the filled gourds around.

"Merry Christmas," he said.

"Merry Christmas," his brothers said, almost together.

Catherine nodded.

"*Mair-creez,*" Sister said, and drank.

"Bonnie Sue would've come down with us, Will, but the snow's deep and she's big as a house."

"That's okay," he said. "Sister made a nice comb for her, didn't you, Sister? Comb," he said, and made a sign with his hands.

"Comb," Sister said, and nodded.

"She's learning a little English. Catherine can't talk, you know, sons of bitches cut out her tongue when she was just comin along."

"Do that again, Will," Bobbo said.

"What you mean? This with my hands? This means comb," he said, and again made the sign.

"*Looks* like a comb, sure enough," Gideon said.

"It sure do," Bobbo said. "Will, *what's* her name again?"

"Sister," Will said.

"Hey, Sister, how you doin?" Bobbo said, and held out his hand to her.

Sister took the hand.

"She knows about shakin hands," Will said.

"Shake," Sister said, and nodded.

"Right," Bobbo said.

"Ain't you gonna open what we brought, Will?"

"Sure I am, you bet I am. Here now, let me get—no, sit down, Catherine, I'll get it. How was your dinner? Did you have a nice Christmas dinner?"

"Oh, yeah, it was real nice," Gideon said. "How about you?"

"I shot us some fine birds—"

"Hey, so did I," Gideon said.

"Yeah?" Will said. "Now how about that?" and he laughed and went to the other side of the tent, where he picked up a basket brimming with gifts. Carrying it back to the robe, he set it down before his brothers and said, "I marked all these with your names. This one's for you, Gideon, and let me see. . . . Catherine, where's—wait a minute. Is this the one for Bobbo? Wrapped here in hide? With the blue thong here?"

Catherine nodded.

"Yeah, take a look at this, Bobbo," he said. "Catherine made it. Well, go on take a look at it. Gideon, open yours, go on now."

"We brought some things for your—for the women, too," Gideon said.

"Thank you, I appreciate that," Will said.

Bobbo slipped the thong off the hide wrapping. The wooden flute was delicately carved, decorated with paint in orange and blue. He looked at it and felt the way he had that time he'd seen Timothy's drawing. Tears suddenly brimmed in his eyes. "Hey," Will said.

"It's beautiful," Bobbo said. "Thank you, Will. Thank you, Catherine. Sister."

"Will, you got to forgive Ma not . . ."

"I understand," Will said. "I really do."

"Open your presents, Will. We want you to please open your presents."

"Yes," Will said, and lifted his drink again. "Merry Christmas," he said.

"Merry Christmas," Gideon said. "Catherine, you too. This one's for you, wrapped here in the polka dot. And Sister . . ."

"*Mair-creez*," Sister said again, and drank.

"Case you don't know it," Will said, "that's 'Merry Christmas.' "

"In Indian?" Bobbo asked.

"Hell, no. In *English!*" Will said.

Catherine laughed. Sister laughed with her. And suddenly, they all were laughing.

•   •   •

Gideon was alone with Bonnie Sue when the first pains came. He'd sprained his ankle in the woods the day before, tripped over a damn root hidden by snow. Hurt like hell now. Bonnie Sue was rocking by the fire. On the mantel the clock ticked. There were times he wanted to pick up that damn clock and hurl it across the room, finish the job the mules had started.

"You'd think he'd have been discouraged," Bonnie Sue said.

"Yeah," Gideon said, and got up, and began limping around.

"Or angry, or whatever."

Still hurt like hell.

"But no, he's been coming back up here every day since Christmas."

"Well, maybe he's daft," Gideon said.

"Do you know what he said just the other day?"

"No, what'd he say?" Gideon asked. *Hated* not being able to move like he normally did.

"He said it was my pride made me refuse him."

"Yeah, he *is* daft," Gideon said.

"Said I thought he'd proposed out of pity, and my pride wouldn't let me accept. I told him it had nothin to *do* with pride, it had only to do with not loving him. You think it's got to do with pride, Gideon?"

"I don't know *what* it's got to do with. It's *you* he's asking; how should I know?"

"Hobbling around that way ain't going to help your ankle none," Bonnie Sue said.

"Well, your *chatter* ain't helpin it none either," Gideon said. "You want to marry the man, then why don't you just up and marry him, stead of—"

"I *don't* want to marry him. I'm only askin do you think it's pride or not."

"What's *my* opinion got to do with it?" Gideon said. "Ain't *me* has to love him, it's—"

"Oh!" Bonnie Sue said.

He turned to her at once. Her eyes were opened wide in surprise. She grimaced, and then clutched for her belly, and then said, "Oh" again, and sat with her arms crossed over her belly, looking straight ahead of her into the cabin.

"Sis?" he said.

"It's all right," she said.

"Sis?"

"It's all right, Gideon. Run on down the fort, go fetch Mama."

"Sis?" he said. He was on the edge of panic now.

"Do what I say, Gideon! Fast!"

He went out the door without putting on a coat. He went limping through the woods on his swollen ankle, stabs of pain shooting up into his leg each time he put the foot down, tripping once in the snow and almost twisting the other ankle, getting to his knees, and catching his breath, and then standing up straight, testing the ankle, and beginning to run for the fort again. He passed the tree where they'd hanged Lester Hackett, whose baby it was, the branches spreading bare and black against the gray winter sky, the sun barely showing as a white ball hidden in the gray.

The river was frozen over almost completely, save for patches here and there where the water ran black through chunks of ice. The trees looked like pencil sketches, black scratchy lines against the gray, everything quiet around him, his footballs cushioned by the snow till he began climbing a small hillock that the wind hit full, and there he broke through crusted snow with each step, crashing into the stillness. He came over the top of the hill and started down toward the fort again, his ankle hurting something fierce, his heart pounding in his chest to burst through his ribs.

The postern gate was open. He came in through the back of the fort and ran past the mules and horses in the corral and then across to the other side, where the kitchen was, and where he guessed he'd find his mother. The cook was dozing on a barrel turned upside down, his back against the kitchen wall, his feet up on a smaller keg. Gideon came in yelling, and the cook sat upright and said in alarm, "*Qu'est-ce que c'est?*" his voice coming out like a squeak, his eyes opened wide in fright, as though he'd been dreaming of marauding Indians.

"Where's my mother?" Gideon said.

"*Ta mère?*" the cook said.

"It's my sister's time!" Gideon said.

"*Ta soeur?*" the cook said, and finally made the connection. This was the brother of the one who'd been made pregnant by the horse thief. He got up off the barrel at once, and looked around the kitchen in bewilderment, as though he'd put Minerva away someplace, perhaps in a bin or a drawer, but could not remember exactly where. Gideon, breathing raggedly, his chest afire, his ankle swollen and throbbing, looked at the man helplessly, waiting for him to say something, to do something. Schwarzenbacher burst into the kitchen just then, having heard the commotion from his office next door. When he saw Gideon, he asked immediately, "Is it Bonnie Sue?"

"*Yes!*" Gideon said.

Schwarzenbacher ran out of the kitchen.

In the courtyard outside, Will was holding up a pair of dead rabbits to an Indian woman who sat cross-legged before a goat. The woman had milk and cheese to sell, and Sister was negotiating with her. The woman shook her head, said something to Sister, shook her head again. Her attention was suddenly captured elsewhere; they turned to follow her gaze. Schwarzenbacher was running wildly across the courtyard, Gideon limping along behind him.

"Will!" Schwarzenbacher shouted. "Where's your mother?"

"What?" Will said.

"Your mother, your mother! She was here a minute ago. Where . . . ?"

Bewildered, Will opened his hands, shook his head.

"Bonnie Sue's having the baby!" Schwarzenbacher yelled, and seized Sister's hand and pulled her toward the main gate.

There should have been a hut apart from the house; *that* was where the baby should have been born. Or lacking such a hut, there should have been a part of the house separate from the rest of it, with a screen of wood and hides constructed to protect the others from the glances of the woman giving birth. It was not permissible for men to be present in the hut or in the house, but here in the cabin were Will and his brother and the clerk from the fort. Sister would not permit it. She went to them at once, and pushed them out, and closed the door behind them.

On the bed against the eastern wall, Bonnie Sue lay

on her back. This, too, was wrong. The proper position for a woman in labor was not flat on her back, where she could do nothing but writhe and squirm against the pains that rippled through her. She should have been kneeling instead, so that she could squeeze the infant from her loins. There should have been a rope attached to one of the ceiling beams, and she should have been holding tight to it, so as not to fall over. Or else there should have been a pair of stakes driven into the floor, one for each hand, to which she could have clung while squatting. But no, she lay on her back jerking with each new pain. Sister marveled at the stupidity of it. She went to her and held out her hand.

"What is it? What . . . ?" Bonnie Sue said. "Oh, *Jesus!*" she screamed, and twisted again in pain.

"Up," Sister said.

"What?"

"Up," she said, and made a rising motion with her hands, lifting her palms toward the ceiling. "Come, up."

"You want—ow!" she said, "Ow!" and squeezed her eyes shut.

"Come!" Sister said, and grabbed both her hands, and pulled her off the bed. Bonnie Sue clung to her, puzzled, and then realized the woman wanted her to squat, was gently easing her into a squatting position. Sobbing, her nose running, her hair wet with tears and perspiration, she knelt before her. Sister pulled on her hands, grunting, grimacing, trying to indicate what she must do to force the child out of her. Bonnie Sue said, "Jesus!" and then, "Oh, Christ!" and then, "Oh, sweet loving mother . . ." and Sister squeezed her hands hard and said, "*You!*"

"What?" Bonnie Sue said, and looked up into her face. "Where's my mama? Please get my—oh, Jesus! *Jesus!*"

"*You,*" Sister said again, and shook her head in anger and again tugged at Bonnie Sue's hands, and at last Bonnie Sue pulled back against them. "Ah!" Sister said sharply, and "Ah!" again, and squinched her face and made the grunting sound again, and said, "You, you," and now Bonnie Sue began to squeeze, screaming, "Jesus, Jesus," pushing. "Ah," Sister said, nodding encouragement, "Ah, ah," and Bonnie Sue said, "Yes, please help me," and pushed again, harder this time. Sister knelt before her, one hand extended to hold both of Bonnie Sue's, the other beneath her to cradle the baby's head as it began to slide from her womb. "You!" Sister shouted, and Bonnie Sue gave a fierce push below, fearing she would soil herself, embarrassed, sobbing, clinging tightly to Sister's hand, and feeling the baby slipping from her loins, feeling suddenly exuberantly joyous, and hearing the baby's triumphant squawl like a bugle on the air.

When Minerva got to the cabin, she found Bonnie Sue in bed with the baby on her belly. Will's Indian woman handed her a rag upon which was the afterbirth, and Minerva immediately threw it into a slops bucket. The Indian woman shook her head violently.

Minerva didn't know what she was trying to say. She knew only that Bonnie Sue and the baby both needed washing, and she began immediately to do that. The Indian woman stood by watching, seemingly appalled, shaking her head. Minerva took the bloodstained bed-clothes from the bed and replaced them with clean ones. The woman scowled. Minerva wrapped the baby in a blanket and handed it to her. "Here," she said, "hold the child," and then helped Bonnie Sue into a clean nightgown, and combed her hair. She took the baby from the Indian woman, and put it into Bonnie Sue's arms. Bonnie Sue smiled wearily.

"That was the hardest thing I ever done in my life," she said.

"And me not here to help," Minerva said, and clucked her tongue.

"I sure did wonder where you were," Bonnie Sue said.

"Took it in my head to stroll up the long way. Came over the hill past where the river—"

"Ma," Bonnie Sue said. "Is the baby . . . ?"

"Sound as can be, child."

"Thank God," Bonnie Sue said, and turned to look at Sister. "Thank you," she said. Sister looked at her blankly. "Thank you for what you done," Bonnie Sue said.

Minerva went to the door and opened it. Schwarzenbacher looked scared to death. Gideon and Will stood with their hands in their pockets.

"It's a baby girl," Minerva said.

Schwarzenbacher nodded. "Is Bonnie Sue . . . ?"

"She's fine," Minerva said. "Come in."

Will hung back.

"Come in," she said, and took his hand. "You must help me thank Sister—is that her name, is that what you call her?"

"Yes, Ma," Will said.

"Come in, son, please," she said.

He went into the cabin and his mother hugged him to her.

•   •   •

Schwarzenbacher was back the very next day.

Bonnie Sue sat up in bed, the baby in her arms. Sunlight streamed through the window, touching her golden hair with a paler wintry light. She asked whether he thought the child was beautiful and he said indeed he thought so. She asked if he thought the child favored her, being quick to add she was not seeking flattery, but thinking only of the fair hair and blue eyes; her own eyes had been blue at birth. He said he thought the child did indeed favor her, in coloring *and* in beauty, and then asked her what she thought to name her.

She said, "What do *you* think?"

He said, "I thought after your sister, unless that would cause the family pain."

"I'll ask them," she said.

They talked of the weather then, of how mild it was for the last week in February. He told her he'd seen wildflowers blooming in the snow by the river, and ventured the opinion that spring would come early this year.

"Bonnie Sue," he said at last, "have you given any further thought . . . ?"

"I don't yet know your name," she said.

"What?" he said.

"Your Christian name."

"Ah," he said.

"What is it then?"

"Franz."

"Franz," she said.

"Yes."

"Franz Schwarzenbacher," she said.

"Even so."

For some reason they both laughed. And then fell silent.

"Further thought . . ." she said.

"Yes, I wondered . . ."

"To what?" she said.

"To what was discussed at Christmastime."

"Ah," she said. "That."

She was silent for a time. She touched the baby where it lay sleeping against her breast. Then she said, "The child's not yours. I don't see how you can . . ."

"I *can*," he said firmly.

"Won't it trouble you?"

"It will," he said. "It troubles me even now that there's been someone before. And I'll tell you, Bonnie Sue, should there be anyone *after*, I'll kill him and you besides. But I love you, and I'd have you if there'd been an army, that's the truth. Now what do you say? I've asked you once, and I'm asking you again. If you refuse me this time . . ." He hesitated. Then he said, "I'll ask you again next week," and smiled so suddenly and so boyishly that he captured her heart in that instant. "Will you marry me?" he said.

"I think I shall," she said.

The way they kept reading from their charts, it sounded almost religious to Hadley. Like in Genesis, where all the descendants of this one or that one were listed. His sons weren't calling off any Schechems or Shobals, though; they were instead naming places and distances from place to place, as if by dividing the trip into segments it would become shorter than it was.

It was thirteen hundred miles, *that's* what it was.

You couldn't change that by breaking it in half or in quarters or in little bitty inches. It was *still* thirteen hundred miles to California, and that was twice again what they'd already traveled from Independence to here. So when he heard Gideon saying it was only a hun' thirty, a hun' forty miles to the North Fork of the Platte, and Bobbo saying they could make it to the upper crossing in ten days or a bit more, he found himself thinking: *That* still *leaves more'n eleven hundred miles to go, lads.* And when they talked about Independence Rock being a scant fifty miles beyond the river, and South Pass but a hundred after that, he realized that in their minds they were already *through* the pass and traversing the three hundred and more miles to Fort Hall, and were past that to Raft River and Goose Creek, and Mary's River—and that was where it began sounding Biblical to Hadley.

Not because of Mary's River, which he didn't think had been named after the Virgin Mother, but only because the names and the distances tumbled one after the other like all the sons of Jacob and Leah: fifty miles to the Truckee, and then across the Forty-Mile Desert, through Dog Valley, Bear Valley, Emigrant Gap, the Sacramento Valley, Sutter's Fort . . . ah, there was the end of it, praise the Lord. But here they went at it again, this time naming the Indians they might meet along the way, Sioux and Snake in the desert beyond Big Sandy, hostile Bannocks beyond Fort Hall, Shoshones on the way to Mary's River, Paiutes beyond that, and afterward only the devil knew what!

It was Gideon alone planning to go at first, and then Schwarzenbacher told them all (as if they didn't know it was coming to pass anyway) that he and Bonnie Sue would be getting married and moving west, and then Bobbo mentioned that he might go along, too. By the second week in March, they were all four of them reciting the route and the distances on each segment, and the names of the Indians, and Hadley said to Minerva he wished to hell they'd hurry up and get *going*.

"No, you don't," she told him.

In the woods, the snow began to melt. Patches of earth appeared, spreading like stains. The ice on the river broke away in chunks that rushed downstream on waters running swift and black and icy cold. In the winter, you could plainly see the cottonwood from which Lester Hackett had been hanged, but the trees around it now were in bright green leaf, and it blended with the rest of the forest, and was invisible.

She walked Hadley down by the river.

She said, "Had, I keep worryin if I done the right thing about the baby's name. I keep thinkin I'm doing all the *wrong* things lately. I'm worried to death I maybe hurt Bonnie Sue's feelings. I tried to explain, but I'm not sure I . . . Had, I *couldn't* let her name the baby Annabel."

"I think she understood."

"You think so? She talked it over with Franz . . . can you get used to callin him that?"

"It's hard," Hadley said, and smiled.

"Aye, it is. Franz," she said, shaking her head. "I think namin the baby for your mother's a better idea, don't you?"

"Yes, Min."

"But I keep thinkin I hurt her feelings. I told her I wouldn't hurt her for nothin in the world, but I wished she wouldn't name the child for her sister cause . . . Hadley, my grief's still . . . Had, I can't think of her yet without wantin to weep."

They walked silently by the river.

Mallows were growing along the banks, scarlet and pink, purple and white. There were wood sorrels yellow as Eva's fine hair, hyacinths as blue as her eyes. Birdcalls carried liquidly on the soft new wind.

"I wish they wouldn't go," Minerva said. "I have the feeling I'll never see any of them again." She turned and looked directly into his eyes. "Had," she said, "do you think we might go with them?"

"West?" he said, surprised. "West, Min?"

"Aye. I'm thinkin you were maybe right. I'm thinkin that's where the dream is, west. Are we yet too old to chase it, Had?"

"I sometimes feel a hundred," he said.

"I know the field's waitin to be plowed. . . ."

"It is," he said.

"And I know you're anxious to start growin things again. . . ."

"I am."

"But, Hadley, I'd like to go with them. I'd like to move on again."

"I'm thinkin it's time myself," he said, and nodded.

They came now with buffalo robes to barter.

They came by the hundreds, on horseback or on foot, the hills alive with them. They came noisily, entire families of them, villages of them, braves and their painted squaws, young children, old men, stray horses and colts, dogs and puppies, descending to the river on the opposite shore, and then crossing close by the Chisholm cabin, pointing their fingers, turning their heads—the cabin had not been here the year before. Seasoned lodge poles trailed behind the horses, robes stacked high on woven baskets hanging between them. The river was running swiftly and children tumbled from their perches atop pyramids of robes, to be rescued by mothers or aunts or scolding older sisters. Yapping dogs reached the shore on which the Chisholm cabin stood, pissed against trees and shrubs, ran barking down to the water's edge again to await the rest of the caravan. The Indians buzzed through the woods like a swarm of bees, their sound moving farther and farther away till they emerged—still noisy, but seemingly silent from a distance—upon the plain behind the fort. The tipis went up, lodge poles first, three of them to form a tripod, the others placed in a circle against the supporting triangle, a dozen or more cut fresh in the forest. Buffalo hides were lifted into place over the skeletons, woven mats scattered, fires started, kettles put to boil. Where an hour before there had been an empty plain, there was now a village bustling with life.

Among the Indians who came to trade buffalo robes that spring was a young brave of the Dakota tribe.

He was there at the fort a full three days before he spied the horse. There was a white man's saddle on it now, but Teetonkah recognized the stallion at once. It belonged to his cousin Otaktay, who had been killed last year during the Moon of Moulting Feathers.

There were several of his nation among the Indians who had camped behind the fort. He went to them now, and invited them to hear him. He talked of a war party. He spoke eloquently and earnestly, and they listened with respect. He told them of what had happened the year before, when he and three others had come across a lone wagon while riding against the Pawnee. He spoke openly and honestly of defeat and disgrace, his cousin and his two close friends slain, three horses captured, he himself managing to escape with both his eyes, though they had tried to pluck them from his head. He had been ridiculed by those in his village, and had thought more than once of taking his own life, so shamed had he been by his failure.

He now wished to regain his lost honor.

He had seen his cousin's stallion, and also the other horses captured that night. There were more horses besides, three belonging to the white men, a total of six horses to be had. He asked now that these warriors of his nation, though not of his village, assist him in restoring his honor.

They listened solemnly.

There was not a one among them who did not understand his request. All ten agreed to accompany him against the white man, and smoked the pipe to indicate accord.

In the woods, there was the constant drone of insects. It was too hot for the beginning of April. Sister dipped her hand into the water and wet her face and the back of her neck. She had lost sight of Will, who'd been fishing downstream of her just a short while before. An insect bit her arm; she slapped at it. She wished now that she had stayed in the tipi with Catherine. She jiggled her fishing line in the water and glanced lazily at the cabin. Will's family were at the fort attending church services. She did not understand this. The religion was not their own, but they went every Sunday morning. She shook her head, and dipped more water from the river, and wet her arm where the insect had bit her. When next she looked at the cabin, a trail of black smoke was racing toward the sky. She dropped the fishing line, and jumped to her feet.

Flames were leaping from the window on the side facing the river. An Indian wearing a wolfskin over his shoulder was running toward the enclosure at the back of the cabin. There were six horses inside the split-rail fence there. A second Indian came out of the cabin, carrying a torch in one hand, a clock in the other. Another was behind him, wearing a white man's coat, and yet another came out with a clay pipe stuck in his mouth. There were four of them then. Sister had counted four, and thought that was all till she realized there were at least a half-dozen more circling the cabin or coming out of it, leaping the fence to rush at the horses from every side. She became suddenly frightened, and was turning to run back toward the fort for help when someone grabbed her from behind, looping his left arm around her throat.

She saw the paint on his arm, black paint like a long glove covering the man's hand and wrist and coming clear up to the forearm. In the instant he looped his arm around her neck, she knew she would have to kill him, and reached behind her at once with her right hand, and groped at his belt above the hanging breechclout and found the bone handle of his knife and yanked it free. He did not even know it was in her hand till she plunged it into the arm encircling her neck, plunged it again and again until, screaming in pain, he

released her. He was reaching with his right hand for
his tomahawk when she shoved the blade into his
throat. His left arm hung in tatters; he toppled toward
her with blood gushing from the open slash in his neck
where she had twisted the knife and pulled it loose.
Sister backed away from him and was again running for
the fort when she saw Will approaching from the opposite side.

He had no rifle; they were not in the habit of carrying weapons here in the vicinity of the fort. She recognized the Indians now as Dakota, whom she hated and
feared. Across the enclosure, one of them threw an
elkhorn saddle onto the back of a mare, and swiftly
mounted the animal. Another opened the gate. They
all rode out then, save the one with the wolfskin, who
was still trying to loop a thong bridle over the stallion's
jaw. The horse wheeled about, reared, pawed the air.
Will grabbed the man by the shoulder. He whirled suddenly and hit Will with his closed fist, knocking him to
the ground.

Sister ran to the fence and leaped it.

The Dakota was swinging his tomahawk downward
at Will's head when she stuck the knife into his back
and ripped the blade down toward his waist. She
stabbed with the knife again, this time cutting through
his leather shirt as he turned. His face was painted with
a wide vermilion band across the forehead; she could
smell the medicine mixed in with the grease. The
thongs of his war whistle were threaded through the
nostrils of the wolf's nose, the whistle was of eagle
bone, it swung across his glistening chest as he swung
the tomahawk at her. She screamed and drew back her
hand, and then stared in horror at her wrist gushing

blood. She heard Will shout, "Sister, oh my God!" and the Dakota struck her again, splitting her cheek with the sharp blade of the hatchet, and then again, bringing it down upon her shoulder, cracking her collarbone and opening a wedge three inches deep. He pulled the tomahawk free and was preparing to strike her again when Will seized him by the throat.

She fell to the ground, bleeding. They struggled above her as if she no longer existed, and perhaps she did not. She knew she was dying. She could hear the stallion whinnying his fright, could see the sky above, a startling blue with black clouds of smoke drifting across it, rising, drifting. One of the men stepped on her face, she did not know which of them it was. His foot slid away into the dust; she choked on the dust, rising. Her head fell limply to the side, and she could see her own severed right hand on the ground, lifeless, the fingers curled against the palm. She wanted to vomit; she felt the blood gushing steadily from her open wrist, drifting. The two men moved like shadows. She could hear them above her, struggling, grunting, the lazy hum of her blood, drifting. Within minutes, she no longer knew which of the men was white and which was Indian. Minutes after that, she was dead.

They stood about the open grave on the field they had cleared and grubbed free of stumps. Hadley spoke the words. His voice was faint, almost a whisper. He said he had searched in his memory and searched in the Holy Book for the right words to say over this woman they'd scarcely known, and had felt forsaken of the Lord, not being able to find what he'd been looking for though he'd stayed awake all night. And then he'd realized the

Lord was only asking him to find for himself what was in his own head and in his own heart.

So he'd tried to do that, tried to summon up words that would express his sorrow at yet another death, searched in his heart for that, and searched in his head for the *sense* of it—but could find only the sorrow and not the sense. He knew it was written that all things are full of weariness and that a man cannot utter it, and that the eye is not satisfied with seeing, nor the ear filled with hearing. And he knew, too, that what has been is what will be, and what has been done is what will be done. He doubted none of this, all of this was written, as were the words "There is no remembrance of former things; neither shall there be any remembrance of things that are to come with those that shall come after." But it grieved him to believe that this woman they were burying today might be forgotten as if she'd never been. If that happened, then it *would* be true what was written about there being no remembrance of former things, which he wasn't doubting, but only hoping to understand a bit more fully. . . .

His voice trailed.

He seemed to have lost for a moment what it was he wanted to say. He looked into the grave. He shook his head, and put his arm around Will and very softly said, "Lord, please bless this good woman, and give us the strength and courage to continue." He nodded as if to say he'd made his thoughts plain at last, and then gently hugged his weeping son to him, and said, "Amen," and brushed the tears from his own eyes.

"Amen," they said.

It was only after they had covered her over with earth that Gracieuse took her husband aside and reminded him in halting French that the Indian custom was to place the body of the deceased on a raised scaffold or in the branches of a tree. Sister might have preferred this to burial, she said, since interring a body made it impossible for the spirit to pass to the other world.

Orliac did not bother translating this for the others.

The Chisholms left Fort Laramie on the sixteenth day of June, in the company of twenty other wagons heading west. The road veered sharply away from the riverbank upon which sat the charred ruins of the cabin. Gideon rode out front on the stallion they'd taken from the Indians almost a year before. Hadley and Minerva were on the seat of the wagon, and Will sat on the tailgate with Catherine. Immediately behind was the wagon belonging to Franz and Bonnie Sue. Bobbo rode with them. Little Eva Schwarzenbacher, wearing a sunbonnet that shaded her blue eyes, sat on her mother's lap and looked off into the distance.

"See?" Bonnie Sue said, pointing vaguely west. "That's California there."